# toad

A *Public Enemy* Standalone
By Cambria Hebert

# A PUBLIC ENEMY STANDALONE

*Aerie Boone is a toad.*
*At least according to every news outlet and online hater*
*imaginable.*


Accusations of lip-syncing.
Rumors of being dropped by my label.
Reports of celebrity feuds and rivalries.
And then there's my personal favorite…
The pending annulment of a marriage I can't even
remember agreeing to.
When you're the sweetheart of country music, being a
headline is a given.
*Living* the headline is more of an uninvited surprise.
I'm barely recognized for the massive success I've had.
Now I'm famous because people love to hate me.
I'm a public enemy, but no one knows my side of the
story.
I'm beginning to think it doesn't even matter.
I'm burned out, hurting, and everyone thinks I have
warts. *Ew.*
Becoming a shut-in is exactly what the doctor ordered.
Too bad my label has other ideas.
They send me a solution…
In the form of a red-haired, green-eyed man who wears
sarcasm like armor.
I don't want a stranger in my house.
I don't want Nate.
All I want is to go back to a time when I wasn't a toad.
When I was country music's princess.
But going back is impossible.
Moving forward will change everything.

*For all the ladies out there who feel like toads…*

*There are plenty of princes ready to pucker up.*

toad

# prologue

## Aerie

A very slim shaft of light beamed through the otherwise inky darkness, disturbing the complete undertow sleep held me down with. It was almost as if the sliver of sunshine was a raft, suddenly appearing to pull me to the surface…

To reality.

As of late, reality was entirely overrated.

I lay still for long moments, content to fool life into believing I was actually still asleep. Reality wasn't one to be put off, however, nudging me awake regardless.

The more "alert" I grew, the more aware of my unawareness I became.

Where was I? What time was it…? And why in the world was I feeling a draft?

Goose bumps prickled my skin and chills raced across my body, leaving behind a wintry stiffness in my limbs. Defeated, my eyes sprang open, and even though it was darker in this room than it was under a sky filled with stars, it was still too bright.

Groaning, I slapped my hand over my eyes, saving them from that damned slice of daylight. The draft was still brushing over my bare skin, so I peeled my fingers away one at a time until my eyes were blinking and adjusting to the room. I gazed across the mattress. The large lump beneath a pile of blankets was clear proof I wasn't in this bed alone.

My nose wrinkled.

Where the hell was I?

It wasn't as strange as most might believe—you know, me waking up and being confused as to where I was. That was the life of a singer. I traveled so much, so often, that hotel rooms blurred together, and quite frankly, I was beginning to forget what the inside of my own house looked like.

I just needed a moment to shove back the heavy curtain of sleep draped over my mind. *And to get another blanket!* How was a girl supposed to think when she was a giant icicle?

I reached for the blankets, but all I got was a handful of a scratchy, sequined dress. Forcing my head off the pillow, I gazed down the length of my body.

Disgust shot through me. Instantly, I sat up, propping myself on one hand. No wonder there was a draft. I was half naked! Yet… also still dressed.

A dull throbbing made itself known in the back of my skull, and the idea of going back to sleep beckoned like long, bony fingers reaching up from a grave. I blinked it back because I was still trying to understand why I went to bed in my sequined mini dress, short, snug, and held up by straps barely wide enough to cover a bra. It was hardly comfortable to wear out, let alone to bed.

Currently, it was even more uncomfortable because it was bunched up around my waist completely exposing my lower half! My underwear was MIA, and I'd been sleeping on top of the blankets, not beneath them.

Strands of my hair brushed the tops of my shoulders when I turned my head to stare at the still-present lump beside me. Glancing down, I noted that my arm was completely out of one of the dress straps, while the other was still in place. The side had worked itself below one breast, the sequins rubbing rather uncomfortably against my skin and pushing up the underwire of my strapless bra.

So.

There I was in a hotel room, freezing from lack of blankets, dress bunched around my waist, bra shoved up over one boob, and a rash forming from the scratching material that looked really good in photos but pretty much felt like sandpaper. Oh, and don't forget the headache.

And reality wondered why I tried to stay asleep?

Sliding off the mattress, I trudged like a zombie over to the wall of curtains. On the way, I passed by a mess of magazines all spread out over the table near the window. Some were open. Some lay cover facing up… All of them boasted unflattering photos and headlines of me.

*Lip-Sync Disaster!*
*Aerie and Will Over!*
*Oh no she didn't! Becky spills the tea on her feud with Aerie!*

What the hell were those rags doing here? I never read that trash. Hearing about it was bad enough.

After sneering at the tabloids, I sent a few scattering off the table and continued on, stepping over them toward the heavy curtain and grasping the edge where that pesky ray of light was coming through. Bracing myself, I drew it back, recoiling from the sunshine beyond.

A very congested, very urban city stared back at me.

Vegas.

Like a floodgate had burst and water quite literally swept over everything, hazy memories from last night flooded my brain.

The ache at the base of my skull was instantly ten times worse. My eyes watered with the memories, the knowledge of what I'd done.

There was no way.

*No* way in hell. It must have been a dream. I was a lot of things, definitely a hot mess… but I wasn't that far gone.

Was I?

Standing there in the window, bathed in the sunlight of a new day, I squinted as nausea rolled over my entire midsection. I didn't even think about the fact that my dress was still around my waist, one boob literally on display as far as the eye could see.

Shoving at my tangled hair and trying to unstick my tongue from the roof of my mouth, I took a breath and looked down. After one second of hesitation, I lifted my left hand, barely noticing how unsteady it was as I held it out.

Sun glinted off the slim silver band around my ring finger. Diamonds caught the light and reflected it back in a way that was most stunning.

*No!*

My right hand slapped against my mouth, and my head shook back and forth as if the denial could somehow erase that ring. Erase what happened last night.

What the hell *had* happened!?

I whirled around so fast I nearly fell onto my bare ass. Before tumbling, I gripped the heavy drapes and steadied myself. Nearly slipping on the magazines as I rushed across the room, I plunged onto the bed, scurrying to the lump still facing away from me.

"Wake up!" I said, grabbing his shoulder and shaking it. His skin was very warm to the touch. It made my nausea worse.

He made a sound, then let me pull him around so he was flat on his back and I could peer down into his face.

"Will!" I said, slapping my palm on his bare chest and giving him a shake.

His body stiffened and his eyes sprang open. "Your hand is like ice," he complained, bucking my touch.

"Will," I said again, undeterred. "What the hell happened last night?"

His eyes opened again, this time still sleepy but with more awareness. A smile pulled his lips upward. "Morning, Mrs. Solberg."

There was a beat of silence. The kind of silence the likes of Las Vegas had never heard before. "What did you just call me?" I whispered, hoarse.

Will groped around until he found my hand, lifted it, and glanced at the band on my finger.

We didn't… *I didn't.*

He chuckled. "Come on now, babe. Don't tell me you forgot the most important night of your life."

I glanced down at the ring. The *wedding* ring.

"We got married?" My voice was still gravelly.

"You can finally get rid of that hick last name you've been saddled with your entire life."

I barely heard what he said. There was a very loud roaring between my ears. I shook it, trying to rid myself so I could think. Will chuckled and wrapped his arm around my shoulders, pulling me down so I was sprawled over his chest.

"You can believe it, babe. It's real. It's you and me now. Forever."

Tears welled up in my eyes, threatening to spill across his very warm chest.

"Your skin is like ice." I felt rather than saw him glancing down at me. "Are you still dressed from last night?" He made a sound. "I know that's your wedding dress and all, but, babe, you really should change. You look a mess."

*Forever.* The word echoed around my brain as if it were the only word in existence. The only thought inside my head.

*Oh my God.* I got married last night.

What the hell had I done?

# Nate

Everybody wants a seat on the Nate Train.

Nonetheless, I was still here. Trudging around campus, freezing my ass off when I knew I could be in sunny L.A. selling tickets, all aboard. Well, not everyone wanted a seat on the Nate Train. Or rather, they didn't like the destination it was heading for.

I stepped out of the music building, my last class of the day finally over. It was Friday, but I didn't have any weekend plans. Same shit, different day. Except, of course, I could sleep in and not sit in classes that threatened to numb my brain until it was rendered useless.

I didn't mind college… at least until lately. This semester made me feel restless. Like I shouldn't be here, but out there. You know, in the world and stuff.

The wind blew uncomfortably, the chill stinging my cheeks. It was almost spring break, but you wouldn't know it by the weather. March in New York wasn't spring. At least not this year. I grabbed the black beanie out of my jacket pocket and pulled it down over my head. The second I tucked my hands into my pockets and ducked against the wind to make the trek to my car, my pants started vibrating.

Kinky, right?

After glancing at the name flashing on the screen, I answered, "What's up, cuz?"

"Dude. You need a manager. Or an agent," Ten said into my ear.

I glanced up, surprised, and got a nice eyeful of a frigid blast of air. "Oww!" I wailed.

"Nate!" Ten said, not at all worried about my eyesight.

"I bet it's a nice eighty degrees in L.A.," I muttered, offended.

"Actually, it's eighty-five."

I gave my cell the finger. Repeatedly.

"Stop flipping off your phone," he said, laughter in his voice.

"I wasn't," I argued, even though I totally was. "I'm much more mature than that."

Ten made a sound, as if he knew I was full of turds, and shifted the conversation. "Becca got another call for you."

"Did she give them my email?"

"Do you even check your email?" Ten wondered.

"I would if she gave it out," I retorted.

"Dude. Big music execs don't just send emails."

"Their people do," I pointed out.

"It wasn't their people who called her. It was the big guy himself."

"Santa Claus owns a music label!" I said, excited.

"We've been over this, Nate," Ten replied, exasperated. "Your dad is Santa."

He was a dream crusher. I pressed an icy finger into my ear. "I can't hear you."

"Do you want the deal or not?"

I dropped my arm. "Hit me!"

"Rolland Solberg, as in Solberg Records, CEO of the second-most-successful label in the industry, called."

"Second only to your label," I said, nodding. I knew all the big players in the industry.

I knew them before my cousin Ten (the hottest thing in pop since like *ever*, and that's even *after* he became public enemy number one) came home and we got close again. Before I started working with him on his new album and a few original songs. Now that his new album wrapped, first single dropped *and* hit number one, and I'd sold a couple other songs to some big-name artists, I was even more fluent in the business.

"Seriously. I hear Rolland had a serious hard-on for the top spot, but he's not going to get it. Not with my album about to drop."

He wasn't even being cocky. It was just the truth.

"So what does this have to do with me?"

"Apparently, they're about to sign Aerie Boone. How the fuck they are managing that, I have no clue, and they want her first single with them to blow up the charts."

A little bit of adrenaline started to fill my lungs. I loved it. It was the most addictive feeling I'd ever known. Music always did that to me. I could sense the words stirring around inside me. Even though I didn't know what words were there yet, I still felt them. I could almost taste them.

"He wants a song?" I asked, my hand tightening around the phone.

"Not just *a* song, a Nate Roth original."

I pumped my fist into the air and shouted. Unfortunately, I used the fist that was clutching the phone, and it fell out of my grip and landed in a lump of snow with a thud.

*Oops.* My fingers dove into the cold, soft matter, causing the skin at the tips to burn, telling me they were tired of being out here.

After I scooped up the phone, I shoved it back against my ear, some of the snow dripping off the bottom and hitting my shoe.

"You still there?" I asked.

"You dropped the phone again."

I shrugged. "I was excited."

"They want a meeting first thing Monday morning. You gotta bring your A-game. If you land this song, a whole bunch of doors are going to open wide for you."

"I have classes Monday. Spring break starts Thursday, though. Think we can book it then?"

"That's not how this works, man. At least not until you are so in demand you can make your own demands," Ten said. "You gotta show up on their time."

I knew that. I did. It was the reason I missed classes at the end of last semester when we were working on Ten's new album, *Butterfly*.

*If he was pissed about it then... this is going to be worse.* The thought taunted the back of my mind, momentarily rendering me speechless.

"Nate," Ten called me back to the present.

"Yeah," I said. "So what did Becca tell them?"

"She booked the meeting. And she's making a bunch of noise about commission for acting like your manager. I'm telling you, man. You don't want to deal with her. You might want to get someone to handle these calls."

I mock shuddered. "Becca the barracuda. Hiring someone might be a good call."

"Look, my plane is already in the air for you. Fly out tonight, and we can prep this weekend."

"You're sending your plane?"

"Like I'd let my cousin and my girl fly commercial." He scoffed.

"Violet?" I asked, glancing around as though I expected her to just appear.

"I haven't seen her in almost a week," he intoned. "Too long. Pick her up on the way to the airstrip, okay? She knows to be ready."

I hesitated just a fraction of a second.

"Is he going to be that pissed?" Ten's low voice filled my ear.

I felt my shoulders sag. "I'm not sure," I replied.

"You want me to have Becca call back and cancel?"

"No!" My answer was swift. "I'll be there."

"You're sure?"

"You better have extra Fruity Pebbles when I get there. Flying makes me hungry."

Ten laughed. "Already sent my assistant out."

Dude had an assistant to get his cereal. Lame.

"This is a really great opportunity, Nate." His voice no longer held laughter, but was more subdued.

"Yeah," I said solemnly. "I know."

"Call if you need backup."

"Thanks."

I disconnected the call and pocketed my phone.

Remember how I said not everyone wanted a seat on the Nate Train? Specifically, I meant my dad.

He definitely didn't want a seat, especially if it was heading to L.A.

# two

## Aerie

The second the little ding of the fancy elevator filled the space, I began moving, the doors just barely opening in time for me to stride out.

I was a woman on a mission.

Tucking the newest tabloid under my arm, I marched with my head high through the wide reception area, the sound of my high-heeled boots reverberating confidence around me. The receptionist looked up, her eyes widening just slightly. Instantly, she clicked the little button on the Bluetooth set against her ear and began to speak rapidly.

Warning them, I was sure.

She stood as I drew closer, a fake smile plastered on her face. She didn't like me. But it wouldn't stop her from kissing my ass.

How two-faced.

Her lips parted, but I held up my hand, silencing whatever she was about to say. The men flanking me, walking just a fraction behind, kept with my pace, knowing I wasn't going to stop.

I didn't have an appointment. I didn't care.

Turning the corner, I marched right up to the double oak doors. One of the men behind, stepped deftly around me and pulled back the door, allowing me to stride ahead into the room.

Walter looked up from behind his desk. He wasn't surprised. Proof that he was indeed warned about my arrival. Or maybe he just knew this visit was inevitable.

"What is taking so long?" I asked, dropping some of the superiority I wore like a winter coat.

Sitting back in his oversized leather chair, he took off the bifocals perched on his nose, tossed them aside, and sighed. "I can assure you this firm is doing everything in our power to get your marriage annulled as soon as possible."

"Maybe the power this firm once had is losing its foothold," I snapped.

He glanced up, partly surprised by my words. There was a spark of offended anger in the depths of his eyes, and I instantly felt contrite. I didn't show it, though. The second I showed any kind of weakness, he would seize the chance to feed me a line of bull, which I would then pretend to swallow because I felt bad about hurting his ego.

Men and their egos.

It was utterly exhausting. And insulting. If a man needed his ego stroked so much and so often, then he wasn't a very good man.

In my humble opinion, of course.

Instead of apologizing, I unfolded the tabloid from beneath my arm and placed it on the desk right in front of him. Then I lowered onto one of the leather club chairs across from him. "This doesn't look like you're any closer to getting me out of that sham of a marriage than you were the last time I was here."

"You mean the time you had an appointment?" he quipped.

"I wouldn't have to barge in like this if I was getting results," I retorted and pointed at the cover of the rag. "Just look at that!"

*Secret marriage leads to huge acquisition for Solberg Records!*

Walter glanced down at the obtrusive headline and sighed. "Will is doing everything possible to delay or even stop the annulment altogether."

"I warned you he would. It was quite obvious the morning I woke up..."—I paused, choosing my words carefully— "married, he wasn't regretful."

"As you said. But you, on the other hand, you were." Lawyers had an uncanny ability to state the obvious.

"I wouldn't be sitting here otherwise."

"You haven't quite said why, Ms. Boone. Why is it you want an annulment so desperately?"

I felt as though my eyes could fall right out of my face. Was he serious? "I did tell you. Quite adamantly. I must have been highly intoxicated when we eloped. I don't even remember what crappy Vegas chapel we did it in. I didn't know what I was doing. I'm not ready for marriage." *Especially to Will.*

"Mr. Solberg claims you were of sound mind and, though you were both imbibing champagne, there was equal consent to the marriage."

My shoulder blades drew together, tension coiling in my upper body. "Will is lying."

Walter leaned forward, placing his forearms over the magazine and regarded me seriously. "You have been publicly dating Will Solberg for nearly a year."

My stomach dipped. It wasn't the excited kind of dip either. It was the kind that made me feel I was going to throw up. "What are you saying, Walter?"

"His legal team is claiming there are no grounds for an annulment. They say they can provide witness testimony that you agreed to the marriage and that you two had discussed the union in the past, during the time you were dating."

I sat back in my chair as though his words were a strong gust of wind I had no chance of withstanding. But the second my body gave in and slumped, I recovered and shot out of the chair. Hands on my hips, I regarded my lawyer. "He's lying. I did *not* consent, and I want out."

"Can you prove you weren't in the right mind to agree?"

I faltered. "My word isn't good enough?"

"Perhaps if you were less high profile. Perhaps if you had married some backup dancer without the limitless resources that come with Solberg Records. But Will is pushing—hard. We're pushing back, but it's not as cut and dry as you want it to be."

"What's the point of being a famous country singer with a lot of money if I can't use it to untangle myself from a mess?" I muttered, dropping back into the chair.

"I'm afraid that in times like these, your status only makes it messier," Walter said, his voice gentle.

I wanted to cry. I would later, but not right now. "What are my options?"

"We could drop the petition for annulment and start proceedings for a divorce."

My breath caught. "If we do that, Will can call himself my ex-husband. Our marriage will be considered legal."

"Yes, and I have to warn you he could make a claim against some of your assets."

My insides turned frigid, despite the anger boiling in my veins. He would do it. Not because he needed anything I had, but just because he could. An annulment would nullify our quick "marriage." It would erase it, as if it never even happened. He could have no claim to me.

Not ever again.

"I can't do that," I whispered. "I want an annulment. It's my right."

He nodded once. "I thought you would say that."

I leaned in, my eyes intent on his. "I didn't want this marriage, Walter."

He didn't offer any sympathy. Did lawyers ever? I wasn't sure. All I knew was it would be nice to feel like he was on my side. That *anyone* was on my side.

"That article…" My lawyer pointed at his desk. "All the headlines about this, it's his way of trying to sway public opinion. Trying to put together a visible case for the hearing."

"Is there a date for the hearing yet?" I asked. The sooner the better.

"No. He's delaying, trying to get the notion of an annulment dismissed."

I swallowed. "And if he's successful?"

"The divorce could take six months to a year to push through."

The words were like bullets, each penetrating my body one and a time. "That's completely unacceptable!" I exclaimed and stood, beginning to pace.

"Forgive me for the personal question, miss," Walter said, clearing his throat. "Have you and Mr. Solberg consummated the marriage?"

"No!" I said, then backtracked. "Well, I'm not sure."

His forehead wrinkled. "I don't follow."

"We haven't since I woke up that morning." I gazed down at my ring finger, which was empty now. The memory of that wedding band wrapped around my finger like a shackle haunted me. "But the night of the marriage… we could have." I lowered my gaze to the floor. "I don't remember."

Walter's eyes narrowed solicitously. "Miss Boone, is there a chance that William Solberg raped you?"

I sucked in a breath, and the action created an empty whistling sound between my lips. I was ashamed. Embarrassed. Utterly mortified. "Possibly."

"But all previous relations before that night were consensual?"

Why did it sound like he was making it my fault? Why did everything always feel like it was my fault?

"I didn't realize that mattered," I stated.

"Unfortunately, it does. Especially in court. Especially since you can't remember. Especially since one of the stipulations for annulment is failure to consummate."

I remembered waking up that morning. No panties. Dress around my waist and one of my girls out to party. Wasn't it pretty obvious we'd had sex?

"I'll push for a hearing to be set. We can let the judge determine if the annulment is valid. But, Aerie, it would be very helpful if you could remember what happened that night. Or find someone who can corroborate that you were too intoxicated to agree to marriage."

I nodded. Glancing down at the paper on his desk, I met his eyes. "Please, Walter. Please do everything you can to get me out of this."

I hoped he understood the plea in my words.

"I can assure you my entire staff is working on this. We'll get it resolved."

I left his room using the same stride and confidence I entered with. I felt as if my world were crumbling. Everything and everyone was against me. I wanted to go back to my place, scrub off this mask of makeup, and succumb to the tears.

I couldn't.

Not yet anyway. I had one more place to be. One more attempt to make.

I was definitely a woman on a mission.

But inside, this woman was exhausted and about to break.

# three

## *Nate*

The distinct sound of the zipper of my duffle filled the bedroom as I finished packing, but it silenced abruptly. I darted into the hall bathroom to quickly jam my toothbrush and a few other necessary items into a small pouch. Once back in the bedroom, I stuffed it into the duffle and finished zipping it closed.

That was a close call. I almost sentenced myself to dragon breath while I was in L.A.

Not exactly the kind of impression I wanted to make when meeting with freaking Solberg Records. As if my career as a songwriter wasn't already off to an awesome start, now I had the opportunity to work with the second-largest recording company in music.

*'Course, ah,* I thought as I literally patted myself on the shoulder, *it's sort of a step down considering my first job was with Ten's album, which is with the number-one recording company.*

I snorted and grabbed up the duffle. The door leading out into the garage from the kitchen opened and closed, my stomach knotted, and all sarcastic thoughts drained from my mind. With the bag slung over my shoulder, I went in search of the sound, finding my dad standing in front of the kitchen table as he sorted through the mail, car keys still hanging from one of his fingers.

He glanced up quickly when I moved into the room, back down at the mail, then back up at me once more. His stare zeroed in on the duffle, and his mouth drew into a thin line.

"Hey, Dad," I said, dumping the bag rather loudly on the floor behind me. There was no point in pretending it wasn't there. "How was work?"

"Spring break doesn't start 'til next week," he said, still shuffling through the mail.

"It's the weekend."

All the envelopes were abandoned to the table, his keys joining them. "Seems like an awful big bag for just a weekend trip."

"I got another opportunity…" I began.

Dad made a sound and shook his head. "What's he need this time?"

I drew a momentary blank, then felt my brow furrow. "Are you taking about Ten?"

Dad paced across the room and began putting on a pot of coffee. We didn't have one of those fancy machines that used those little pods. Dad thought they were frivolous. He was so old-school. We had a coffee pot that had most likely been my grandma's.

"Ever since he stayed here last semester, he's depended on you a lot."

I felt my eyes sharpen on his back. I was hearing a lot of words he wasn't saying. "We're family. We drifted apart, but it's good to have him back. You know we were more like brothers growing up." *He was like a son to you.*

He cleared his throat and turned as the coffee started to brew. The rich scent filled the small kitchen, and I inhaled. "He's changed a lot since you guys were kids."

I considered his words instead of retorting a quick denial. "Yeah. I guess he has. I think fame would do that to anyone. He's still a good guy, Dad."

He measured me for a long moment, then relented. "Yes, he seems to have gotten his head on straight again. I think you had a lot to do with that."

"And you. And Violet," I added. After a heartbeat, I said, "And he doesn't depend on me, not in the way you mean. But it's nice to have people in your life you can trust."

"Ten get you this new opportunity?"

My hackles rose. What the fuck was his problem? He was acting like I was fourteen and trying to watch porn on some channel that we didn't get and came in fuzzy. I admit I used to turn on that channel and hope for a boob shot. Sometimes I got lucky.

Crossing my arms over my chest, I asked, "You saying you don't think I have enough talent or ambition to get my own opportunities?"

"Of course not, Nate," he grumbled.

"Sure as hell sounds like it."

He glanced up. "So who called you about this?"

"Don't you even want to know what *this* is?" I challenged.

He nodded. "What is it?"

"Solberg Records—you know, the second-biggest music producer in the business—wants me to write an original song for Aerie Boone."

His brow furrowed a second, then smoothed out. "The country singer?"

"The most famous country singer. She's practically Ten with boobs."

Dad smirked, then turned around to pour some coffee. "I can't say that's a ringing endorsement. She's been in the media a lot, just like my nephew."

"And what did we learn from that? The media lies."

Dad turned, mug poised at his lips. "Actually, I'm pretty certain the stuff they said about Ten was accurate."

"Some of it." Then I flung out my hands. "Who freaking cares? I'm writing a song for her, not marrying her!"

"Pretty sure she's already married, to a Solberg," he quipped, sipping his coffee. It reminded me of that meme with Kermit the frog making observations that were "none of his business."

"Which means they want the best for her, and they called *me*." I puffed out my chest. "If I do this and the song is as huge as I know it can be, my entire career will be set."

"She's a bad influence."

I laughed.

"So what? You're going to just give up on the last couple years you've been working toward your degree?"

He shook his head. "You can't just go to L.A. on a whim, son. It's a fickle business. They'll eat you up and spit you out just like they did Ten."

I didn't get pissed off very often. I was a chill guy. But I did have red hair.

That meant I wasn't completely free of a temper. I had buttons. And right now, dear ol' dad was pushing them like a game of Whack-A-Mole.

"I'm not going out there on a whim," I snapped, holding on to the anger. It stung, actually. It stung he really thought so low of me. I almost felt betrayed. "I got a job opportunity. One that could make me a lot of money. One that could pay for the rest the degree you're so intent on me earning."

"Your tuition is free, Nate. You know that."

"Because my dad works for the college. You want me to depend on you forever? I gotta be my own man."

"By dropping out of college and running off to L.A.? That's not a very manly choice."

"Are you fucking kidding me right now!" I snapped.

"Watch your tone." He warned.

I shoved my hand through my hair. "I never said I was dropping out of college, Dad. I said I got an opportunity in L.A. I have a meeting on Monday. I'm coming back. I know how important it is to finish my degree." *Important to you, not so much to me.*

"Spring break doesn't start 'til Thursday," he pointed out.

"So I'm going to miss a couple classes. I already talked to my professors. It's cool. I'll make sure I'm caught up."

"Your education and honoring the commitment you made to Blaylock is important." Spoken like a true father... with a gigantic stick up his ass.

"Relax, Dad. It's not like I'm TP-ing the school and going to jail in my hoodie." I pointed to the university hoodie I was currently dressed in. "Think how good it will look if one of your students makes it big in the music industry. It will make your music department even more prestigious."

He didn't say anything. I didn't figure he would. He didn't seem impressed at all by the extra recognition the music department at Blaylock University was getting because Ten composed most of his upcoming album there.

"I'm going," I said, final.

His displeasure permeated the room and stunk like a dead body. "I figured."

He knew he couldn't stop me. I was twenty-one years old. I might live at home still, but legally, I was an adult.

"Well, thanks for the support," I said, gruff and oddly hurt. I wasn't about to show that, though. "I'll be back before spring break is over, and I'll tell Ten you said hi."

I grabbed up my bag and flung it over my shoulder. Dad was still standing there drinking his coffee, watching me.

I started toward the door, the tightness in my chest not easing at all.

"Son?"

I stopped, but didn't turn back.

"Call me when the plane lands."

The side of my mouth kicked up in a smile he couldn't see. Pissed or not about my choices, he was still gonna worry about me. Knowing that took away a lot of my anger.

I glanced over my shoulder. "Will do."

I headed out in the driveway toward my old Ford Focus and threw my bag in the hatch before sliding behind the wheel.

I wasn't quite sure why he was so against me following my dream, but he made it crystal clear going to L.A. was not something he approved of.

I never really defied my dad. Ever.

I guess I'd never wanted anything bad enough.

But now I did.

"Are you okay?" Violet asked.

I paused midway through shutting off the engine, then continued, snatching the keys out of the ignition and turning toward her. "We're taking off for sunny L.A. No more cold weather or classes for a week. Of course I'm okay!"

She gave me a look that said she'd been friends with me long enough that she knew better.

Girls. They always knew, didn't they? Even when they didn't know, they knew.

"Derek wasn't happy about the trip, was he?" she asked, quiet.

The sun was already sinking in the sky, making the air outside feel even cooler. Her blue eyes held a note of understanding that made me slightly uncomfortable. It was kinda crazy how fast we grew close. Besides Ten, I would say Violet was my best friend. One day she was just a girl Ten had a boner for, and the next, she was a permanent fixture in his life… and mine.

Sure, Ten asked me to watch out for her when he wasn't around—he was beyond overprotective—but I hung out with her because I liked her. Violet was pretty cool.

I sighed. "He definitely wasn't giving me the warm and fuzzy feeling when I left."

She nodded. "Between you and me, I think it bothers Stark a lot more than he lets on."

"That my dad doesn't want me to come to L.A.?"

She laughed and shoved my arm. "No, that Derek isn't as supportive of Stark's career as he hoped."

"He hasn't said anything to me."

Violet smiled, tucking a strand of blond hair behind her ear. "Me, either."

See? She just, like, knew stuff.

"My dad will get over it," I replied, shoving open the door, allowing cold air to rush inside.

"And if he doesn't?" she asked, leaning over the center console to look at me through the open door.

My chest tightened, reminding me of how I'd felt when I left the house. Girls talked too much.

"He will." I slammed the car door and opened the hatch.

Violet ran around the back of the car, ducking beside me and blowing on her bare fingers.

I frowned. "Where's your gloves?"

"We're flying to L.A. I'm not bringing gloves."

I shrugged and grabbed up both our bags.

"I'll take mine."

I ignored her and motioned to the hatch. "Close that for me." Then I continued toward the plane that sat near the hangar I'd parked beside.

"I can carry my own bag," Violet said, rushing to catch up. I noticed her carrying the small backpack she always had with her and nodded toward it.

"You have one."

"You and Stark act like I'm an invalid."

"Do not," I shot back.

"Do so."

Truth was we knew she wasn't an invalid. But yeah, maybe we were a little more eager to do stuff for her because of her rheumatoid arthritis. It was only because we cared.

The set of stairs was already folded out for us to board. Movement at the top of the steps caught my attention, but I was slower to look up because I figured it was just the pilot.

Beside me, Violet gasped. "Stark!"

Violet didn't call my cousin by his first name. She called him by his last name (long story).

It was as though our argument hadn't even happened. One minute she was telling me she wanted to carry her own crap, and the next, she was tossing that backpack of hers at me.

"I'm pretty sure that doesn't go there!" I announced even as she hung it around my neck.

"Did you know he was coming?" she exclaimed, her eyes bright.

"There's my girl," Stark called from the doorway of the plane.

She made a sound of impatience and darted away.

"Be careful!" he scolded her.

Violet's laugh floated behind her as she fumbled up the stairs in her Adidas.

"Next time you want to carry your own bag, I'm going to remind you of this!" I yelled behind her. "She better tip me," I griped as I kept walking.

At the top of the stairs, Violet launched herself at Stark, and the pair fell backward, disappearing out of the doorway.

This was going to be a long flight.

I heard him laughing inside. When I reached the top, his hand shot out and relieved me of Violet's bag.

"You're spoiling her, man," I told Ten. "She thinks I'm her personal valet!"

"Do not!" Violet rebutted.

I pointed to the backpack hanging around my neck. "This isn't a fashion statement."

We had a good brother-sister relationship happening. I liked to help foster that along by arguing with her.

Ten pulled it over my head and tossed it on a nearby bench seat along one side of the plane. It looked like a cream-colored leather couch. Soon as I was relieved of all the baggage, Violet filled his arms again, and he grinned at me from over her shoulder, holding out his fist. I pounded it out and then went toward a table with some chairs around it.

"You called from the plane," I mused.

"Like I'd sit at home and let my girl fly out to L.A. without me."

"What am I, chopped liver?" I scoffed.

"Of course not," Violet replied instantly. Then she turned to Ten. "No security this trip?"

"They'll meet us at the strip when we land. It's family time now."

Partway through the flight, Violet fell asleep in Ten's lap, and I was staring out into the dark sky.

"How bad was it?" Ten asked.

I knew he was talking about my dad.

"Could've been worse."

After a few moments of silence, Ten's voice reached across the plane once more. "Is this what you want?"

I looked at him then. His gaze was steady. The point-blank question sort of caught me off guard. I hadn't really thought about it like that. Black and white. Probably because it wasn't just black and white, but I appreciated the perspective Ten brought in that moment.

Songwriting was my dream. But was this what I wanted? Reaching for it despite my father's strong reservations—the man who had always been there for me?

I rummaged deep down in my gut. Past the place where the Fruity Pebbles and corndogs went. Past the sarcasm and the jokes.

I swallowed before replying. My cousin didn't rush me or interpret my silence as indecision. That was the thing about Ten, the thing I think my dad never quite realized.

Ten's fame didn't ruin his life. Or the man he could have been. It could have. If he'd let it.

The business he chose (or the one that chose him) didn't define him. He defined it. And all the struggle to get to where he was right now, with a sleeping blonde in his lap, shaped him. Made him stronger.

"Yes," was all I said, despite all the words working through my head.

Ten nodded. "Then we'll work it out. Uncle Derek will come around."

I glanced back out the small window.

I sure hoped he was right.

# four

## Aerie

Solberg Records was in the heart of Los Angeles. It was a tall building shaped like a cylinder made almost entirely of windows. The very top of the building boasted the family name in massive illuminated letters.

Rolland Solberg liked to make his presence known. And so did his son.

After the black SUV with excessively tinted windows stopped near the entrance, I was escorted into the building by my bodyguards. The press was staked outside, likely hoping for a glimpse of me. Or my darling husband Will.

It was almost enough to keep me away. Giving these vultures anything they salivated for was pretty much worse than death these days. At least in death, I'd be away from all their dramatic lies.

Actually, wait.

There was something worse than death—remaining married to Will.

I know. I know. I married him. Before that, I dated him. For too long.

I have an explanation. One I never gave. People would just call it an excuse.

Anyhow, that was why I was here, keeping my head down, avoiding the paparazzi and taking comfort in the fact my bodyguards were trying to shield me. Sometimes it cut me like a well-sharpened knife that the only true shielding I ever got was from paid employees.

We whisked through the building, securing an empty elevator, and as soon as the doors slid closed, I hunched in on myself just a little. The reprieve lasted all of two seconds, and then I was back to wearing my armor and holding my chin high.

Here, all the high-powered execs had their own receptionist, not just one for the entire floor. To me, it was just another way Rolland Solberg liked to show superiority. I had to hand it to him on the business side, though. Presenting the allusion his execs were all so busy they needed their own assistant sure made his business look booming.

Will had a corner office (like that surprises you), and the second his assistant (who was no more than twenty-one, with a boob job, lip injections, and head full of fake hair) saw me, she lurched to her feet.

"Mrs. Solberg!" she said, and my stomach literally lurched. "Will didn't tell me you were stopping by."

I gave her a glare out of the corners of my eyes as I swept by. "I wasn't aware I needed an appointment to see my *husband*." I enunciated the word, reminding her I was the one in charge here. I didn't bother telling her what I thought of the fact she was calling him by his first name.

Wasn't that cozy?

"I'll just tell him—" She began, as if she had the power to stop me.

I hesitated long enough that the clipping of my heels over the polished floor paused and silence fell around me like snow. The dark strands of my sleekly blown-out hair whipped around like a satin curtain as I turned my head, saying nothing, just lifting one perfectly sculpted dark brow.

The assistant's mouth clapped shut and her throat worked.

With a small sound, I spun around as my bodyguard pulled open the door.

Will glanced up in surprise, his expression morphing even more when our eyes collided. He was lounged back in his posh leather chair, feet propped on top of his glass desktop, ruby-red tie tossed over his shoulder, a crystal tumbler of dark liquid at his elbow, and a phone mashed to his ear.

Was this work or drinks at the club?

Upon seeing me, he jolted up. His feet hit the floor, and the tie slithered back over his chest. "I'm gonna have to call you back," he told the person on the line, then promptly disconnected the call.

"Babe!" he said, flashing a smile that used to fool me into thinking he really was happy to see me. "I had no idea you were coming by!"

"Really?" I muttered darkly and pointedly stared at him.

He cleared his throat as both hands slid into the pockets of his very black, very tailored designer dress pants. The action drew attention to the strength of his thighs, and I knew if I looked in the windows behind him, I would be able to see the reflection of the material pulled taut over his well-defined ass.

I didn't look. I held his stare instead.

"Mind if I have a moment alone with my wife, gentlemen?" Will said, glancing at my two bodyguards who were just inside the room.

I could tell by the look on his face that they didn't do his bidding immediately. Anger flared in his eyes. He despised being challenged in any way.

What a tell that was. If only I had realized it months ago.

My stomach coiled a little at the countenance brewing in his blue stare, so I turned around to meet the eyes of my guards. "I'll be fine."

Both of them hesitated until I nodded.

"We'll be just outside." Mac assured me, but he glanced at Will when he spoke.

"Thank you," I said as they shut the door softly behind them. The latching noise was very definitive. It almost made me wince.

*Hold it together, Aerie.*

"You're holding up the annulment," I said, not mincing words.

He plastered what I was sure he thought of as a charming smile on the lower half of his face. "No. I'm just giving you some time to realize what you're doing is a mistake."

Folding my arms across my chest, I regarded him. "Getting married was the mistake, Will."

He smirked. "Funny, you were all for it the night we said I do."

"I don't even remember that night," I snapped. "And there is no way I would have agreed to marry you."

Annoyance flashed in his eyes but then disappeared. Turning, he walked around his bulky, glass-topped desk, pulled open a drawer, and withdrew a file folder. Coming back to stand in front of me, he made a show of opening the folder and turning it around so I could see the single sheet of paper inside.

The room tilted a little when I realized what it was. Our marriage license. Right there as undeniable proof. "But you did agree," he quipped and clapped the folder shut quickly.

"Why?" I asked, abrupt.

He frowned, his stupid smile—the one that made him look like he belonged in a wax museum—falling away. "Excuse me?"

"Why did I marry you?"

"I'm insulted you're asking me."

My voice was dry. "More insulted than when I filed for an annulment?"

That look, the kind that pulled back the curtain on all the anger he banked behind the mask that was his face, appeared again. The urge to take a step back was so strong I literally rocked on my feet.

I resisted, however, refusing to back down. If I retreated now, if I gave in at all, he'd win. Like all the other times he'd won before.

And then?

And then my life would no longer be mine.

Despite the urge to flee, I stood my ground.

Will stepped forward, almost as if he knew his presence was more than I could tolerate. He loved intimidating people. It was a sport to him.

He reached out, caught a strand of my hair, and slid his fingers down it, letting go to caress the side of my chin. My stomach clenched. I didn't breathe.

"You've embarrassed me quite a lot over the past few weeks." His voice was calm, almost amused.

Chilling.

"Then sign the papers. I'll go away quietly and never embarrass you again."

"No," he said much more forcefully and turned his back to me.

I let out the breath I'd been holding, deflating like a balloon with a gigantic hole. "I saw the headline."

His chuckle filled the room. Goose bumps broke out over my skin. "Is that why you're here?"

"You leaked that rumor to the press, didn't you?"

"You joining me and Dad here at Solberg? That's not a rumor. That's inevitable."

"My lawyer says you're trying to say there isn't even any case for an annulment."

He stopped at the corner of his desk and turned back. He had authority about him. The kind that pulled in a girl, that made her drunk and stupid. By the time the hangover was over and she smartened up, she was in far, far too deep.

*Claw your way out, Aerie. Do it.*

"Might as well drop this now, babe. We both know I always get what I want. No point in making me any more pissed than I already am."

I'd have asked him if he was so pissed, why even bother fighting me on this, but I knew the answer.

It wasn't love.

He didn't know what that was. Another lesson I learned far too late.

"Even if, by some divine act of God, we stayed married, I still wouldn't sign with Solberg Records."

He chuckled again—the sound I'd hear in my nightmares for years to come. "Now how would that look? A wife not joining the family business?"

"It's not my family."

Impatience flashed across his features, and within seconds, he was back in front of me. He was bigger, broader. He loomed over me in a way that was not protective or desirable.

His breath was hot on my face when he leaned in to speak low. "You're my wife. That makes us family."

"I don't know what you did, how you managed to get me to sign that marriage certificate, but I know it's not something I did with a clear head. Annulment or not, Will, we are *not* staying married."

His hand shot out, wrapping around my upper arm, and he yanked me into his personal space. His fingers bit into my flesh, squeezing so hard I felt them grind against bone. Blinking back the tears, I forced myself to stare up at him, refusing to look away.

"If you try and divorce me, I will take half your bank account and make you waste what's left on legal fees. You're mine, Aerie, and I never give up what's mine."

"Let go," I ground out.

He squeezed tighter. I bit the inside of my lip to keep from flinching.

His eyes flared and so did his nostrils. "I don't know where this sudden... *defiant* streak is coming from, but I suggest you drop it before you really piss me off."

I ripped my arm free, nearly falling back on my ass. Straightening, I glared at him, putting some distance between us. My chest was heaving, my breaths coming in short gasps.

Will advanced, and I moved back instinctively until my back hit the wall and he was caging me in with both arms. "Let me tell you how it's going to be from here on out," he intoned. "You're going to drop this silly lawsuit and move to my house in Beverly Hills. We're going to attend events and walk red carpets together and become the music industry's newest king and queen. You will walk away from your current label and sign with Solberg, and by this time next year, we're all going to be much, much richer. Solberg Records will no longer be number two in music. We'll rule at the very top."

He should just add world domination to his plans, because he sure was sounding like some kind of maniacal tyrant.

I stood there, completely numb, for long moments. Fear coursed through my veins so thickly it robbed me of my own thoughts.

Then something happened.

Clarity.

Clarity so strong I swear I grew a pair of golden balls right then and there.

Yes, my knees were quivering. My hands were clammy and my stomach felt as though I had day-two cramps, even though I wasn't on my period. (Seriously, day two is the worst!) I knew Will wasn't bluffing, and I knew I was walking the edge of the anger I'd always managed to not instill in him before…

But how dare he?

How dare he try and rule me like I was less than? Like I was nothing but a piece of arm candy. A piece of property to be bought, sold, and traded. A business transaction with boobs.

No.

*Oh, hell no.*

All that fear coursing through me morphed to rage. White-hot, self-serving fury.

I lifted my hands between us, planting them firmly on his chest, and shoved. He moved back enough that I was able to slip out from beneath him.

Squaring my shoulders, I spun on him. "I don't know who you think you're talking to, but I am *not* one of your daddy's minions. I might have let you do this to me in the past, but *never* again. The only reason you're so desperate to keep me is because I have what you want. Power." I took a step forward, lifting my chin. "You can't have it and you can't have *me.*"

My balls shriveled up just as fast as they grew because the look on his face was emasculating.

"Mac," I yelled out the second Will took a menacing lunge forward.

I fell back, the door burst open, and Will teetered in his designer shoes the second his payback was cut short.

"Ms. Boone," Mac implored, rushing to my side as my other guard filled the doorway. "What happened?"

I glanced quickly at Will, who was trying really, super hard to conceal the sheer vileness of his true face. The thing that seemed most shocking was how convincing he was. One would never have realized the violence with which he was about to come at me if they hadn't personally witnessed it.

But I'd seen. More than once. Enough that it was almost all I saw when I looked at him now. Ever since that morning I woke up shackled to him.

His eyes narrowed, Will's stare became beady and hawk-like. I heard the threat, though none was voiced.

My balls were still shriveled, my brain going numb. I'd had just about all I could take. These last few months, which bled into these last few weeks, had nearly drained me.

I wasn't kidding when I told myself to claw my way out. There was no way in hell I was going to walk. My balance was too unsteady.

"Ms. Boone," Mac said again, moving so his large frame was between me and Will, blocking him from sight. It didn't matter, though. I still saw him. I still felt the air around me vibrating with threat. "What happened? Why are you on the floor?"

Mac carefully helped me up. Even after I was on my feet, I held on to his wrist just a little longer than was really necessary.

"Did he strike you?" Mac asked, his voice low and serious.

His eyes implored me to tell the truth.

Unfortunately, at this moment, the fear in this room outweighed the rest.

"Oh, no!" I said, feigning shock and surprise. I released his wrist instantly. "It's these damn heels. They might be designer, but it doesn't make them any easier to walk in."

Mac frowned.

I smiled, dazzling him with my professionally whitened teeth. "I'm fine, really."

Will laughed. "I gotta admit she looks gorgeous in those heels, but she never could walk in them." He appeared over Mac's shoulder, warning and approval ripe in his gaze.

I cleared my throat, averting my eyes. "I called for you to ask you to please call downstairs and have them bring my car around. I'm sure the press is still lurking out there, and I'm tired."

"Of course." He inclined his head and gestured to my other guard in the door. Once that was done, his eyes searched mine again, and I smiled.

He stepped aside, but didn't leave the room. Thankfully.

"I have places to be," I told Will.

"Of course. Everyone wants a piece of my wife." Will held out his arms for a hug.

My stomach clenched so hard I nearly doubled over. I stepped forward because it was easier than making a scene and let him wrap his arms around me. He lifted me off my feet and twirled me. I made the dutiful sound of a happy squeal and let my fingers bite into his arms a little too hard.

When he stopped, he made sure he was facing away from the door, his back to my guards. Then he put me down and squeezed tight, wrapping himself around me. "The harder you fight, the worse it's going to be for you, babe."

It was as though he didn't even know my name. Or he thought he was above using it.

"When I'm done with you, all you'll have left is me."

I yanked away from him and brushed past. "Good-bye, Will."

"See you later," he said, satisfaction in his tone.

I exited without looking back. The second we were in the elevator, I let out a shaky breath.

"Are you okay, Ms. Boone?" Mac asked.
"Never better." I lied.
Truth was Will scared me.

# *Nate*

The black Lamborghini pulled up in front of Solberg Records, sliding right up to the curb near the entrance in a no-parking zone. The doorman at the huge glass double doors glanced out, but didn't exit to tell us to move.

"You're so famous you can park in a no-parking zone and not get towed?" I asked, partially awed.

"This from the guy who parked my Jeep on a sidewalk in front of the music building. At least I'm still on the road," Ten cracked.

"That Jeep is so ghetto people probably saw it and thought it broke down there. This Lambo? Not quite as pathetic."

Ten smirked. "True."

"Want me to open my door and fall out? Make a big scene, act like I'm injured and we're gonna sue? Free parking for life then."

"You're here for a job interview. I think trying to blackmail free parking isn't the best way to get hired."

I sighed and muttered, "People are so touchy these days."

"I'm not coming in." Ten went on.

I turned in the seat to face him. "What?"

"If I go in there with you, it's going to look like their direct competition is scoping out their business plans. I told you Rolland Solberg wants my record label's top spot, and I'm the main reason he can't get it."

"Maybe I shouldn't take this deal," I replied, thinking about what he said.

"Why?"

"Because this banger I'm about to write might kick you out of the top spot."

Ten gave me the finger. With both hands.

I held up mine. "Down, boy. We can't afford any accidental angry whizzing. I didn't bring an extra shirt."

Ten dropped his hands. "You piss on an audience one time," he mumbled.

"So I'm going in alone." I glanced back at the giant shiny building. I wondered if birds ever flew by just to check themselves out.

"Not exactly."

I raised an eyebrow at him, and he sighed. "Becca's meeting you inside."

I made a horrified face.

Ten laughed. "I know, but she insisted. Not only does she want to rep you on the deal, but she wants info."

"What kind of info?"

"The kind that tells her what Solberg is up to with Aerie. I'm sure Becca will report back to my label with the 4-1-1."

"Business rivalry." I pursed my lips.

"Well, considering Solberg is trying to steal Aerie right out from under us…"

"Aerie is with Time Track?" I asked.

"Yeah, so why on earth would she ditch them to sign with number two?"

I held up my hand and pointed to my ring finger. "Bling-bling."

Ten made a noise. "Maybe. Anyway, she'll meet you upstairs. You're going to the executive level."

"Maybe I should've worn a tie," I commented.

"Do you own a tie?"

I nodded. "It has Darth Vader on it."

"Probably good you didn't, then."

My voice was sage. "Yeah, maybe they only like the Light Side."

"Get out of my car, Nate."

"Luke, I am your faaa-ther," I said, doing my best deep voice and heavy breathing.

"Out," he ordered again, but he was laughing.

The second I was on the sidewalk, he pulled back out into traffic without missing a beat. It was like everyone on the road just sort of paused to make room for him on the pavement.

I had no idea how long this meeting was going to last, but I was a little more nervous because of what Ten said. Was Solberg trying to steal an artist from his label? Was that legal?

It probably was legal. Anything in this business seemed to be if you threw enough money at it. I wouldn't exactly call it ethical, though.

Come to think of it, they probably would have appreciated the Vader tie. They seemed to be part of the Dark Side.

I made a sound. The man in a suit walking beside me glanced over. "Should have worn a *Star Wars* tie with that," I told him.

He hurried away.

Maybe he wasn't a *Star Wars* fan.

The doorman opened the door for me, and I stepped in, the AC blasting me instantly. There were several rows of elevators, all labeled with different floor numbers. Off to the side, there was one elevator with golden paneled doors and a plaque above it with the words *Executive Level*.

I went to the doors, about to push the button, when a white-gloved hand reached out to stop me.

"Ah!" I said, shocked because this dude came out of nowhere. I glanced around. He was wearing a funny hat and jacket. "Were you hiding in that plant?" I demanded, jabbing my finger at a gigantic green thing nearby.

"I do not hide in plants," he responded. He was British. "You walked right by me. You were distracted by the shiny door."

"Think that's real gold?" I asked.

"This goes to the executive level."

"I can read." I pointed to the sign.

"I was beginning to wonder," he muttered.

My eyes narrowed, and I shoved his hand away and hit the button for my ride.

"You cannot go up there without an appointment."

"I have one."

He gave me a withering stare. "Name."

"Nate Roth. To see Rolland Solberg."

The man seemed surprised, then spoke into some kind of phone/walkie talkie. A second later, his eyes slid to mine, still surprised. "Identification, please."

I fished it out and handed it over. "I was having a good hair day in this pic."

The man rolled his eyes, glanced at it, then cleared his throat. The elevator opened. "You may go."

"Dilly, dilly," I said in my best Brit accent. I waved at him as the doors closed between us.

The cart chimed when I arrived on the executive level, and I emerged into a small hallway with an intricate tile medallion on the floor. Ahead of me, out into the main room, a sparkling crystal chandelier hung from the ceiling. I couldn't help but wonder who they paid to clean that.

*Oomph.* I knocked into something and bounced back. Something else hit the floor with a thud, and lighter, scattering sounds filled my ears.

There was a loud gasp. "Watch it!" a woman practically shrieked.

"Careful," I told her. "You screech any louder and that light fixture's gonna crack."

Her dark eyes rounded so wide I was worried I might see her brain. "Did you just nearly run me over and then insult me?" She glanced down at her bag, which had toppled onto the floor and spilled out like twelve pounds worth of crap.

"Are you moving?" I asked, bending down to pick it up.

"Here, Ms. Boone, let us help you," said a bulky man in a dark jacket and jeans, appearing at her side.

"I got it," I said, waving him back. My hand closed around a metal thing with handles. "Is this a torture device?"

"Give me that!" She snatched it out of my hand and dropped down beside me to grab the bag and shove it inside.

"Ms. Boone—"

"I got it, Mac. Thank you," she said.

I grabbed a glitter-saturated notebook with the word *Sparkle* on the cover and sat back. "I've always wanted to know what girls write in their diaries," I quipped and started to crack it open.

She gasped and lunged at me. I was expecting it, so I jolted backward, holding the book out of reach. We both went down right there on the lobby floor, my body under hers.

"Don't you dare read that," she gasped out, wiggling up my body and reaching for the notebook I was holding over my head.

All her squirming was making me forget about the book. She smelled nice. Light and fresh… with a hint of fruit.

Sort of like an upscale version of Fruity Pebbles.

Did I mention Fruity Pebbles is my favorite?

I was so distracted that she ripped the book out of my hand and made a triumphant sound. "Ha!"

I grabbed her by the waist and rolled, pinning her beneath me.

"Hey!"

"You smell like my favorite cereal," I told her.

Her eyes widened. "Mac!"

I was hauled off her in seconds, my hands restrained behind my back as Mac towed me backward. She scurried to her feet, pulling down her cute little skirt. It was kinda flouncy; it floated out around her hips like a giant red ruffle.

Her top was hot-pink lace and her sneakers weren't actually sneakers, but heels.

Aerie Boone was hot. Way hotter in person than in any tabloid.

She bent to pick up the rest of her scattered stuff.

I started to move forward to help her, but Mac tightened his hold. I glanced over my shoulder at him. "You can let go now."

"I'll let go when security gets here."

"If you mean that British guy that's in charge of the elevator, he's not going to be much help."

Mac's lips turned upward as he fought a smile.

"Just let him go," Aerie said. "Clearly, he's a moron."

Mac released me, and I bent to pick up a lipstick and a roll of Lifesavers near my feet.

"How did you even get up here?" she asked, flustered.

I opened up the candy and pulled out a green one. I made a face and offered it to her. "I prefer red."

She stared at me, dumbfounded. I shrugged and stuck the Lifesaver in my pocket, then fished out the red one that had been beneath it. After popping it in my mouth, I folded the end and handed it to her along with the lipstick.

She took the items. "You just ate my candy."

I grinned.

Becca turned the corner at that moment and spotted us. "What's going on here?"

"She dropped all her stuff," I explained.

"I dropped my stuff because you weren't watching where you were going," Aerie snapped.

"Maybe you're the one who ran into me," I pointed out.

She gasped, surprised I would suggest such a thing.

"We're going to be late," Mac announced.

Aerie tucked the handle of her bag in the crook of her arm and spun away. I watched her go, that red skirt bouncing with every step.

Becca cleared her throat. "Pissing off the woman you're supposed to work with is not a smart idea."

"I didn't do anything," I answered.

Ten's manager made a sound. "You don't argue with girls like that."

"Girls like what?" I asked.

"Girls with money and power."

I cocked my head to the side. "You talk about Ten like that when he's not around?"

Her eyes widened a fraction. "What?"

I held her eyes, my stare steady. "You do know that girls like that, and men like Ten—hell, any celebrity or artist—they're just like everyone else, right? They're people. Maybe they wouldn't have chips on their shoulders if people *like you* didn't talk about them or to them that way."

Becca opened her mouth, then closed it, then opened it again. I could tell she was surprised. Surprised I'd opened my mouth and nothing stupid or benign came out. Surprised I didn't make a wisecrack or buckle under her she-devil attitude.

I might be a goofball, but that wasn't all I was.

"We need to get in there." She gestured ahead.

"Lead the way."

On the way to Rolland's office, we passed by his personal assistant who motioned us forward. "He's expecting you."

"Thank you," Becca replied and kept walking.

Before she could pull open the large wooden door, I caught her hand. "I'm assuming they don't know you're here digging for info for Time Track?"

Her gaze sharpened. "I'm a talent manager. I don't work for any certain label or company."

"Except the one who employs your highest-paid client. And the one who offered you a fat check for intel."

"That would be unethical." She countered.

I smiled. "Don't worry. I won't tell."

"You're a lot smarter than you let on."

I pulled open the door and motioned for her to go ahead.

# Six

## *Aerie*

I did not want to be here.

At all.

I tried to get out of it.

When a major record label calls your manager for a meeting—and that label happens to be the one spreading rumors about you signing with them—there isn't a "getting out of it" option.

At least my manager was here. And my security.

Frankly, I'd be glad if the janitor were in the meeting with me. So long as I wasn't alone with Will.

He scared me.

For lots of reasons I didn't care to think about right then. Or like ever.

There wasn't a "getting out of it" option for that either.

My manager was waiting outside Rolland's office when I walked up. "Aerie," he said, standing from the chair he was in.

"Seth," I said, leaning in to kiss his cheek. "Do you have any idea what this is about?"

"Judging from the rumors all over the papers…"

"Which rumors?" I said, sarcastic.

He barely blinked at the remark, then carried on. "I'm thinking they're going to come at you with a contract and a hell of a lot of money to dump Time Track and sign with them."

I put my hands on my hips. "I can't just dump my record label. I have a contract."

"You can go in now," Rolland's assistant said, approaching.

Seth nodded and started forward. I grabbed his arm, and he turned back. "Just to be clear. I am not changing labels. And the *marriage* to Will isn't valid. My lawyers are working on the annulment as we speak."

"My office has been getting a lot of calls," he murmured.

"He's going to try and use this marriage as a way to get me signed here. I won't do it."

Seth frowned, nodding slowly. "Gotcha."

I knew he wanted to ask for details about my sham of a marriage. Everyone wanted details. So far, I'd been putting it all off. Avoiding it. I didn't want to tell anyone anything. I just wanted out.

I just wanted to stop feeling ashamed.

The door to Rolland's office opened, and a man in his fifties stood dressed a pair of dark dress pants, sneakers, a white V-neck T-shirt, and an open blazer.

His hair was an ashy blond, the kind I was sure he got from a bottle. The grayer he got, the more silvery-blond his hair became. It worked on him, though, giving him an on-trend look suitable for the head of a record label.

"Ah, good. You're here."

"Mr. Solberg." Seth went forward and shook his hand with gusto.

"Good to see you, Seth," the man returned. He called everyone by their first name, but few called him by his (to his face, anyway).

"There's my beautiful daughter-in-law," he said when he saw me, holding out his arms.

My skin crawled. His affection for me was as fake as his hair. As I moved closer, I braced for the hug and tried not to recoil from the wiry-looking chest hair sticking out from the edge of his too-low V-neck.

"Lovely to see you, Mr. Solberg." I lied.

He began to shut the door before my two guards could enter, and I nearly panicked. "They're with me," I said quickly.

"You'll be perfectly safe in my office."

I was saved from having to argue because Mac and Ben slipped into the room while Rolland was tsking at me. When he turned back to, no doubt, order them away, the pair were already positioned at the back of the room, folded hands in front of them, and staring ahead.

"Dad, is she here?" The familiar voice on the other side of the threshold made my stomach lurch.

Will.

"Of course, son," Rolland replied and stepped aside so Will could enter.

"My beautiful wife," he announced, sweeping over to me. His palm slid around my waist, and he leaned in for a kiss. I turned my head so his mouth grazed my cheek. "I prefer you in blue," he whispered in my ear.

I drew back, meeting his gaze. "That's why I wore pink."

"I'm intrigued," Seth announced, drawing everyone's attention. "What is this meeting all about?"

"Surely it's not that much of a mystery, what with the recent rumors and the marriage of my son to your biggest client," Rolland retorted, stepping around his huge walnut desk and taking a seat.

"I know you are aware of her current contract." Seth slid a glance at me.

"A contract that is up for renewal."

I gasped. "How do you know that?" I swung around on Seth and shot daggers out of my eyes. For real, if looks could kill, he'd be a dead man on this carpet.

"I would never divulge private contract information." He assured me.

"It doesn't matter how I found out. I have the information. And since you are recently wed to my son, it seems only natural that you would change labels and join us here."

I arched a brow at him. "You do know I'm getting an annulment?"

"Now why on earth would you want to go and do something like that?" he puzzled.

Like he didn't know. Yeah right. I was sure he knew every last detail of Will's life, right down to the color of the boxers he wore today.

"I like my label just fine. But thank you for the offer." I stood from the couch, ready to leave.

Will caught my hand, lacing our fingers as if we were an actual couple, then gave me a warning squeeze. I tried to tug free, but his grip only tightened.

"I'm sure you are very happy with them." Rolland went on. "But what are you going to do when they don't offer you a renewal?"

My head whipped around. "What?"

"I know you are well aware of your… reputation in the press as of late."

I bristled. "Most of which is untrue."

"Yes, well, unfortunately for you, the general public doesn't know that. Record sales and downloads prove it. There's been quite a decline in the past six months."

I glanced at Seth. He looked like a deer caught in a pair of headlights. He shot up from his seat as well. "I have no idea where you are getting this information, but it is unequivocally false."

Rolland turned his full, direct gaze to my manager. "Don't insult me by lying."

The room swam a little in front of me. The shapes and people started to blur together and look like big lumps.

Will's previous words echoed through the back of my mind. *When I'm done with you, all you'll have left is me.*

The office door opened with a great whoosh. I swear with it, oxygen—which had sorely been lacking—flooded the room. I sucked in a deep breath and blinked my vision back into focus.

"Becca," Rolland said abrupt. "I assume you brought your client?"

The woman in a fierce-looking pantsuit stepped farther into the room, and then right behind her followed her "client."

"You," I intoned, zeroing in on the red-haired, green-eyed troublemaker.

"You know him?" Will demanded.

"We go way back," the guy from the hallway replied.

Will gave my hand an impatient squeeze.

I slid him a glance. "We met out in the hall."

"Good, then you've already been introduced." Rolland cut in.

"Not really," I said, but he ignored me.

"I like the work you've done recently. You have a knack for being on trend yet somehow original," Rolland said, gesturing for the candy stealer to take a seat.

"It's the red hair. Gives me an edge," he replied, not missing a beat.

"Funny," Rolland said in a way that guaranteed he was *not* amused. "I want you to work with Aerie, our newest country music sensation. Write her a song or two that will be a surefire hit. I want this song to get stuck in the head of every person who hears it."

"What!" I interjected, shocked.

"I want it done ASAP. Get it written. We'll move into production and have everything ready to go this summer."

"I haven't agreed to anything," I demanded. "I'm staying with Time Track."

"And when that's not an option?"

"With all due respect, I have heard no indication that Aerie's contract will not be renewed." Seth put in.

I nodded, adamant.

"This is all very premature," Seth added.

"It's business," Rolland barked. "If you don't understand that, then what the hell are you in this office for?"

"Should I just come back later?" the guy with red hair wondered aloud.

I stifled a sudden laugh that bubbled up inside me. I was going delusional. Guy whose name I didn't know turned his green-eyed stare on me, and I was hit with the same zing I'd felt (and ignored) before when I'd fallen on top of him and he'd palmed the sides of my waist.

For some reason, I felt a little less suffocated, a little less on the verge of a massive panic attack, as I looked at him. He was dressed totally unprofessionally in a pair of green board shorts and a T-shirt with a palm tree on the chest. He told me I smelled like cereal.

He was weird.

Yet his eyes looked like uncut emeralds and his hair like the dying ember of a fire, which to me was the strongest part of a flame. It was the part that went out last. The part that hung on, stayed hot the longest, until the fire inexplicably burned out.

"I'll give you half a million dollars to get me a hit song in two weeks." Rolland dropped the words like a bomb.

"What?" everyone in the room except Will and his father exclaimed.

I felt the loss of the calm I'd found when my eyes left the redhead. When he was no longer focused on me.

"Did you just offer me five hundred G's?" emerald eyes asked.

"Do you take it or not?" Rolland demanded.

Becca stepped up beside emerald eyes and put a restraining hand on his chest. "You know my client can't verbally agree to anything. I'll need to see it in writing, with a signature attached. And there better be something in there regarding royalties."

Will pulled out a stack of papers from the folder he had tucked under his arm and extended them toward Becca. "The contract."

Becca flipped through it while he leaned over her shoulder and watched.

Seth cleared his throat. "Even if he signs that, Aerie isn't obligated to any of this."

"I won't do it," I announced, on the edge of hysteria. "I'm not signing with Solberg and I'm not writing a song for them!"

"Aerie," Will said, a note of warning in his voice.

"We're done here." I concluded and stormed toward the door. "Seth! Let's go."

Mac had the door open when I got there, and I shot him a grateful look as I strode past.

"We aren't done here!" Will trilled from behind.

"Let her go, son," Rolland interjected.

*Yeah. Let me go.*

Once the door was closed and my team was out in the hall, I spun toward Seth. "What the hell was that?" I hissed. "How did he know so much about my contract and sales?"

"I don't know." He frowned. "He must have someone over at TT that he pays for information."

"Is my future at my label on solid ground?" I could feel the ground shifting and shaking beneath me.

"I—" Seth opened his mouth, but the office door opened and closed again. This time it was Becca and her client.

On impulse, I marched across the tile, my Converse heels clapping. "Don't waste your time signing that useless piece of paper," I told him. "It's not going to happen."

I expected him to come back with something sharp. Some kind of rebuttal that would make my blood boil more.

He didn't.

Instead, he gave me a lopsided smile and stuck his hand between us. "I'm Nate."

My belly dipped a little.

He shook his still-waiting hand around, reminding me it was there. I smacked it away. "I'm not working with you, Nate."

Damn. I liked the way that sounded on my lips.

The color of his eyes deepened a shade, reminding me of a secret forest of thick moss. My goodness, what was with me? Every time I looked at him, I thought of moss, or flame embers… calmness washing over me.

Maybe I needed to go to the doctor.

Becca stepped up to our little group. She was still holding the copy of Nate's contract.

Funny how his contract somehow signaled the end of the world as I knew it.

Becca leaned in and whispered, "My office. Now."

# seven

## *Nate*

Five hundred grand.

For one song.

Can you hear the Nate Train whistle blowing? I sure as hell could.

Ten was at the curb, you know, in his no-parking zone parking spot.

I slid into the buttery soft leather seat and smiled. "A guy could get used to riding in style like this."

"I take it the meeting went well?" Ten mused, pulling out into L.A. traffic.

"Dude, Solberg offered me five hundred G's to write that song."

Ten's eyes left the road to gape at me, then went back to the windshield. "Are you shitting me?"

"Nope."

"That's a lot of cash up front, man. Songwriters can make some serious bank, but for a rookie and for only one song?" He whistled. "What about royalties?"

"Not sure. Becca seemed adamant they be in the contract."

Ten seemed surprised. "You didn't sign?"

"No. It was a bunch of drama up in there. Like *Real Housewives* shit, but with men. Aerie seemed kinda blindsided, and not in a good way. She flat out refused to do the song or sign with them. She stormed out with her entourage. Then Becca went all Darth Vader in the hallway." I lowered my voice to mock Becca. "*My office. Now.*"

"You're supposed to go to Becca's office?"

"I didn't already say that?"

His curse filled the interior, and he swerved abruptly into the nearby lane and took the exit just before we passed. "What's Becca want to meet for? To go over the contract?"

"I don't think so, considering Aerie and her manager are supposed to be there, too."

"All this drama is taking time that I could be spending with my girl. In bed," Ten growled.

"Just drop me off and go home. I'll catch a cab back to your place."

Violet was totally onboard with Ten's career, but it wasn't her favorite thing about him. She usually stayed away from all business stuff, unless she was at a concert or some event.

He made a noise. "I'm coming in. I want to know what the hell is going on."

I shrugged and settled back into the seat. My mind instantly turned to Aerie, her red skirt and long legs. I liked pressing her buttons. It seemed pretty easy to do. She definitely was uptight, standoffish, and probably hella high maintenance.

There was something else, though, something beyond how it felt to have her wiggling around on top of me. I wasn't exactly sure what it was about her, but I anticipated seeing her again. I wanted to know if the air would crackle, if my body automatically rotated toward her when she walked into a room.

A few minutes later, Ten turned into a parking garage and then into a spot with his name on it.

"So Aerie seemed pretty pissed about the offer?" he asked as we walked through the garage.

"Oh yeah, I got the feeling there was a lot more going on than I realized."

"She has a rep for being a handful."

A sour flavor coated my tongue. Abruptly, I stopped walking, at the same time grabbing Ten by the shoulder, jerking him to a halt, too. "You actually putting stock in a bunch of shit the media's saying about her?"

His eyes rounded and he held up one hand, surrendering. "Who peed in your Fruity Pebbles?"

I felt my eyes narrow. "Seriously, man. You of all people know it isn't always what it seems."

"I do know." He agreed. "I wasn't insulting her. I was just saying the rumor mill has been working overtime lately."

"You know her?" I started walking again. I felt my cousin's eyes, but I didn't bother to look at him.

"I've met her a few times."

"And?"

"Why you want to know about Aerie Boone?"

I pushed a hand through my hair. "'Cause I'm supposed to work with her."

"You sure that's all it is?" Ten pressed.

"What else would there be?" I countered.

"She's pretty hot,"

I spun and shoved him. His back hit the wall of the elevator we'd just boarded. We stared at each other for long moments, neither saying a word.

"So that's how it is," Ten finally said.

"You shouldn't be looking at other women. Not when you've got Vi."

A low growl rumbled in his throat. He hated when I called her Vi. That was his nickname for her and no one else's. I knew it.

I said it on purpose.

I waited for him to get pissed and issue some warning for suggesting he was anything other than one million percent faithful to his girl.

He did issue a warning. But it wasn't about Violet.

"All I'm saying is be careful. I don't think Aerie's a bad person, but fame does something to you. And all those stories and rumors I mentioned? I know firsthand that the avalanche of it all started with a little snow."

"What the fuck does that mean?" I asked.

"A lot of the shit in the tabloids about me? It all started with a grain of truth. She's not going to be any different."

I didn't answer, and we rode the rest of the way in silence.

Aerie was already in Becca's office when we arrived, her two security guards outside the door. I thought it was very interesting that they weren't *inside* the office, like back at Solberg.

I nodded to Mac, the one who'd yanked me off her earlier, and went ahead of Ten into the office.

Everyone looked up when we walked in.

I learned something.

My body did in fact rotate toward Aerie. My eyes went right to her, my upper body angled so my chest was open to the space between us.

The first thing about her I noted was the tightness in her shoulders. The way they were pulled up toward her ears. She was gonna have a hella sore neck later if she kept holding herself like that.

Almost the instant we walked in, she jolted in her seat, teetering on the edge as she spun around. Our eyes collided, and the tension in her shoulders went down.

Not a lot, but enough that I noticed.

I felt.

I winked at her. For no other reason than to acknowledge her presence, to somehow show that she was the first person I sought out in this room.

Not the deal. Not the money.

Her.

I had no idea why that suddenly seemed so important. No girl had ever been before.

There'd been tons of them, too. Tons. Women everywhere.

It's true.

Fine. It's not true.

Truth was women thought I was a giant goof.

Maybe I was. But I didn't want to be just that to her.

Aerie's cheeks flushed a little, and she rolled her eyes. But then she glanced back at me, and the tiniest of smiles curved her lips.

"What took so long?" Becca admonished.

"My driver was slow," I told her and hitched my thumb toward Ten as he shut the door.

"Ten! I didn't know you were coming," Becca exclaimed.

"Like I wouldn't sit in on my cousin's deal."

"Cousin?" Aerie wondered.

"We're related," I told her, motioning between me and Ten. "He's totally jealous I got the good looks in the family."

"How ya doing, Aerie?" Ten said, nodding, then dropping onto a nearby black leather couch.

"You know how it is," she said, and I sensed with that reply, she told him a lot more than the rest of us.

"That I do."

"You're Nate Roth?" Aerie's agent, Seth, asked, recognition coming over him. "The one who wrote some songs for Ten and another for an artist over at KJ Studios."

I nodded. The extra song I'd sold was actually one I'd written for Ten, but it didn't fit with the rest of the album. But the producer liked it enough that he sent it over to another artist, who liked it, too.

Bam. Sold.

"So you got the job because of who you're related to," Aerie quipped, turning back in her seat.

"Yeah, but I'll keep getting jobs because I'm good at what I do." I countered.

"This is fun and all," Becca said in a voice that pretty much proved this wasn't any fun. "But we have actual business to discuss. And I'd rather not have an office full of sniveling children when the head of TT walks in here."

"Byron Ryan's coming here?" Ten perked up.

"I told you. We have business," Becca snapped. "Now let's all get on the same page before it happens."

Quickly, Becca pointed to me. "Nate, meet Aerie Boone, mega country star. You two will be working together on a song. If all goes well, maybe more."

"I haven't agreed to anything," Aerie snapped.

I'd been on my way over to Aerie to, you know, be formally introduced, when she glanced over her shoulder and spoke with a look and a tone meant to freeze me in place.

I wasn't the kind of guy to get the hint very easily, so I kept walking. Without hesitation, I laid my palms on her overly tense shoulders and gently pushed them down, beginning to knead the stony muscles. "You will," I intoned as I used my thumbs to work a knot in her shoulder.

She lifted her hand to smack me away, and I increased the pressure. She melted back into the chair and dropped her hand.

Did I mention I was good with my hands?

Behind me, the office door sprang open again, and Byron Ryan strode in. He was a tall, wide man with dark, smooth skin and close-cropped hair. He was dressed in a pair of dark jeans and a tucked-in dress shirt in a silvery shade. The sleeves were rolled up to his elbows, and there was a silver Rolex around his wrist.

Byron was a cool guy. I'd met him once before when I was working with Ten.

I stepped back from Aerie and offered my hand as he entered.

"Good to see you again, Mr. Roth," he greeted and accepted the shake.

I turned and gave Aerie a look as if to say, *See, I'm legit, and the head of your label knows my name.*

She wasn't looking at me. Instead, she was looking at him and then away, as if she were nervous.

"Ten!" Byron said and grinned a blinding white smile. "Didn't expect to see you, man."

"Hey, B. Had to come out to support my fam."

"How's your girl? She in L.A.?"

Ten smiled at the mention of Violet. "Yep, flew out with Nate."

"Sweet. Tell her I said hi. I like that girl."

"Will do."

After he greeted Seth and Becca, he turned to Aerie. "Quite the mess we got here, Ms. Boone."

"I know."

He shifted his gaze to Becca. "Fill me in."

"Little Miss Country here went and got herself married to Will Solberg, and now Rolland thinks he has the rights to her career. Basically, he brought in Nate, who recently just had a number-one hit with Ten." She motioned to Ten. "Because you know Rolland. If Time Track has it, then he wants it, too."

Byron made a sound and motioned for Becca to continue.

I thought it was interesting how Aerie, who seemed to be the loud, outspoken type, was sitting here allowing Becca to call her Little Miss Country. If anything, she appeared subdued.

"He seems to think he can poach your top-selling country artist, match her up with your newly discovered songwriter, and pair them together for the song of the summer."

Byron turned to Aerie and her manager. "And where do you stand in all this?"

Seth cleared his throat. "I'd heard the rumors up until today, but I thought it was just tabloid gossip. I had no idea Solberg was actually trying to sign Aerie. He never reached out with a contract or anything until today."

"Aerie?"

She lifted her chin, squaring her shoulders. "Will mentioned it to me, and I told him no. I do not want to sign with Solberg." Her eyes slid to me. "And I had no idea they called in a songwriter."

Byron seemed skeptical. "Why would they do that if you were clear with your refusal? Don't you talk to your husband?"

She shot up out of her chair. Anger and something else vibrated off her. "He is *not* my husband! I'm getting an annulment."

Byron pressed. "Annulments happen fast. You've been married a couple weeks."

Her face tightened and her shoulders inched their way back up toward her ears. "He's fighting it."

"Why?" Byron asked, bold. He didn't even seem to feel bad about it.

"I'd rather not talk about my personal life in front of people I don't know."

I felt my eyes narrow, all my attention condensed only on her. She was afraid of him. Of Will. She tried to hide it, and she did a good job.

But I knew.

"Seth needs to be privy to everything that's happening, like it or not. He's your manager, and as such, it's his job to issue statements, etcetera, on your behalf. It keeps things like this from happening."

"I don't know how any of this happened," she muttered and sank back into the chair. The edge of her skirt draped over the side, and I wanted to go over and tuck it beneath her.

This girl was fierier than me, and I had red hair. Still, she incited in me a need to shelter. A need to shield and protect. It wasn't a feeling I was very familiar with. At most, I'd only ever felt it with Violet, in a brotherly way. This? There was nothing brotherly about it at all.

"Rolland knew about her slipping sales," Seth interjected. Aerie rubbed a hand across her forehead. "He also knows her contract with your label is up for renewal."

"And he thinks she's ripe for the picking," Byron mused.

"Do you have plans to not renew my contract?" Aerie said abruptly.

"This is not a contract meeting." Byron countered smoothly.

She stood, drawing up to her full height, which couldn't have been more than five feet five (without heels). After she brushed the glossy dark strands of hair away from her face, she regarded Byron as though he wasn't the one in charge in this room.

"With all due respect, why are we here? I haven't put out an album for a year, no new one is in development, and the press has literally been eating me alive for at least six months. My last live appearance, I got hit with rumors of lip-syncing. Everyone thinks I'm jealous of Becky Lane, and we have a fierce rival, something she's happy to *not* deny.

"Then there's Will… and this farce of a marriage. I'm done being controlled by a bunch of men. Rolland and Will act like I'm some toy they just purchased, and you called us in here for what? To belittle me before booting me off the label? I'm tired. I'm done. If you're firing me, I'd rather know now than in a few months."

You could have heard a pin drop when she was done. Everyone stared, sort of in shock, which, if you asked me, was probably a hard thing to do. Shutting up the egos in this room was practically impossible.

I glanced at Ten, and he lifted an eyebrow at me. Then he glanced at Aerie, and a look of recognition slammed onto his face. She was falling apart, heading down the same path he did.

In the stillness her words left behind, I pushed off the wall and went over to her chair, flipped open her bag, and stuck my hand in.

She glanced around at me, her hands hitting her hips. "What are you doing?"

"Looking for your Lifesavers. I figure I should at least get something out of this meeting, because clearly, I'm not going to be getting a job."

She made a rude sound and looked at Ten. "Is he seriously always like this?"

"Pretty much," Ten remarked. "Sometimes he's worse."

Aerie came forward and smacked my arm so I would stop digging. "It is so rude to just go rooting around in someone else's private bag."

"I want some candy."

She pulled out the roll of Lifesavers in two seconds flat. Like she knew exactly where everything was in that black hole of a bag.

"Here." She handed it over. "And do not throw the green ones back in my bag. Eat them."

How did she know I was going to do that? "Green ones are gross."

She snatched the candy back. "Do you want this?"

I sighed, forlorn. "Fine. I'll eat the green ones, too."

Her lips tugged upward, the darkness of her eyes sparking with humor.

It was a far better look on her than the one she'd been wearing just moments ago.

She watched me unwrap the candy and pop one in my mouth. I grinned, holding it between my teeth. "Thanks."

The silence in the room pressed in. I glanced up. Everyone was staring at us.

"Candy anyone?" I offered.

Ten was looking at me like I was insane. I shrugged.

"I'm not dropping you," Byron said, pursing his lips. His eyes went back and forth between us, a shrewd glint coming into them.

"You're not?" Aerie asked, surprised.

He chuckled, tucking his hands into the pockets of his jeans. "No. That would be bad business, and I'm not in the habit."

"But my sales are down."

"As you pointed out, you haven't had any new music for a year. A decline in sales is natural at this point. That's partly the label's fault. We should have had you in the studio already. At least had a couple singles out."

"You seriously want to keep me with all the bad press going around?"

Byron laughed. "Any press is good press. You should know that. It actually works to our advantage that you've been fairly quiet on your personal life. We can use that as a way to promote the new album. *Everything Aerie has to say is in the music.*"

"It's good marketing," Becca mused. "The press will eat it up. Dissect every song, every line, and try to speculate who it's about."

"You want me to use my personal life to sell records?" Aerie wondered.

"It works." Ten cut in.

I nodded sagely and popped another Lifesaver in my mouth.

Byron pointed at Ten and nodded. "It does. We can apply the same style of marketing we used for Ten's to your next album. Go underground for a while, stay out of the press, work on some new music. An entire album. By the time we start releasing some promo, people will be frothing at the mouth."

"I'm not going to be able to stay out of the press. Will is going to make it impossible."

Byron shrugged. "Let him say what he will. Let the media report what they will. You give no comment. Perhaps get out of town. You have a house that isn't in L.A., right?"

"I could go home."

Oh, the wistfulness in her tone caught me like a right hook in the gut.

Seth cleared his throat. "I'm assuming this is all going to be put in writing. With a number attached to it."

Byron waved his hand. "Of course. I'll have something to you by the end of the day." He walked over to stand directly in front of Aerie, putting his hands on her shoulders. "You. You need to sit down with Seth and let him know where you'll be and the details you don't seem to want to give anyone."

She hesitated.

"What is it?" he asked.

She ducked her head for a moment, then looked back up at him. "Will and his father… they aren't going to let this go. Will can be very… demanding."

"That means he's a giant dick," I put in.

Aerie burst out laughing, then slapped her hand over her mouth.

"You leave Rolland and his son to me." Byron patted her on the shoulder. "They'll drop the idea you're signing with Solberg the second we announce you've resigned and are going underground to work on the new album."

Aerie clasped her hands in front of her and nodded once. I think I was the only one who noticed the way her fingers trembled.

There was more to this. So much more.

Byron turned to me. "How much did Solberg offer you to write for him?"

"Five hundred grand."

Byron's eyes widened, and he glanced at Becca.

"It's true." She held up the contract she'd been given.

"He must really want this," he mused.

"Nate's good at what he does," Ten put in.

"I'll give you five hundred grand to help Aerie write her new album. Then I'll pay you another five hundred once the album is wrapped."

"What?" she shrieked.

I nearly choked on the Lifesaver. "What?" I croaked. "An entire album?"

"Yeah. That'll teach Rolland to try and poach my artists." Then he pointed at me. "But you can't sign any deals with Solberg."

I shrugged. I didn't like that guy anyway.

"I thought I was supposed to go underground to work," Aerie rushed to say.

"You are."

"But I was going to go home. I can't do that if I have to work with him."

"Take him home with you."

Aerie gasped. "I don't even know him!"

"I'm a peach." I assured her.

"Absolutely not! No."

Byron pinned her with a stare. "You wanted to know if I was going to drop you. I made the decision. This is it. These are the conditions. Make it work."

With that, he checked the fancy watch on his wrist and strode from the room.

# eight

## *Aerie*

What was worse: being alone or being surrounded by people who were paid to be there?

Everything I was, everything I had—it was all wrapped up in Aerie Boone the star, the musician. It was as if who I was before I was famous was completely gone. Everything I was came down to my music career. Without it, I would be completely alone.

Will definitely helped isolate me further. I could blame him for a lot of this. The reality, though? I was the biggest one at fault. I made a mess of everything.

A mess I didn't even know how to clean up.

All I knew was exhaustion. I was tired and afraid. I was a strong woman, but even the strong could become weak.

After Byron dropped his little bomb and left, I followed suit. I couldn't sit there any longer. I had to think. To really ask myself what it was I wanted.

How bad did I really want my career?

That was the question.

The answer?

I wanted to go home. To be away from Will, Los Angeles, and all the tabloid bullshit.

I loved my job, though. Creating music and watching a crowd light up when I performed. Right now, I had a unique opportunity to go home and work on some new music. I could have both.

There was a catch, though. Wasn't there always?

Nate Roth.

Actually, he wasn't a catch. He was a freaking headache. A headache that would likely turn into a raging migraine. The fact that Byron ordered me to work with him, knowing it was what Solberg wanted, put me in a *very* awkward position. As if it hadn't been precarious enough to start.

I was caught in the middle of a power struggle between two giant music producers. Just a pawn on their chessboard but feeling more like the spark about to start a fire.

On one hand, I was so relieved Byron wasn't going to drop me from his label. On the other, this turn of events was going to make Will even angrier. He would hold even tighter to our sham of a "marriage," lording it over my head as punishment. As payment for a debt.

A debt he would never let me repay, because with Will, it didn't matter how many payments I made. The balance never seemed to go down.

And here I was. Damned if I did. Damned if I didn't.

I sat on my white sofa, not even seeing the million-dollar view out the enormous windows, as I considered my options. Did I really have any?

It felt like I didn't.

Even if I wanted to quit music, disappear into the unknown, I couldn't.

He would never let me. And I'd given my word.

How long did a verbal agreement last? A promise?

When did it turn into emotional blackmail? Was emotional blackmail even a thing?

I'd been so stupid in the past. Stupid and naive. I'd grown up since then. Unfortunately, the mistakes of my past still kept me from my future.

*I'd still do the same thing today.* I guess that was something. Right?

The cushion beside me vibrated, and I glanced down at the screen and groaned.

"Seth," I said, answering the call. "Didn't you see enough of me this morning?"

"It's always a pleasure, Aerie." His reply was smooth. "I'm calling because I have the contract from Time Track."

"Already?" I practically squeaked. My goodness, we'd just met this morning.

"I've been going over it since it came through. Everything is in order. Byron was very generous."

"How generous?"

"Two million up front. Better-than-average royalties and a clause that states the majority of the album will be produced in the studio of your choice, which we are all assuming is your place."

I sat back, almost stunned. "Seriously?"

"You shouldn't be surprised. Your first album went platinum. You were nominated for country artist of the year."

"I lost." I reminded him.

"You won't next year."

"Does it say anything in there about Nate?" I asked, mulling over all this information.

"There is a stipulation that you work with him for the songwriting. Byron is determined to use Rolland's idea against him."

I sighed. "It's so juvenile."

"It's business. That's why Byron's on top."

I didn't say anything because, deep down, I knew Seth was right. The music industry was nothing if not cutthroat.

"Look, Aerie. I know you don't want to work with him. I know Will is putting the screws to you, and honestly, this is just going to piss him off more. But it's a good deal—hell, a great one. You're not going to get better."

"I know." I sighed. "Do you think if I signed it, Byron would let me have some time at my place to myself? You know, before I start work on the new album."

"I can ask."

I hesitated a moment longer, then relented. "Fine. Send the contract over to my lawyer so he can go over it. If he says everything is in order, and once I read it, I'll sign."

"Awesome!" Seth exclaimed, a smile in his voice.

I couldn't blame the guy for being happy. He was getting a good payday off this.

"I'll forward you a copy of it now. Go ahead and read through it tonight. Then when you talk to your lawyer, he can answer any questions you have."

"Sounds good."

"Hey, Aerie?" Seth said.

"Yeah?"

"Try to sound a little excited, huh? You just scored a deal that's going to make you millions of dollars."

*Money isn't everything.*

*But having it means you can take care of yourself.*

I smiled. "I am happy. Thank you for working on this and for being so patient with all the tabloid rumors lately. I know your phone has probably been ringing nonstop."

"I changed the number," he quipped.

I laughed.

He cleared his throat. "Speaking of, I can't keep saying no comment forever. The speculation about you and Will is huge. One minute, it's being reported you're joining Solberg, and the next, the press has pics of you out and about without your wedding ring."

"As soon as my signature is dry on the contract with Time Track, I'll release a statement."

"Any idea on what the statement might entail?"

"Seth," I drawled. "Even you are curious about my personal life?"

"I gotta tell you, Ms. Boone. The past few meetings I've had with you have gotten me quite intrigued."

"I should have kept you in the loop." I admonished myself, lifting a strand of hair and twisting it around my finger.

"Probably. But I understand."

"The truth is I don't remember marrying Will. I woke up with a ring on my finger one morning, and ever since then, I've been horrified as hell. I don't want to be married to him. He asked me months before, and I turned him down flat. My lawyers are working on an annulment. Have been since that day. But he's stalling them. Pushing back."

"Will definitely isn't going to want to let go of anything that could make him more money," Seth mused.

"I'm not a paycheck," I snapped. "I'm a person."

He cleared his throat. "Of course. I won't say a word to the press until you're ready to release a statement. Until then, read the contract."

Some of my anger drained away, but not enough to make me apologize. "Thank you, Seth."

"I'll call you tomorrow."

Once we hung up, I shut off all the lights in the main room and locked myself in the bathroom for a long, hot bath.

The difference between my reaction to this contract and the euphoria I felt when I signed my first one was remarkably different.

It wasn't the only thing different, though. Everything else was, too.

Loud, obnoxious pounding woke me. I shot up from my pillows as if I were being attacked. Blinking back the sleep, my heart raced as I clicked on the bedside lamp and scurried out of bed.

The banging was definitely not a dream, and neither was the yelling of my name.

My stomach cramped as I ran in a circle at the foot of my bed, worrying about what to do.

"Aerie!" he yelled.

*Bang. Bang. Bang.*

Maybe if I ignored him, he would go away.

"I'll break this fucking door down!" he wailed.

I felt the blood drain from my face. *Or maybe he will indeed bust down the door and the neighbors will call the cops. What a nice headline that would make.* Not.

Peeling away from the circle I was making, I ran through the condo and to the front door. My bare feet slapped on the cold tile, and the silk of my pajama romper made me feel exposed and vulnerable.

The second the sound of throwing the locks echoed, Will stopped acting like an ass. I yanked open the door, only enough for me to look out at him and glare.

"It's the middle of the night!" I hissed.

He didn't seem to get the hint that I didn't want him to come in. His hand slapped against the white wood and shoved so hard I stumbled backward.

He strode in, his suit rumpled, jacket long ago removed. His tie was also missing, the sleeves of his dress shirt rolled up to his elbows. Will's hair was disheveled, his eyes dark and stormy. I watched with bated breath as he stalked into the room, kicking the door shut behind him.

"Did you think I wouldn't hear?" he rasped. Sometimes his voice sounded that way. Like he had a sore throat. Really, he didn't. He was just angry enough it vibrated his vocal chords.

"Hear what?" I asked, wrapping my arms over my chest. I really wished I wasn't standing here in silk pajamas.

He rushed close, shoving his finger in my face. "Don't you play stupid with me, you little bitch."

My mouth ran dry. Pushing his finger out of my face, I answered, "I told you I would not sign with Solberg."

"I thought we made it clear you didn't have a choice."

"I have a choice. You're never going to take choice from me ever again."

It happened fast.

One minute, I was standing there with my heart nearly thumping out of my chest, and the next…

I was on the ground.

He'd slapped me across the face. With an open palm. So hard it knocked me down.

My bare legs lay against the tile floor. The cold was sort of shocking, yet I was grateful for it. It kept me alert. My head drooped toward the floor and strands of hair fell like a dark curtain over my face, providing me with something to hide behind.

My hand shook as I reached up and felt my cheek. It was warm to the touch, the skin burning and tingling. I prayed to God there wasn't a mark.

Lowering my hand, lifting my head, I stared up at Will.

"Babe…" He began, a hint of regret in his voice.

I lost my shit.

"Don't call me that!" I screamed and shoved up off the floor. The thin strap of my outfit slid down over my shoulder, but I ignored it. "Don't you ever call me that again."

His eyes narrowed.

The sting in my cheek kept me from backing down.

"You will not sign that contract. You're my wife. And as such, you will do what I tell you to do."

"I already signed it." I lied. "The deal is done."

His hands balled into fists at his sides. I braced myself, going on high alert. That was the first time he'd ever hit me, and so help me God, it would be the last.

I couldn't believe I was married to this. *To him.*

*Why would I have done that?* Sure, we'd been together, but I would never have married him.

He knew that. I'd told him as much.

He'd been pissed that night, too.

"And the songwriter? He signed, too?" Will's hands flexed.

I swallowed. "Yes."

He lunged forward, and I retreated. I would have fallen, but he caught my arm and yanked me up. Will dragged me through the condo, into the living room. My eyes slid to the contract that was spread out on my dining room table, unsigned.

If he saw that…

"You have betrayed and humiliated me in every possible way," he said, shoving me away. I came up against the sofa and stood there, using it as a prop.

"First, you file for an annulment, wanting to erase the fact that we're married, that you've spent two years with me."

"One year." I corrected.

His jaw jumped. "*Two.*"

I nodded.

"Then you tell your label about the deal we got for you, our plans for your summer song, and let them poach it!" He fumed. "Let them poach our songwriter!"

"I didn't tell them." I defended myself. I should have just stood there and taken credit for it all. I wanted to. But I was afraid. "They already knew."

"Roth?" He seethed. "He went behind our backs and used our offer as leverage to get a better deal for himself."

"No, I don't—" I refuted. The thought that Will was directing any portion of his anger at Nate… My stomach cramped, and I nearly doubled over.

"Shut it!" he demanded, then paced over to the windows that looked out over L.A. It was beautiful. But right now? Not so much. Will stopped to look outside, clasped his hands behind his back, and went motionless. "After everything I've done for you…"

The cramps in my stomach were suddenly joined by a terrible, terrible ache in my heart.

"I appreciate everything you've done for me, Will. But enough is enough."

He turned, eyes stormy. "You owe me."

"I've paid ten times over," I said, quiet, automatically fingering my cheek.

"No." His voice was gentle. The distance between us closed until he was standing right in front of me, staring down.

I swear he was bipolar. Or had multiple personalities. Like Jekyll and Hyde. One minute he was angry and fuming; the next he was gentle and sweet.

He cupped my face. I turned away. He wouldn't let me go, though. I found myself in his arms, against his chest. He smelled like perfume, and it disgusted me.

Even married, he couldn't be faithful.

(Not that we were actually married. Kinda. You know what I mean.)

"This is what it's all been leading up to, babe," he said, stroking the back of my head. "Everything I've done for you. For us. To bring us here." He pulled me away from him, holding me out like a rag doll. "And you ruined it."

"Then just let me go. Clearly, I'm not what or who you want me to be. Focus your energy on some other up-and-coming star."

He made a tsking sound. "It doesn't work like that, Aerie. I'm invested in you. In us. We can still salvage this. We can still be the king and queen of music."

"I don't want to be a queen."

He laughed and let me go. Taking the opportunity, I moved away from him. "Well, your princess title is all but gone. It wouldn't take much to rip it away completely. And then who would you be, Aerie? No more crown, no more royalty."

I opened my mouth, but no words came out. Was there really any point in arguing with a man who didn't even listen?

He pushed a hand through his hair and chuckled. "Without me, babe, you'll be back where you started. You'll be nothing but a toad."

His words hurt just as much as his hand had. I marched past him, practically ran to the front door, and yanked it open wide.

"Get out. Get the hell out now, or I swear to God I will call the cops."

He walked at a painfully unhurried pace, then leaned down to whisper in my ear. "And who do you think the cops will believe? Will Solberg, prince of Solberg records, or Aerie Boone, *toad*."

Stubborn rage filled me. I refused to concede to his torture. I turned my head and met his stare. "I think they'll believe the handprint on my face."

Judging by the way his pallor went ghostly, I knew there was indeed a handprint.

He stalked out into the hallway. I slammed the door in his face, but it didn't latch. He hit it before it could, and the door bounced back open, forcing me to look at him some more.

"Sign the annulment papers, Will," I intoned. "If you don't, being a toad will look like a luxury when I'm done with you."

"You just made a huge mistake," he half growled.

This time, the door latched when I slammed it. I made sure of it by throwing my body against it and then latching every lock and arming the alarm.

I gave myself less than a minute to lean against the door and breathe with a hand pressed against my chest. Without any hesitation, I rushed back into my living room, past the couch, and toward the dining table.

I fished around the papers spread about and then picked up a pen. My signature scrawled across the line without the pen lifting once.

Once that was done, I ran into my home office and faxed the entire signed contract straight to Byron Ryan himself.

Then I faxed a copy of it to Seth and my lawyer. Screw waiting for miniscule details to be ironed out. This deal was my only option now. My only protection.

The second everything was sent off, I took the original contract into my walk-in closet. It was the first thing I packed in my suitcase. I randomly tossed in items on top of it, without really paying attention.

Before exiting the room, I pulled on some plain clothes and a trucker hat, then wheeled my suitcase behind me to my cell.

I called down for a car, then dialed LAX. "I need the first flight out of L.A."

# nine

## Nate

What do you do when you have to go where you aren't wanted?

Bring a gift.

Too bad I had no idea what to get a famous, rich country princess who already had everything except, of course, for me *not* to show up.

I could have turned down the job, I guess. But come on. Five hundred G's times two. Credit on an entire album, an album that would be heavily promoted and probably rock the country charts?

I couldn't pass that up.

Plus, I wanted to see her again.

She was grouchy. Bossy. Kinda self-righteous.

Oh, and she clearly hated men as of late.

Aerie was also gorgeous, talented, and I had a hunch beneath that crunchy exterior of hers was a center made entirely of creamy, smooth ganache.

My stomach growled at the thought of ganache. I was starving.

I was currently driving a rental that was provided by the label. Byron Ryan wasn't kidding when he said he wanted Aerie to take me home and he wanted some songs STAT.

After only getting to spend a few days in sunny L.A., I got back on Ten's plane for Tennessee, the place Aerie had so longingly called home.

I really wasn't even sure she knew I was coming. At least not this fast... I hoped someone told her. No one would give me her number to call and tell her myself. Hell, they wouldn't even give me her actual address.

I didn't even know the plane was going to Tennessee until the pilot told me before takeoff.

The second I landed, I was greeted with a set of keys to a black Tahoe with windows tinted so dark I wondered if it would feel like nighttime inside.

PS: It was dim in here for sure.

The second I got into the rental, my phone beeped with the address so I could plug it into the GPS. I sat there and looked around for a while, wondering how the hell they knew to text at the exact right moment.

Was I working for a music label or the mafia?

*Fa-reeaak-yyyy.*

So here I was. Driving my mafia-qualified SUV down some back road in the mountains of Tennessee. I just hoped the GPS signal held. If it didn't, I'd probably be lost for days.

My stomach rumbled again, and I grimaced. Remembering the protein bar I had in the pocket of my duffle, I reached over into the passenger seat to grab the bag and fish around.

I glanced away from the empty, hick-style street for like ten seconds. Twenty tops.

A loud sound filled the air and made me jolt upright. The SUV sagged crookedly, and suddenly, I felt I was in some old rap video the way the truck was bobbing around on the road.

"Plot twist!" I yelled.

Slowing down, I didn't bother to pull to the side. I highly doubted anyone else was going to happen along on this road, so I just stopped right in the center.

Leaving the car running and the driver's door open, I jumped out and stared down at the flat tire. Shoving a hand through my hair, I gazed off in the direction from which I came, wondering what in the hell I'd hit that would blow out my tire like that.

It was probably bones. From the dead body of the man who last drove this road.

*Where the fuck am I anyway?*

The sun was already beginning to sink low in the sky. The temperature was cooler than I expected it to be in the South, so without any hesitation, I went to work changing the flat.

It only took me about thirty minutes, maybe a little more, to get the job done. My fingers were stiff from the cold, and the sky was definitely darker than it was when I started. As I was packing up the tools, a sound, familiar yet not one I would think to hear right then, caught my attention.

Pausing, I cocked my head to the side as I wiped my greasy hands on the front of my T-shirt.

I heard it again.

Quickly, I finished up and closed the back of the Tahoe and turned toward the sound. It was off to the side, not on the road, but off toward some bushes about thirty yards away.

Walking toward it, I fully expected to see it dart away. I mean, my presence here wasn't exactly normal either.

Maybe that's why it didn't move. Because we were both in a foreign, unexpected place.

The closer I got, the quieter it became, and when I finally crouched down and looked into the shrubs, it was there, hunkered and shaking.

"Hey there, little dude." I kept my voice low. I stood back up, did a full three-sixty, looking for any nearby houses or anything I might have missed.

Nothing.

Nothing but open space and a single road that wasn't even paved. A chilled wind kicked up, pressing against my bare arms. My skin prickled with bumps.

I glanced back down at the bush and shrugged. "Finders keepers."

Then I slowly crouched back down and reached for my discovery.

As I walked back to the SUV, I grinned. Guess I wouldn't be going to Aerie's without a gift after all.

# ten

*Aerie*

It was full dark when the buzzer went off.

I nearly jumped out of my socks when it happened. With a rapidly pounding heart and breaths coming in short gasps, I questioned my decision to send the staff home. I'd only wanted to be alone. To have some peace. To not worry about who was looking at me, and what they might (or might not) see.

I got what I wanted.

Solitude.

And now someone was buzzing down from the gate, wanting onto my property.

I made the decision to ignore it. I didn't invite anyone over, so therefore, they weren't welcome and shouldn't be here. That meant the gate stayed locked.

It buzzed again.

And then again.

The fourth time, it was for an extended amount of time.

I was good and irritated when I got up and marched over to the command panel installed on the wall. After a few quick taps, I had the camera feed from the gate pulled up.

I frowned when I saw the giant black SUV with bright, glaring headlights.

I hit a button and spoke. "What?" I demanded, hoping I sounded like I had a gun. A big one.

"'Bout time! Geez, I thought you were in there passed out or dead. Good thing you answered or we would have both been embarrassed when the cops got here."

My mouth went slack. His was the last voice I expected to come out of the heavily tinted windows. I barely knew him, but he was the only person I'd met that could go on and on in such a ridiculous way.

"Go away, Nate," I intoned, released the button, and started to retreat.

The buzzer went off again. And then again.

Racing back over, I yelled into it, "Stop doing that!"

"I have to pee!" he whined.

I blew out a frustrated breath. "Pee in the bushes, then!"

He gasped. "That's unsanitary."

I rolled my eyes. "Like you care."

All the charm in his voice evaporated. "Open the gate, Aerie," Nate intoned.

A shiver worked its way up my spine, and I *wanted* to open the gate. The intensity of that caught me off guard. The sudden intensity of him.

I wanted to be alone.

*Didn't I?*

I punched in a code and watched on the monitor as the large wooden gate swung open. The second it was wide enough for the SUV, it drove through and out of sight. My stomach fluttered as I watched the gate close.

Pressing a hand to my middle, I blew out a breath. The softness of my sweater made me glance down. I grimaced instantly, a note of panic washing over me. Oh my God! I looked a mess! Having alone time meant being comfortable.

Being comfortable = wearing whatever I wanted.

And what I wanted was to wear no pants.

Or makeup. Or a bra… *Hell.* I slapped my hand over my head and felt around my hair. Crap. I hadn't even brushed it.

As I stood there and nearly hyperventilated about how my appearance was lacking, I realized something. This was stupid.

I didn't want him here. This was *my* house. I could dress (or not dress) however I wanted. And furthermore, he wasn't staying!

Upon that internal declaration, I marched out of the sunken living room, away from the welcoming fireplace, my book, and blanket, toward the front entry. Flipping on the large overhead fixture that looked like a lantern, the entire entryway lit up. Light spilled out all the front windows and stretched across the wooden decking that led to the wide steps leading to the front door.

Absentmindedly, I pulled at the oversized, baby-pink sweater, making sure it was covering my bottom.

It was all I had on, except for panties and a pair of chunky-knit gray knee socks.

Headlights from his SUV bounced around out front. I opened the wood and glass front door and stepped outside. Night air brushed over the backs of my thighs and my knees. Shivering a bit, I crossed my arms over my chest and glared at the car.

The engine shut off and lights went out, leaving us with only the light from the interior of the foyer.

"Am I even still in the United States?" Nate quipped, getting out.

"The drive isn't that bad," I spat.

He walked around to the front of the car. I could practically taste the smart-alecky remark he was ready to deliver. Then he looked up. Did a double take.

No words passed his lips.

"What are you looking at?" I said, hands on hips, suddenly very shy about my unkempt appearance.

"You forgot your pants," he replied, eyes lingering on my legs. Then as if by sheer force, his gaze averted to his feet.

Something about that reaction totally endeared him to me. Instead of staring, making a lewd comment, or even mocking my lack of put-togetherness, he looked away. Like he was shy. Like he wanted to respect me.

I didn't feel the cold air in that moment. Not at all.

It scared the shit out of me.

"I didn't forget," I replied, tart. "I thought I was going to be *alone.*"

He looked up. "They didn't tell you I was coming?" The wind shifted again, blowing his deep-red locks onto his forehead.

I anticipated the action of him pushing it out of his face, but he didn't. Instead, he kept his left arm anchored at his middle.

"It doesn't matter," I said. "You aren't staying."

"I'm pretty sure the closest hotel is like in the next state." His arm moved, and then he jolted. "Ow!"

I opened my mouth to ask him what the hell he was doing, but he yelled again.

"Shit!" Nate squirmed, trying to get away from whatever his issue was but at the same time, still keeping his arms close around his middle, as if he were holding something.

"I don't know what you're trying to pull right now, but it's not going to work. Might as well get back in that ride and be gone."

Nate was still wiggling around and glanced up. "Excuse me?"

I watched, part incredulous, as he spun, putting his back to me, and hunched forward. I leaned up on my tiptoes, wondering what on earth he was doing, but from my position, I couldn't see. I heard him, though.

"I know we just met and all, but, dude, I thought we had an understanding." Then… "I'm pretty sure I'm bleeding. Not cool."

"Look, I know you're a weird guy…" I began. "But this is weird, even for you."

He finished what he was doing, then straightened, but didn't turn around. "Sure I can't stay?" he asked.

"Negative."

He spun. "What about this little guy?"

I gasped and rushed down the stairs. "Oh my God," I said, trying to keep myself from squeeing and scaring what Nate had just produced.

It was a kitten. A small, fluffy little thing. He was orange with bright-blue eyes and a tiny little head.

My hand moved out, hovering near where he was tucked against Nate's chest. I wanted to stroke his fur so much, to see if it was as soft as it appeared.

"Where did you get her?" I asked.

"It's a boy. I looked."

My eyes shot up to his, and he grinned. My God, his eyes were so green. And this close, I could see some light-red stubble lining his jaw. He was rumpled, as though he'd been traveling all day to get here.

I tore my gaze away from him and back to the little bundle in his arms. The kitten was squished against him, peering at me like he wasn't so sure if I was good or bad.

"Where did you get *him*?" I corrected.

Nate hitched his thumb over his shoulder. "A while back. On that damn Oregon Trail I had to drive down to get here."

I glanced up. "You saw him and stopped the car?"

"No, I had a flat. When I stopped to change it, I heard him crying in the bushes."

I made a stricken sound without even trying and reached for the kitten. "You poor little baby! You must be freezing." Nate surrendered the cat instantly, and I cuddled him close to my chest. His tiny little claws flexed into my sweater and gripped on, but I didn't mind.

He was soft.

"Let's get you inside," I crooned. "Poor baby."

I was almost to the front door when Nate called out, "Hey! What about me? I'm cold, too!"

I stopped and glanced over my shoulder and sighed loudly. "Fine. Come on."

I heard him scrambling up the stairs behind me, but I didn't wait. I just went on into the house, leaving the door open for him. I walked back down into the sunken living room where the glow from the fire and a single lamp illuminated the room. I sank down into the oversized chair I'd been reading in and looked down at the kitten.

He meowed at me. I made a sound and stroked his fur. "Here we go," I murmured and lifted the blanket, tucking it around him like he was a baby.

He began to purr almost immediately.

Movement across the room pulled my eyes up. Nate was standing just inside the room, watching me. I couldn't make out the expression he wore because it was more shadowed where he stood. "I guess you like cats," was all he said.

"I like all animals."

"Figured you might."

I tilted my head. "Why?"

He shrugged and moved across the room toward me.

"I need to get him some food. And water. He's probably starved."

"Probably."

His voice was very near, but not much louder than before. That intensity I felt earlier emanated off him in waves. It was almost warmer than the heat coming off the fire.

I looked up. He was so close I had to tip my chin back to meet his eyes. I swallowed thickly, not sure what to say. What to do.

Nate crouched in front of the chair. His body was so close it almost bumped my knees. He wasn't looking at me, though, but the cat. His long fingers stroked over the kitten, and I noticed the bright-red scratches all over the back of his hand and giggled.

Nate glanced up swiftly, then down at his hand. "Feisty little fella."

"Does he have a name?" I asked, unable to pull my eyes away from his face. His irises were so green. So rare.

"I've been calling him Cheeto."

"Cheeto," I echoed.

"Yeah, cause he's orange like one."

I laughed.

The cat squirmed, and I struggled to hold on to him. My knees brushed against Nate's chest, and a jolt of awareness went through me. His hand shot out, palming the side of my leg as he balanced.

My teeth sank into my lower lip. Then I jerked back. "I need to get him some food," I spoke, abrupt. My voice was like a needle popping a giant bubble.

"I'll hold him." Nate shifted back and stood.

I handed over little Cheeto, careful not to let our hands brush, and then practically ran from the room under the guise of finding food for the kitten.

# eleven

## *Nate*

Her house wasn't really a house.

It was basically a ranch with a giant, fancy log cabin perched in the center of it.

With a gate (obviously).

It wasn't what I was expecting. Well, aside from the fancy part.

It was the kind of fancy that was throwing me off. And the location.

I expected Aerie to be a city mouse. Hollywood and L.A. through and through. You know, the kind of girl who liked shopping, coffee, and restaurants all in close proximity. All the conveniences at the touch of a finger. I expected sleek lines, white paint… chrome.

This was the complete opposite. There was land for miles, mountains, and reaching modern conveniences would require significant time in the car. The house itself was warm and comfortable. It was a place you could live in, not just look at. I wanted to settle in and watch football on a Sunday, play my guitar by the fire, and eat Fruity Pebbles on the couch.

What surprised me more was that she fit in. Aerie didn't appear out of place at all in this country setting… I didn't know her well, but I was willing to bet a corndog that she looked more herself here than anywhere else.

It didn't hurt she wasn't wearing pants either.

What a fucking test that was, not to stare at those damn long legs sticking out from beneath that soft-looking sweater.

There was attraction between us.

Don't tell anyone, but it shocked the hell outta me.

Not that I was attracted to her. Um, she was hot.

But her attraction to me. I know I often say how much the ladies love the Nate Train… but you know, I might be overestimating a bit.

Or a lot.

Truth was I was kinda awkward. Goofy. Definitely not the smoothest when it came to women or talking to one. Maybe that's why I adapted such a sarcastic personality. It was easier to have a woman laugh and roll her eyes at me than turn me down flat.

I wasn't the best-looking guy in the room either. Definitely not like the kind of guys Aerie was used to hanging with.

Still, she was interested in me. She hated it (which oddly made me like it more), and she definitely tried to hide it, but you couldn't hide energy. She definitely didn't hide it by avoiding my hands earlier and then rushing from the room as though her ass were on fire.

I don't know how the hell I managed to catch her attention, but I wanted to keep it. I probably wouldn't. I mean, I couldn't keep something if I didn't even know how I attracted it in the first place.

Cheeto was a good move, though. He at least got me in the door.

*You aren't here for a date, man. You're here for a job. For a job that will pay a shit ton of money.*

"Here we go." Aerie's voice broke into my thoughts. She was carrying a large tray with a handle on each end.

The pink bows at the top of her socks practically teased me, but I forced my attention up to her face.

"From the bushes to dinner by the fire," I told Cheeto. "You're moving up in the world, buddy."

Aerie laughed and set the tray on the brick hearth near the fire, then sank down on the rug beside me. "Can I have that blanket?" she asked, motioning behind me.

I reached into the chair and grabbed the blanket, handing it over to her. She tucked it over her lap, then adjusted her legs so she was sitting Indian style under it. When she was done, she set a small white dish on the floor between us. On it was chopped-up chicken. Beside that she placed a bowl of water and then a small bowl of what looked like milk.

"You aren't really supposed to give cats milk, but he's had a rough night," she explained.

Cheeto went to the food immediately and started scarfing it down.

"He's going to be sick!" She worried.

"He'll be all right," I replied. "Though, you might want to find him a litter box."

She frowned. "I don't have any cat litter."

"We can shred up some paper," I suggested.

She nodded. Her hair, which I'd only ever seen sleek and straight, bounced around her head. It was wavier and rumpled-looking today. More natural.

And her skin was completely free of makeup. No red lips tonight. But her cheeks were pink, maybe from the cold. Maybe from excitement.

She looked younger like this. Vulnerable.

"I'll have some supplies picked up and brought out for me tomorrow morning," she said, thoughtfully.

"You have a staff here?" I asked, curious.

"Not a big one. I have someone who takes care of the house and land. Kind of like a foreman, I guess. And I have a housekeeper who cleans and stocks the fridge. Sometimes she cooks for me. A few other people who do things like that. But no one's here now. I sent everyone home. I meant it when I said I wanted to be *alone*."

"Well, now you're alone with me." That didn't come out nearly as sarcastic and nonthreatening as I intended.

She cleared her throat and then turned and grabbed something off the tray behind her. "I made you a sandwich." She held out a white plate with a chicken sandwich, chips, and a pickle on the side.

"You made that for me?"

She nodded.

I snatched up half the sammy and shoved the end into my mouth. "*Omigoood*," I said around a bite of the food. "How did you know I was starved?"

She gaped as I shoved another bite in my mouth. "You're always hungry."

I paused. "How'd you know that?"

"Because both times we met, you stole my candy."

"This is good shit. It's trending in my mouth," I said as I chewed and pointed to my lips.

"It's trending in your mouth?" She wondered.

"If this sandwich was a Facebook post, it would have thousands of likes."

She laughed. I liked the sound. And by the way, she still smelled like Fruity Pebbles. It was nearly addicting.

I took the plate and finished the food in record time. Although, Cheeto was faster than me. After he ate and drank, he settled beside Aerie and began licking his paws.

"They did tell me you were coming." Her quiet voice admitted, her gaze trained on the kitten. "I told them I wasn't ready. I guess they didn't care."

"Not ready to work on new music? Or not ready have me around?"

She kept her eyes turned down, but I stared at her anyway. The firelight played across her features, creating shadows on her face and streaks of gold in her dark hair.

"Both." I watched her throat work after she spoke. Noticed the slight tremble in her lower lip. It was one word, but it held a lot.

I felt bad for being here, bad for showing up without calling. For basically putting my paycheck above her.

"Hey, uh…" I said, clearing my throat. "I'll go. I can put the label off a little, tell them I had a family emergency at home and buy you some time."

Her eyes lifted. "You would do that?"

"Sure. It's not like my dad wants me to be here anyway."

"Your dad?"

"Yep, I still live at home," I said. *Way to sound like a loser, Roth.*

A little inkling of interest sparked in her eyes. "Where is home?"

"Upstate New York."

"You don't live in L.A.?"

"L.A. couldn't handle all this." I gestured to myself.

She gave me a look that basically said to knock it off.

I sighed. "No. I'm not that established in songwriting. I'm a college student. Who lives with his dad and drives a crappy Ford."

When she didn't say anything, I figured that was her way of being nice and not laughing me out onto the porch. I got to my feet and adjusted my shirt. "You mind taking care of Cheeto? I think he'd like it better here than a car ride back to New York."

"Of course."

"Cool." I stood there awkwardly for a few painful seconds, then started from the room.

"Did you want to use the bathroom before you left?" she asked.

I gave her a lopsided smile over my shoulder. "Nah, I peed in the bushes a few miles back."

"I knew it!" She gasped.

I laughed.

My hand closed around the large wrought iron handle on the front door when I heard her behind me.

"Nate!"

I turned to see her at the top of the stairs of the living room, Cheeto cradled in her arms.

"Aerie?"

Her teeth sank into her lower lip when I said her name, and my hand tightened around the handle. I didn't say anything else. I was afraid if I opened my mouth, a bunch of stupid would tumble out.

Finally, she released her lip. "Will you stay?"

"U-uh, uh," I stuttered. I cleared my throat, rubbing the back of my neck. "Uh, yeah."

"Just for tonight," she rushed out. "Maybe we can talk in the morning? About work."

I nodded.

"Help me find a litter box for this little guy, and then I'll show you to your room."

I blinked after her as she went from the room, my eyes drawn back to her legs. She was almost out of sight when I heard her call out, "You coming or what?"

I rushed to catch up.

#  twelve

## Aerie

The second I hit the top of the staircase, music floated through the air. The melodic tunes of a guitar wrapped around my senses and propelled my feet a little bit faster, even though I'd yet to have any coffee.

I didn't know the tune, but I knew my ears liked it. It was a little haunting, a little melancholy, but at the same time, it held an undertone of hope.

There was something about music, wasn't there? No matter what kind you listened to. It just had this indescribable way of making you feel *something*.

The second my foot hit the bottom of the steps, I was almost transfixed. My footsteps were soundless as I went in search of the music.

I knew Nate was a songwriter. But I had no idea he played guitar. I didn't know much about him at all. His melody made me hungry for the information. For any detail I could garner. I wondered if the piece was something he wrote. Something autobiographical. If it wasn't, I wondered where he got the inspiration.

Just as my foot hit the top step into the living room, a quiet voice began to sing.

*"Sometimes it feels like you were just a dream,*
*"A wish floating through reality.*
*"At night, I wait for sleep to claim me,*
*"To hear your voice, remember your face,*
*"But when I open my eyes, you're gone without a trace."*

I swallowed. My throat was dry, my eyes oddly damp. That was beautiful. And his voice…

"Shit," he swore and stroked the strings, then lifted his hand.

I moved into the room, unable to hang back. Unwilling to pretend I hadn't heard. I wasn't normally very polite. I wasn't about to start now.

"Play it again," I said, padding across the large plush rug toward where Nate sat on the hearth.

He'd built a fire. The sound of the wood crackling and popping behind him only added to the atmosphere.

Maybe it was the early-morning hour. Maybe I was just lonely from being here in solitude. Or maybe it was the way his voice still haunted the chambers of my heart… making me feel as if the reason it beat was more than just to keep my blood pumping.

His head came up quickly. Red locks fell onto his forehead, and he shoved them away, making it all stand out around his head. "You heard me?"

I nodded, drawing closer. Gesturing with my hand, I urged, "Play it again."

His eyes flashed with a little bit of shyness, and I sank down on the brick ledge beside him. I bumped my knee into the side of his leg.

He didn't glance at me, only down at the guitar balanced in his lap. Music filled the room again, and I watched his fingers nimbly move over the strings. He sang the lines again. Then when his voice fell away, he played what I assumed what was left of the chords.

I picked up where he left off.

*"Lost in the past, nonexistent in the future.*
*"Which is worse? I'm just not sure.*
*"Looking in the mirror, a reflection gazes back,*
*"But it isn't me.*
*"It isn't me.*
*"It's how I know you weren't a dream,*
*"A wish floating through reality.*
*"Memories are hard to keep,*
*"But you're always there, aren't you?*
*"Buried down deep,*
*"Always there when I've had too much reality."*

When my words fell away, so did his music. The final chord ebbed away softly, leaving nothing behind but the crackle and hiss of the fire.

Nate's emerald eyes lifted, glittering like precious gems. "That was amazing."

The rise and fall of my chest was heavy, just like the air between us.

"It's like you knew what I was saying. You understood." He went on.

I did understand.

"Who did you lose?" I asked, not holding back.

He set aside the guitar, leaning forward and placing his elbows on his knees. "My mom died when I was a little kid."

I reached out without thought, sliding my hand over his clasped ones. He stared at where we touched for long moments, then parted his grip and tugged my hand between his. "What about you?"

Pain lanced through my chest. "My grandmother."

"You're a lot like her, then?" he asked, the corner of his mouth kicking up.

I smiled, thinking of her. Then my smile faded away. "She was much more than I will ever be."

His hands tightened around mine, and he looked over. "I don't think that's true," he replied, soft. "*Looking in the mirror, a reflection gazes back. It isn't me.*" He repeated my words. "You see her in you."

I wished I did. But really, when I looked in the mirror, I thought of how disappointed in me she probably was.

Tugging my hand slowly out of his, I was sort of sad when he let me go. But I pushed the feeling back and stood. "Have you had coffee yet?"

He shook his head. "Are you kidding? I got lost twice just trying to find this room. I was afraid if I went in search of the kitchen, you'd never see me again."

"The house isn't that big." I scoffed.

"Where's Cheeto?" He wondered, as if he just noticed I wasn't holding the kitten.

"Curled up in my bed. I didn't want to bother him, he looked too cozy."

"If I was in your bed, I wouldn't want to leave it either." He wagged his eyebrows at me.

I gave him a *forget it* look, then turned away, hiding the smile trying to take over my face. "I'm gonna need some coffee to put up with you today."

He appeared soundlessly behind me as we went, leaning over my shoulder. "Does that mean I'm not leaving?"

"I haven't decided." I sniffed.

"You like me." He teased.

"I do not."

"Like me," he whispered.

I ignored him. He was annoying.

But as we entered the kitchen, an insistent little voice spoke up in the back of my head.

*Maybe I do.*

# Nate

She finished my song as though she knew all the words.

*I* didn't even have the words.

Aerie did.

She walked right into the room without pause, sitting down beside me as if I were a book and all she had to do to continue the story was turn the page.

I wanted to work with her. Now more than ever. Not for the challenge, the money, or even the recognition. Hell, at this point, I didn't even care about proving to my dad that I could handle this career.

I wanted to sit beside her some more, let her voice become my pulse, let all the little details about her become my air.

Ten and I worked well together. The songs we collabed on for his album were epic.

This could be more.

I felt it. If she was already finishing my sentences, combining my melody with hers… what would it be like when we got to know each other?

She was gun shy, though. Oh so cynical. People (mostly men), it seemed, had burned bridges with her—while she was still standing on them. First-degree burns took a long time to heal. But yeah, I'd like to be the aloe to soothe her.

"Earth to Nate!" Aerie's voice cut into my thoughts.

"Huh?"

"Do you want coffee?" she said, enunciating each word like she was talking to a two-year-old. As she did, she waved a pod for the coffee machine in front of my face.

"Is that even a question?" I scoffed, then turned my attention to the room.

The ceilings were high and pitched. Huge wooden beams soared overhead, and a large wrought iron fixture hung from the center. There was a huge marble-topped island, a farmhouse-style sink, and a double refrigerator big enough to hold food for a year.

Windows lined the wall, looking out onto the property, which was wooded with trees. Sunlight shone through, lighting up the room.

"Cream?" Aerie asked as I stared back up at the ceiling.

I nodded, and her body disappeared behind the open door of the fridge. Curious, I moved behind her and peered in, wondering how much food she had. It was only partially filled.

Aerie handed me a bottle of creamer over her shoulder then reached back in, her fingers snatching a cup of Greek yogurt.

I made a face. "Ew. What's that for?"

"Breakfast," she replied, shutting the fridge behind her.

"That is not breakfast," I retorted. "That's nasty."

Her brows shot up. Her hair was rumpled again today. Not messy, just not as straight and sleek as it was the day we met. Instead, it waved around her face and skimmed her collarbone when she moved.

She had on more of those socks again. The kind that reached just below her knees. These were gray with two thick white stripes at the top of each. They reminded me of a jersey, except on her legs.

Sadly, she was wearing pants. They were black and tight. Violet called them leggings. Her light-blue top was cropped, but not so much that I could see her belly. Though, I bet if she reached over her head, I'd see a glimpse of skin.

"You don't like yogurt?" she seemed surprised.

"Does anyone?" I wondered. "It's like swallowing slime."

Aerie wrinkled her nose. "That was graphic."

"I know." Going over to the pantry (it was a distressed-looking door that literally had *Pantry* written on it), I stuck my head in. "Where's the Fruity Pebbles?" I called out to her.

"At the grocery store…"

I gasped. "You don't have any Fruity Pebbles!"

"I thought only four-year-olds ate that."

"You offend me." I told her, backtracking to the mug she was lifting off the Keurig. I took it out of her hand. "Dibs."

"That was mine," she growled.

"I called dibs." I added a generous amount of cream to my coffee.

"You can't call dibs on coffee."

I lifted it and took a sip. "Just did."

Muttering under her breath, she turned away to brew another cup.

I stuck my tongue out at her.

"I saw that!"

I grimaced. "I can't believe you don't have any Fruity Pebbles. I don't know if I can stay in a house like this."

She turned and smiled sweetly. "Should I show you to the door?"

Carrying my coffee back to the fridge, I started pulling things out and laying them on the expansive island.

"What are you doing?"

"Since there's no decent breakfast, I'm going to have to improvise." I slapped an unopened pack of bacon on the counter beside the eggs.

Her voice was incredulous. "You cook?"

I looked around the large open door and lifted one brow. "You don't?"

Her chin lifted a fraction. "I don't have time."

"So that's why you eat slime." I concluded.

"It's healthy!"

"So's Brussel sprouts." I pushed the door closed and added the rest of my ingredients on the counter. "But I don't eat those either."

Without another word, Aerie carried her mug, the slime, and a spoon over and climbed on a chair at the island. With her chin propped in her hand, she regarded me. "You're really going to cook all that?"

"You're going to help me," I informed her.

She blanched.

I spread out my arms. "You have all the time in the world this morning."

"I'll just have this." She poked at the container with her spoon.

I leaned a hip into the counter and crossed my arms over my chest. "You don't know how."

She shot up straight. "I do, too!"

"Prove it."

Aerie jumped off the stool and came around the island, pushing up the sleeves on her T-shirt. "Fine."

She stood there for long moments, staring down at all the stuff on the island without saying a word. When her dark-brown gaze finally peeked up at me, she asked, "Well, what were you going to make?"

I laughed. "I knew it!"

Aerie's expression darkened, and it was like this veil—no, a wall—came down over her features. Her mouth flattened, and she shoved back away from the counter.

"Whoa," I said, catching her wrist. "Where are you going?"

"If you think I'm going to stand here and listen to you make fun of me for something I don't know how to do—"

*Yikes.*

I hit a nerve.

Clearly, Aerie was used to someone poking fun at her, and not in a nice way.

"Hey, *hey*," I said, towing her back around. "I'm not making fun of you."

She gave me an angry, hard stare. The need to flee was so prominent inside her I felt her hands shake with it.

*What did he do to you?*

I wanted to pull her across the rest of the distance between us, to fold her against my chest and rest my chin on top of her head. I never wanted anything so much.

I settled for stroking my thumb on the inside of her wrist. "I was joking. Not laughing at you. I would never do that."

Her eyes lifted. I couldn't stop myself. I reached out and tucked a strand of hair behind her ear. "You like omelets?"

"What kind?" she replied begrudgingly.

"Veggie. Gooey cheese. With bacon and toast dripping with butter."

"I'd have to work out for three hours if I ate that."

I snorted. "You're on vacation. And you don't need to work out." After a brief pause, I took a chance, lowering my voice. "I think you look perfect the way you are."

The wall on her features crumbled. Her entire body relaxed. "Really?"

"Really."

"I've never made an omelet before." Her voice was hesitant.

"I'll teach you."

Before she could say anything else, or think of another reason to run, I plopped a bowl down in front of her and then a carton of eggs. "Here. Crack some eggs into this bowl."

She gave me a blank stare.

"No wonder you live on slime," I muttered and stepped up close to grab an egg. With her watching, I cracked the white shell on the side of the bowl, opened it, and dumped the contents inside.

I watched with some amusement when she picked up the white porcelain mug and took a sip of her coffee as though she needed fortifying to crack an egg.

When she was done, she took the egg and followed what I had done just moments before. Some of the white squirted out of the shell and toward her. She made a small sound and jerked back.

I moved forward, grabbing her hands, still around the partially cracked egg. "The goal is to put it *in* the bowl." I reminded her, guiding her back over.

She giggled. "Sorry,"

"It's all good," I told her, staying close as she dropped the shells on the counter beside the one I had discarded.

"There," she announced, as if she were good and accomplished. It was freaking adorable.

I picked up another egg and handed it over. "You aren't done yet, princess."

She made a disgusted sound. "Princess."

"You look like one from where I'm standing."

She rotated her head enough that our eyes could connect, just barely. I settled a little more firmly at her side, nudging my hip into the island and delivering a crooked smile.

"Is that supposed to be an insult?"

"Far from it," I said low. "And I think you know that."

A beat of attraction passed between us. Then she pulled away. Her stare went back down to the eggs.

"Yeah, well, maybe I once was a princess, but I'm sure as hell not anymore."

I cocked my head to the side. "No?"

She shook her head definitively. "According to some, I'm a toad."

I laughed.

She glanced up sharply.

My laughter died away. "You're serious?"

"As a heart attack." She glanced down at the egg, avoiding my gaze.

"Shit," I swore. "Someone actually called you a toad?"

"It doesn't matter."

I lifted my hand, poised to stroke down the back of her head. I stopped just before I made contact, suddenly aware of my actions. "That why you came here so fast?"

She shrugged. "Partly."

"And the rest?"

She stiffened. "That's none of your business."

I dropped my hand from her and stepped back. "Fair enough." I pointed to the eggs. "Finish those."

I started to move off in search of a pan but suddenly faltered. I stood there debating if maybe what I was thinking was wrong, if it would only push her away further.

I wasn't one to overthink things—much—so I spun back around.

She squeaked when I clasped her gently around the top of her elbow. The egg she had just cracked slipped out of her hand and into the bowl, shell and all.

She gasped and started to reach for the pieces.

"Hey," I said, pulling her around.

Whatever she heard in my voice made her forget the food.

Her round, dark eyes collided with mine, bouncing between them.

"You're always gonna be a princess to me, princess."

She made a scoffing sound, but I caught her chin and held it. "Always."

Her soft exhale was all the reply I needed.

"C'mon," I said, breaking the moment, not wanting it to be too heavy, but needing to make a point. "You clearly need assistance. Me showing you once was not enough."

"You made me do that!" she announced, pointing at the shell mixed in with the eggs.

"It's really not nice to blame other people for your own faults," I informed her.

She gasped. She did that a lot. She was an indignant little thing.

It was sort of a turn on.

"Look," I said right against her ear as I moved behind her, stepping so close her back came into contact with my chest. I put my arms around her, basically caging her in from behind, and reached into the bowl to pick out the shells.

She froze, went quiet, and just stood stock still while I surrounded her.

When I was done with her mess, I picked up an egg and held it in front of her. "C'mon, help me."

Aerie put her hand over mine, and I smacked the egg into the side. Together we cracked open the egg, some of it squirting out and making her squeal and jerk back. My body was there to catch hers. The second she came fully against me, I heard her intake of breath, but said nothing.

She fit against me just right. Her hair felt like strands of silk brushing against my cheek every time I moved. Her hands were small compared to mine, her skin a warmer shade.

"Another," I whispered into her ear, and we repeated the same thing with a fourth egg. "You try," I said when I picked up number five. Instead of moving back, I stayed where I was.

You know, in case she needed help.

This time, Aerie mastered it by herself.

"Ha! I did it," she said, spinning around and looking at me with a triumphant glitter in her stare.

"So you did," I murmured, glancing down at her lips, then back up. Normally, I would have made some wisecrack...

But my brain wasn't on full power.

"Now what?" she asked.

I snapped out of it and stepped back. "Can I trust you with a knife?" I half joked.

She nodded.

Ah... better not.

I handed her a fork instead. "Here whisk up the eggs."

While she was doing that, I found a skillet and placed it on the stove to heat. Then I got the bacon cooking (microwave for the win!) and dropped some toast in a giant-ass toaster on the counter.

After that, I sent her to wait for the toast so she could butter it, and I began dicing up bell peppers, tomatoes, and mushrooms for the omelet.

"Where did you learn to cook?" she asked, watching me.

I smirked. No one ever expected someone like me to be able to eat anything other than cereal.

It was really quite insulting.

"Mom died, remember? It was just me and Dad growing up, and you have better skills in the kitchen than he does. So it was learn to cook or starve." She didn't say anything after I explained, so I glanced over my shoulder.

"How did she die?" Aerie asked softly.

My stomach tightened. "Cancer."

"Cancer is vile," she said, passion in her tone.

I was about to ask her about her reaction, but the toast popped up and she busied herself with it and the butter. Watching her move around the kitchen was sort of like watching a four-year-old on Christmas. All wonder and excitement in her eyes.

Made me want to cook with her more.

After I had everything chopped, I poured the eggs in a pan and sprinkled in the toppings. I let it do its thing for a few moments while I found a spatula. Turning back, I noticed Aerie right near the cooktop, looking at the pan.

"C'mere," I said, drawing her body back in front of mine again. Positioning my arms around her, I held the spatula out for her to take. Once she did, I closed my hand around hers and held onto the handle of the pan. "Like this," I instructed.

I showed her how to lift the edges of the omelet to allow more egg to cook. I moved the pan while she practiced. The only conversation was when I was telling her how to do it.

I was tempted to let the damn eggs burn, anything to keep her in my arms like this. But I figured burning breakfast would make me a terrible teacher, and the next time I pulled her into me to show her how to do something, she would think I was just putting on the moves.

I kinda was. But she didn't need to know that.

Once the omelets, bacon, and toast were plated up, we both sat at the island to eat. After a couple bites in silence, she glanced up. "It's good."

"I know."

"So humble," she quipped.

"Same time, same place tomorrow?" I asked, chewing extra loud.

"You are so annoying." Ah, the fondness in her tone made me chew louder.

After a moment, she put aside her fork and dragged her coffee in front of her, wrapping her hands around it.

I stopped chewing like a mule and swallowed. "Princess?"

She winced, just barely, when I called her that.

"If you want me to go, I'll go."

"We made a good team..." She began. "Before, with your guitar."

I smiled. "I think we could make some good music together."

She frowned and looked back at her partly eaten food. I ate a few more bites, waiting for her to speak again.

What? I was hungry.

Gazing into her mug, she said, "I've been burned a lot by men in the past year."

"I know."

Her face jerked up. "You do?"

I shrugged one shoulder, eating another bite of egg. "It's not hard to see. All I had to do was pay attention."

"To the press?"

"To you, Aerie. I paid attention to you."

"But you still called me princess."

I set down my fork, meeting her probing stare. "Always."

She nodded slow, then swallowed. "I'd like to work on the album with you."

I smiled wide.

Her lips tugged upward. "But that's all it is. Work."

I tilted my head. "Friends?"

She considered it. I batted my eyes—you know, to make me look innocent.

I don't think it worked.

But still she said, "Okay. Friends."

I did a mental fist pump.

Friends. I could work with that.

# fourteen

*Aerie*

Oh, it was easy.

Being around Nate took barely any effort at all. More than once, I felt my guard slip away completely. It made for good songwriting. Vulnerability always created the best music.

Well, that and butterflies.

I seemed to have an abundance of both when Nate was in the room.

Every morning, he made me breakfast; every morning, I helped. That was four days of standing beside him with the scent of coffee and eggs in the air. Four mornings of listening to him crack stupid jokes and chew so charmingly obnoxiously. Cheeto would play at our feet or sleep on one of the barstools. Nate sneaked him bacon.

If I wasn't careful, I would get used to this.

If I wasn't careful, I would remember what it was like to have a real home.

Still, I couldn't stay away.

I was already in the recording studio when Nate strolled in. I'd come to realize he didn't really walk anywhere. He strolled. He swaggered. It was like there was a beat playing in his head that only he could hear.

Glancing up from the notes in front of me, I gave him a look. "Why are you still wearing your pajamas?"

He didn't answer at first. Instead, he grabbed a bottled water out of the nearby fridge, uncapped it, and then took a long drink before rubbing his stomach.

His pajamas didn't even match. The army-green plain T-shirt and blue plaid flannel bottoms definitely didn't go together. Yet somehow, he made it work. And the deep green of the shirt made his eyes stand out all the more.

"It's casual Friday," he finally said, capping the water.

"You've definitely mastered the casual part," I quipped.

Cheeto perked up the second Nate entered. He was curled up in a ball on the furry papasan chair in the corner. He was so small he practically got lost in all the fluff, but his triangular orange ears poked up like little beacons.

"Cheeto, my man," Nate announced and went toward the kitten. "Give me five." He held out his palm to the cat as if he really was going to give him five.

To my surprise, Cheeto put his paw in Nate's hand, who, of course, swiveled his face around and gave me a smirk. "And you thought he would leave me hanging."

"You're a nincompoop."

"Thank you."

"It wasn't a compliment."

"If you say so, princess."

He called me that pretty much all the time. I was never one for pet names. Or nicknames of any kind. Being called anything other than my actual name always felt somehow mocking.

I didn't mind when Nate did it, though.

Just one more thing I was going to get used to but shouldn't.

"So…" He pulled out the chair near me at the round wooden table and flipped it around so he could straddle it. "You still liking everything we've come up with so far?"

I glanced down at the sheet music, our notes, and ideas and nodded. "I actually really do. For the first time in a long time, I'm pretty excited about music again."

The green of his eyes sparkled, white teeth flashing. "My work here is done."

"Actually, it's not," I returned, dry. "But I think in a few more weeks, we will definitely have a solid draft and we can work more on recording. I'll call Byron and get a small crew out here to start with the studio time."

"About that…" Nate began, his voice becoming a little more serious.

My phone went off. "Hold that thought," I said and picked up the cell.

"Hey, Seth," I said into the line.

"I'm judging by the carefree tone of your voice you haven't heard."

*He thinks I sound carefree?* Whoa. I couldn't say I felt carefree, but I definitely did feel a lot less frazzled. The second those thoughts went through my head, the rest of what he said caught up.

"What happened?" My voice was sharp. Nate's eyes flew to my face, but I kept mine averted.

"It's not life or death. Nothing like that." He assured me quickly but added a heavy sigh. "However, it's not good news."

"Just tell me," I half growled.

"There's a new story going around in the press today."

"What else is new?" I muttered, shifting uncomfortably.

Nate was in the background, telling me to put it on speaker, and I mouthed the word *no* at him.

"Considering the amount of time you've spent in the press lately, it's not. I wanted to give you a heads-up, though. Today's headline is grabbing some traction. It's being circulated at a faster than normal rate, and a few copycat articles of speculation are popping up."

The palms of my hands grew damp. Nerves bunched in the back of my neck.

"I know you don't want to, but I think it's time you put some serious thought into what kind of statement you want to release."

My lips pressed into a firm, thin line. "This is about Will."

"It involves him."

Well, there went my less-than-frazzled demeanor. "Thanks for cluing me in. I'll get back to you, okay?"

"Just remember, no one believes that tabloid BS anyway."

I winced and didn't bother saying good-bye. Instead, I disconnected the call, then went right to the web to find the newest headline.

It took all of two seconds. Seth wasn't lying when he said it was going viral. All the blood drained from my face, leaving me lightheaded. Black spots swam before my eyes, making me blink.

Even the black spots couldn't stop me from reading and rereading the headline.

*Princess to Toad?*

*The Fall of Aerie Boone*

The article wasn't very long and included several unflattering pictures of me and a few better ones of me and Will. I felt my cheeks burn as I looked through it. I was in the press a lot. Sometimes it felt very invasive, and the speculation about me was usually so far off the mark.

But this…

*Sources tell us that the marriage to Will Solberg was just a last-ditch attempt at salvaging her unraveling world and reputation. When we reached out to Will himself, he told us exclusively, "I love Aerie. So much so that I suggested we get married so I could protect her better." <pauses> "But you can't save someone who doesn't want to be saved. I was more than willing to go the distance with her, but every man has his limits. The affair was mine. I might have been able to forgive it, but she wasn't safe… and I can't put my own health at risk."*

*We asked for further details, perhaps a name… but Solberg, being the gentleman he is, declined to comment further. We can't say we'd be as mum, especially after the new wife brought home an STD.*

*Seems Aerie Boone really has fallen from grace. We can't help but wonder what Time Track Records was doing when they re-signed her. A toad on the payroll… But even worse? A toad with a raging case of warts.*

I slammed the phone down on the table and brushed rapidly at the tears streaming down my cheeks.

Thought was barely possible. The shock rippling through my brain and filtering down into my limbs was almost incomprehensible.

The entire article had been a slam piece… but those last couple paragraphs? The worst thing that had ever been printed about me.

Ever.

All at the hands of Will.

The chair nearly fell back when I stood abruptly.

"Aerie," Nate said, concern thick in his voice. I'd forgotten he was here.

The reminder of his presence was like a right hook in my kidney. It made this even worse.

I ran from the room, ignoring his pleas to stop. I couldn't face him, the article… not even myself.

Will hadn't been lying when he said I'd regret this.

# fifteen

## Nate

Well, that escalated quickly.

I picked up the phone she left behind as she ran from the room, catching the screen just before it went dark.

That red-headed temper that I didn't often display? It rushed to the surface faster than it ever had. What the actual fuck was this shit? It must have been a hella slow news day, because this was all kinds of made up.

The fact that Will Solberg (aka the guy who most definitely *wasn't* winning husband of the year) was quoted in this article, literally calling Aerie a toad and claiming she cheated and tried to give him an STD, was utterly ridiculous.

And it made me want to punch something. *Hard.*

I'd only known Aerie a week. There was lots of stuff I didn't know about her… including what was up with this dipshit. But there was something of which I was absolutely certain—she was not a love 'em and leave 'em type of girl.

She was a bring home to Momma kind of woman.

You know, if a guy had a momma…

Anyway, now I understood where the toad comment came from the first morning in the kitchen. Why the hell had she married him?

What the fuck kind of man would literally trash his girl in the press?

*She's not his girl. Over my dead body.*

I had lots of questions about their marriage, their relationship. It seemed, as the days passed and the more hours I spent with Aerie, the list grew and grew.

She wrote like a woman with a broken heart. Like a woman with a past that wasn't easy.

*Like a woman without much hope for the future.*

As I stared down at the screen, hand fisted beside it, I realized this article just answered all those questions. Without me having to voice even one.

Suddenly, being here for the album was secondary. Work didn't really seem to matter.

I cared about her. *A lot.*

It really seemed as though within the walls of this house, the time we'd been isolated here, I got to see a side of Aerie that not many people ever did.

I wasn't a hugely successful businessman. I wasn't rich, didn't wear designer clothes or have any type of influence. Hell, I used sarcasm like most people used Chap Stick.

I was the kind of guy who plucked strays out of bushes, ate an entire box of cereal for dinner, and could live out of one duffel bag for weeks.

But I didn't mistreat women. And I wasn't about to stand around and watch someone else do it either.

Especially not her.

The sound of my phone went off. I hit the button on the screen, and a giant picture of Cheeto stared back at me.

"Agh!" I said, dropping it on the table. "Wrong phone."

It was totally cute she had a picture of the cat I gave her as her wallpaper, though.

As I was digging my phone out of my pajama bottoms (casual Friday rules!), it went off again. Two unread texts from different people.

"I'm a popular guy," I told Cheeto.

The first text was from Ten. *The news this a.m. is harsh. Better keep her away from it.*

I made a sound. *Too late,* I typed back.

Ten: *Shit. How bad is it?*

Me: *She ran from the room crying.*

Ten: *Where are you?*

Me: *Studio*

Ten: *Go after her, you moron!*

*Duh,* I shot back.

I scooped up Cheeto with one hand and tucked him against my chest. As I strode from the room, I pulled up the last unread text message.

The second I read it, I sent the screen dark and shoved the phone back into my pants.

I'd deal with that later. Right now, I had a princess to attend.

# sixteen

*Aerie*

I shouldn't be surprised. Yet I was.

I didn't even like Will, not anymore… but his power to hurt me was still unmatched. I shouldn't care what he did or said about me.

Words and actions hurt, though, even if they came from someone who didn't even matter.

I knew Will wasn't necessarily a nice person, but *this*? This was harsh even for him.

Seth wanted me to issue a statement. The thought was laughable. How was I to respond to the fact the press was referring to me as a toad with warts?

*Don't worry, I have cream for that.*

Or…

*Thank goodness green is my color!*

Better yet, I should just go running back to Will with my tail between my legs.

No, no, and, um, triple no.

I thought regretfully of the contract I'd just signed. If I hadn't, I could just hide here forever, let my career and stardom fade into nonexistence, and just move on with my life.

It was cowardly. I knew it. Being a coward was something I was unfortunately used to.

The sound of a tentative knock on my bedroom door made me freeze as if I were caught in the act of something foul instead of being sprawled across my bed, bawling. When I said nothing, the knock came again.

"Go away!" I shouted, then put my face back in the pillow.

"Aerie." Nate's muffled voice came through the thick wood. "Talk to me."

I ignored him.

He'd go away eventually. Once he realized I wouldn't do what he wanted, he'd go.

After several minutes, he knocked again.

I ignored him again.

It was really quite annoying. It was hard holding back the deep sobs racking my body, trying to stifle them into the pillows. The only thing worse than crying your eyes out was when someone heard you.

Finally, everything went silent once more. My body sagged into the mattress, and I moaned into my pillow. I thought I'd be relieved when he was gone.

I wasn't.

I cried anew.

But then the sound of the door unlatching and the disturbance I felt in the air made me stop. Whipping my head up and around, I peered over my shoulder through blurry eyes.

Nate strolled into the room, closing the door behind him.

"That door was locked!" I gasped.

He was holding Cheeto against his chest, shrugging one shoulder. "I picked the lock. It's not hard."

Letting out a wail, I face dived into the pillow. He was unbelievable. Stubborn. Insubordinate.

I wanted him to hug me.

I was a freaking mess.

"Get out!" I flung a pillow in his general direction.

"You almost took out the cat!" he exclaimed.

I gasped and sat up. "Oh, I'm sorry!" Scrambling on my hands and knees across the bed, I went toward Cheeto. "Poor thing, come here."

Nate smirked.

I gasped again. "You liar!"

"You could have hit him." His voice was all kinds of reasonable. It made me want to kick him.

"Give me my cat!" I held out my hands.

He handed over the kitten, and I snuggled him into my chest and rubbed my damp cheek across his fur. He purred, then scrambled out of my arms to lie on one of the pillows. It was feather filled, so he sank down in until all I saw were the orange triangles of his tiny ears.

I rubbed my cheeks with the backs of my hands and sniffled. "I'd like to be alone."

"No."

I jolted. "What did you just say to me?"

"I said no. I'm not leaving you in here alone to cry."

"It's *my* house!" I exclaimed like a spoiled child. I couldn't think of anything better to say.

"Well, you're *my* princess," he countered angrily.

Everything froze. I blinked widely. His declaration vibrated my insides… my heart.

I waited for him to take it back. To make some stupid crack or joke to make light of what he said.

He didn't. Instead, he raked a hand through his deep-red locks and sighed.

"I don't think you'd still call me that if you read what I just did."

He made a sour face, produced my cell phone out of his pajama pants, and held it up. "You mean that piece of trash some 'journalist'"—he actually made air quotes around the word as he spoke—"wrote to suck Will's ass?"

"You read it?" I asked, mortified.

"You think I would watch you fall apart with that phone in your hands and then not look to see what caused it?" He made a tsking sound. "Not bloody likely."

I groaned and fell back on the bed dramatically. More tears leaked out from beneath my lids, and I covered my face with one hand.

"Hey." Nate spoke soft, his voice right above me. I sensed his presence, how he stood towering over the side of the bed, staring down. I didn't have to look to see him. I *felt* him.

I began to roll away, but he caught me. His hand palmed my hip and tugged so I wouldn't be able to roll. I fell back on my back, the hand covering my face dropping to my side. Nate pulled back from my hip but laced his fingers with my hand and reached out with his other. After a moment of hesitation, I relinquished my other one and allowed him to fold it into his.

Slowly, he pulled me up off the bed. I didn't want to move, so I made it extra hard on him. But he didn't give up. Instead, he released my hands and palmed my hips to steady me.

The panic and pain in my chest began to recede, a little bit of tingly warmth battling it back.

"That article fucking sucks," he said.

My chin wobbled, and I nodded. "I'm so embarrassed."

"Why would you be embarrassed?"

"I thought you read it? Will told everyone I cheated on him *and* I have an STD!"

"Will's about to have a fat lip and a black eye," he muttered.

I sucked in a breath. "You can't!" My hands grabbed at his T-shirt in handfuls, and I tried to make him pay attention. "Just stay away from him. He… he's mean."

Nate's voice was all rumbly when it came out. I actually felt his chest vibrate when he spoke. "You worried about me?"

I started to make a scoffing sound and pull away.

"No, you don't." Nate reacted instantly, pulling me in and wrapping his arms around me.

He was warm. And his shirt smelled like him, a scent I didn't even know I recognized until now. I took a deep breath, and one of his palms slid up my back in a soothing motion.

My breath hitched.

"It's okay, princess," he whispered.

The dam broke again, and I cried into his shoulder, tucking my face in the crook of his neck while tears rained and my back heaved with sobs.

He rocked us both back and forth, keeping the strongest of holds on me as we moved. I felt so secure like this. So safe. I couldn't remember the last time I felt safe...

My hand curled around his side and fisted his shirt at his back. He held tighter. I felt his lips move in my hair.

Suddenly, I needed him to know. I had to tell him.

I ripped back so forcefully he had to steady me again. "It's not true," I rushed out. My voice was hoarse. *Great.* Now I *sounded* like a toad. "Everything he said... it isn't true."

He used a thumb to brush some fresh tears off my cheeks, and my stomach dipped. "I know."

I blinked. The heaviness of my wet eyelashes seemed to make the action take longer. "You do?"

"Contrary to popular belief, I am not a moron."

A smile tugged at the corners of my lips.

"There it is," he murmured.

"What?"

"That smile of yours. Favorite part of my day lately."

I wanted to believe him. To take those words, swallow them down, and ingest them. I wanted to not fight the butterflies he always gave me.

I wanted to believe he meant what he said.

"What do you want from me?" I asked, my voice small.

"Right now, I'd really like you to stop crying."

"I'm sorry." I sniffled even as another tear tracked down my cheek.

"I'm kidding. Though, I really hate to see you cry." Nate cupped my face with his palms and tilted my face up. I never really realized I had to look up when I stared at him.

"I don't want anything from you."

I searched his emerald eyes. "I don't believe you."

"Fair enough. I lied anyway. You have good instincts."

I gasped, my eyes going wide. I would have jerked away, but his hands were warm. Comforting. And they spasmed on my jaw as if he anticipated the move.

"I do want something from you. A lot of somethings actually."

"I don't—" I started to pull away.

"Aerie." The intensity with which he said my name made me stop. There was something utterly commanding about him, but not in a scary way. "Don't pull away from me."

I listened.

He shifted, just his hips at first, but the rest of his body followed, coming close, nearly pressing our chests together. "I want your smile. I want your laugh. I want to know all the unanswered questions swimming around in my head about you. I want you to know that nothing anyone ever says or does could make me doubt what I've learned about you in the past week. Most of all…" His mouth lowered closer to mine. So close my breath caught and held. "Most of all, I want to kiss you."

My heart skipped a beat. Then two. "All those wants will go away when you get all the answers to those questions."

He shook his head slowly. "I don't think so."

His lips were so close. So near I was pretty sure it was his air I was breathing and not the room's. Nate had a hypnotic air about him, sort of as though he were his own force of gravity, and the center of it all was his jewel-toned eyes.

"It's almost sinful for a man to have such beautiful eyes."

His lips curved up. The smile reached the eyes I so loved.

I hadn't meant to speak out loud.

Gently, his thumb stroked over my cheek, then again.

My eyes drifted closed. I took the comfort he so casually offered. Will had never been big on affection or even comfort. Maybe in the beginning... before I realized what he really wanted. Before it was too late.

Thoughts of Will jolted me back into the present. Nate pulled away, putting some of the distance I thought I wanted between us. I really thought he was going to take that kiss he said he wanted. I was low-key anticipating it.

*Now isn't the time for kisses,* my head demanded.

*It's always time,* my heart sang back.

"I don't know what to do," I whispered. The confession ripped right out of me.

"I feel that way a lot," he told me. "Usually, I'm just hungry."

I giggled.

His voice turned serious. "There's something I really need to know, princess."

You would think that stupid nickname would remind me of how I "fell" from royalty to a toad with warts. You would think the nickname would make me think he didn't even care enough to bother with my name.

It didn't.

If anything, it reminded me of how Nate saw me when the rest of the world was the complete opposite.

"What?" I was anxious, afraid of what he would ask.

"Are you married or not?"

I frowned. "You know that Will and I…"

He made an impatient sound. His finger shot out, tapping me right above the heart. "Are you married or not?"

"No."

Sweeping forward in a graceful rush of movement, his hand slid effortlessly into my hair to cradle the back of my head. Before I could even think, his mouth collided with mine.

My eyes shot open as a feeling I'd never experienced blew through me like a gale-force wind. He felt it too because his eyes also widened. We stood there frozen, lips locked, staring at each other.

"Whoa," he whispered. Then he kissed me all over again. Two first kisses in the span of a single heartbeat.

He kissed like he was starved, as if I were a full bowl and he wouldn't stop licking into my mouth until he'd gotten every last drop.

And, *oh*, I'd let him lick me dry.

My God, could he kiss. Nate Roth was one surprise after another. Maybe he was so skilled at kissing because he constantly ran his mouth.

It was amazing. Absolutely stunning.

I gripped the front of his shirt and hung on, one of his hands snaked around my back and yanked me against him. I sighed. His tongue danced over my lips, teasing. When I opened, he retreated, sucking my bottom lip between his and coaxing a moan from deep in my throat.

My head fell back, but his palm supported it. Nate lifted his mouth only enough to change the angle and drop a kiss on the corner of my lips. I sighed at the sweetness in the middle of the frenzy. His tongue stroked into me like a jolt of electricity in a blackout.

I met his fever with my own, for once giving instead of allowing someone to just take.

Too soon, he started to retreat. I made a sound and grabbed his ears, pulling him back down again. He laughed in his throat, but it turned to a groan when his lips covered mine again.

My heart was pounding when he finally stepped back. I could barely catch my breath. My head was fuzzy. The second he was gone, I covered my mouth with my fingers, holding in the heat he left behind. Holding on to the feeling no one else had ever inspired.

"That was better than Fruity Pebbles," he quipped, swiping at his lower lip with his thumb. I couldn't help but note the way his eyes had transformed into a deep shade of moss.

"You just compared our kiss to cereal," I pointed out.

He opened his mouth, no doubt to say something else that was ridiculous yet somehow also utterly charming.

I held up my hand, stopping him. "I need some time. To think."

"Thinking is overrated."

I gave him a stern look.

"Yeah. Okay." He nodded. His red hair flopped around with the movement.

*Damn. I should have run my fingers through it when I had the chance.*

I chewed on my lower lip and nodded.

"Don't lock the door. I'll just pick it again."

I narrowed my eyes.

"No more crying."

I crossed my arms over my chest.

"And I'm keeping your phone because you'll just look up more online trash."

"I will not!" I declared. Who was he to boss me around like this?

He raised an eyebrow. "Didn't I already tell you I'm not a moron?"

I let out a huff and went back to glaring.

"I'll be in the living room, working, if you need me. Or if you don't."

I watched his pajama-clad self go and sort of wished he would stay. But I knew time alone was the best thing. He made it hard to think, and I definitely needed to.

"Oh, princess?" he said, turning back around in the doorway.

"What?" I growled.

"Just in case you're wondering, Fruity Pebbles is my favorite thing ever, and you just beat them out."

He left me standing there wondering why I asked for time to think.

# seventeen

## *Nate*

My room wasn't as close to Aerie's as I would have liked. As aforementioned, I am not a moron. Therefore, I never told her I would have preferred to share a wall.

Since I got here, she never so much as came to the door, let alone walk right in, so imagine me shocked as shit when I opened my eyes to find her hovering over me, staring down with wide eyes.

"Princess?" I exclaimed. Not even my shock could conceal the thick sleep in my voice.

It was dark as hell in this room, had to be the dead middle of the night. Yet here she was, her dark hair blending in with the shadows, the whites of her eyes standing out exceptionally. She danced back and forth from foot to foot as she hovered near where I lay.

"There's someone in the house," she whispered, clutching Cheeto against her chest.

I jerked up, the covers falling down around my waist. "What?"

Aerie's head bobbed. "We need to get out."

My brain was tripping to catch up, even though adrenaline was already pumping through my veins. "Why isn't the alarm going off?"

She moved closer to the mattress, so close her body came into contact with it. "Because someone cut the power. I have an alert on my phone that tells me if something like this happens."

"You're sure someone cut the power and it just didn't go out?" Even as I asked, I shoved the covers back.

A loud bang from somewhere in the house caused my head to whip around.

"I already called the police. It's going to take them a few to get all the way out here," she whispered.

I leapt out of the bed, not self-conscious at all of the fact all I had on was a pair of boxer briefs.

"Get in bed," I demanded, pointing at the spot I'd just vacated.

"What?" she stammered. "No. We have to go."

"He's already in the house, A. I'm not risking your safety by lurking around this house for the door. Get in the damn bed." My heart was thundering, my mind already calculating. I really hoped there wasn't more than one or two men.

"What are you going to do?"

My eyes flashed up to her scared face.

"Get in the bed, princess." Gently, I shoved her in and pulled the covers up over her bare legs. "Don't open the door for anyone. Not even me."

"What?"

"Do it," I said, no room for argument in my tone. "You'll be safe in here 'til the cops come."

I started to rush from the room, but her urgent voice stopped me. "Nate! Don't do this!"

"Keep this locked." I reminded her, locking the handle and then slipping out into the hallway, shutting it behind me.

After a quick check to verify the bedroom door was definitely locked, I moved down the hall, keeping my back against the wall as I crept.

I knew someone who wanted in that room could get through the lock. But they'd have to get through me first. I might not be as big as her bodyguards, or as skilled, but I wasn't completely lacking. I had what it took, at the very least, to keep the them fuck away from her until reinforcements showed up.

What the hell was going on anyway? Who had balls big enough to bypass Aerie's very elaborate security system and waltz right into her estate? Why?

*Overzealous fan?*

*Stalker?*

*Someone who didn't know she was home and wanted an easy payday?*

*What if she was here alone?*

My blood ran cold at the last thought. Technically, she was supposed to be here alone. If I hadn't showed up and basically conned my way in, she would be running around this house right now, alone in the dark, against unknown opponents.

"Toss the place," I heard a deep, low voice command as I crept to the top of the stairs. It wasn't quite as dark here because of all the large windows at the front. The moonlight filtered in, giving me some sense of the space.

There was more than one man.

A few other muffled thuds and the sound of shattering glass echoed through the night.

"This is pretty nice shit," another said. "I'm keeping this."

I slinked down the stairs, hoping they were too busy with their felony to come out and notice me. At the bottom, there was a piece of furniture tucked against the wall with some oversized, wooden candleholders in various heights. The second my bare feet left the last step, I crept to the holders and silently picked up the biggest, heaviest one.

It wasn't a gun, but I was better at baseball than shooting anyway.

"C'mon, next room. Then we'll go find her."

Goose bumps raced over my skin. That temper in me exploded like an erupting volcano. Trashing this house was one thing. Going after my girl?

Fuck no.

Bubbling anger made me move faster, rushing across the cold floor. I didn't look down, but toward the living room.

Sharp pain sliced through the pad of my foot, and then more stinging pain followed. I bit down on my lip and stuttered to a stop, but it wasn't a silent sound. My sudden movements sent broken glass shards sliding over the tile and clinking into each other.

A few things happened instantly:

1. I noted the giant windowpane that was smashed in near the door.

2. My presence was no longer secret.

3. We all stopped, silently trying to sense each other out.

After I stood frozen for all of the span of several heart beats, I burst into action. Ignoring the pain in the bottom of my feet, I rushed into the room, brandishing the candleholder.

"Who the hell are you?" one of the men exclaimed.

Barely noting how trashed the room was, I rushed toward the closest man. There were two of them, all in black, ski masks covering their fuckwad faces.

I used the element of surprise I had going and lunged, swinging the heavy wood and clocking him on the side of the head. He dropped onto the floor like an anvil and didn't move.

I crashed stares with the second man, but then he took off deeper into the house. No longer attempting to be any kind of quiet, he grabbed and pulled things as he went, leaving a trail of shit for me to maneuver around as I chased.

Just when I thought he was going into the kitchen, he veered off, ducking into a small hallway that led back out to the front of the house near the front door.

I picked up the pace, thinking he was going to try and run out the front door. As I rounded the corner, he jolted up the first step.

*Holy fuck, he's going for Aerie.*

"You mother fucker!" I yelled. "Don't you touch her!"

He laughed as I scrambled after him. Dropping the candlestick, I took the stairs three at a time, catching his out-of-shape ass at the top. With a running leap, I jumped on his back, and he fell onto his knees. I punched him in the side of the head, and he grabbed me, flipping me over his shoulder.

I landed on my back, sprawled out in front of him.

He grunted as his fist came down like a hammer. I rolled just before he caught me in the face.

Scrambling up to my knees, I lunged, knocking him backward. With him on his back, I leapt on top of him and decked him in the face. Then I did it again. The sound of the bones in my hand crunching didn't make me pause as I drew back my fist a third time.

The man rolled, using his weight and hands to shove as we went. I hit the wall with a thud. The painting hanging there rattled loudly. The man stood, and I rushed to do the same.

"Nate!" Aerie screamed, her voice muffled from behind the door at the end of the hall.

"Don't you open that—*oomph*." With my distraction at hearing Aerie call out, the man buried his fist in my gut. I folded over, grabbing my middle, but then jerked upright again.

We stood there, measuring each other, chests heaving. I should have ripped the mask off his face when I had the chance, though at least I got in some good hits. His mouth was bloody and so was his nose.

Aerie screamed for me again, and the man's mouth curved into a slow, sadistic smile.

I lunged, throwing all my weight into him, slamming us both into the wall behind him. His head bounced off, and I took a cheap shot, kneeing him right in the balls.

I didn't give a fuck. Any man who would break into some defenseless woman's house with the intent to do her harm didn't deserve a pair anyway.

Douche.

He doubled over with a whimper, and I stepped back, wiping at the side of my mouth. Preparing to launch myself at him one more time, I lurched forward.

The burglar snapped upright, suddenly more confident than before. The muzzle of a gun glinted in the dark, and the sound of it cocking made me stop.

"Step aside," he slurred, pointing the weapon at the center of my chest.

I kept my eyes trained on his, not giving the gun a glance.

"You're not going down this hallway," I growled.

"We'll just see about that."

# eighteen

*Aerie*

The sounds of shattering glass echoed in my ears.

Muffled thumps and shouts weren't totally kept out by the door Nate shut me behind.

I paced, desperate to know if he was okay.

"You're not going down this hallway," I heard him intone.

He was literally putting himself in front of me, this man who compared me to cereal and kissed like a god.

I couldn't just sit here. I couldn't just allow him to protect me.

Who would protect him?

I glanced back, making sure the kitten was still in the bed, then reached for the lock.

The sound of a gunshot reverberated through the house.

# nineteen

## Nate

Never rush a man with a gun.

It was probably Self-Defense 101.

I never took that class.

And I meant what the hell I said. He wasn't going down this hallway, bullet or no. The second he made his little declaration, *"We'll just see about that"*—seriously, he couldn't give a better one-liner?—I burst into action.

His eyes widened when he realized I didn't give two little shits about his threats, but it was a second too late. I slammed into him, and the gun went off.

We both went down. The bullet tunneled into the wall, and the pistol fell from his grip.

Aerie was near hysterical in the background, but I didn't look back.

We scrambled for the gun, and I came up the winner. Lurching up, I cocked it again and pointed it down where he was heaving on the floor.

"Get up," I intoned, pointing it with a steady hand. He hesitated.

"I'm a terrible shot, bro," I told him. "So when I pull this trigger, there's no telling where the bullet is gonna go."

"Nate!" Aerie collided into my back, nearly taking me down.

"I told you to stay in the bedroom!" My eyes didn't leave the criminal, even as her soft arms wrapped around me from behind.

"Are you hurt? Oh my gosh!" Small hands patted me down, reminding me I had no clothes on.

"I'm fine." I assured her. "Now go back to the room. Lock the door."

The man thought I was distracted and tried to rush me. Aerie screamed, and I wrapped my free hand over her arms where she held me, then fired off a shot.

It whizzed by the man, barely missing him. He stopped short.

"Next time, I won't miss."

He retreated for the stairs. I took off after him, grabbing a handful of the black jacket he was wearing. Taken off guard, he lurched forward, and I let go. He went tumbling down the stairs like an actor in a bad movie.

"Watch your head!" I told him as he rolled.

Now *that* was a one-liner.

He landed with a thud at the bottom, staring up at the ceiling, his chest still heaving. Police sirens filled the silence, and I casually walked down the stairs, stood over the man, and pointed the gun directly down.

"Just stay there," I told him. "Cops are here. Their aim is better than mine."

He made a pathetic moaning sound.

I heard Aerie behind me, and I held out one arm, not glancing away from the man. She rushed into my side, burying her face into my neck as I tucked my arm around her.

"I told you to stay in the room." I scolded, kissing the top of her head.

"I thought you got shot." She sniffled into my neck.

"His aim sucks, too." I assured her.

Police cars skidded to a halt in front of the house, and I noted the way the front door swayed open in the breeze. The man I clocked with the candleholder must have skipped out.

"Looks like your buddy left you to take the fall," I told the thug.

He groaned.

"I hope you're feeling chatty, 'cause I've got some questions."

In my arms, Aerie trembled, and I tightened my hold.

# twenty

## *Aerie*

Nate was willing to take a bullet for me. Without being paid to do so.

I literally couldn't say that about anyone else. I could scarcely wrap my head around the fact, but as I watched the sky lighten as the last police officer drove away, the darkness couldn't conceal the truth anymore.

"I should have shot him," Nate muttered, watching the car go.

I glanced at him, slightly amused. My stomach fluttered as I took in his rumpled hair, shadowed jaw, and shrewd expression. "I thought you were a bad shot?"

He snorted. "I'm not that bad. Asshole was right in front of me."

"Maybe once he's spent the night behind bars, he'll talk." Much to Nate's disliking, the intruder said not one word about his intentions or even how he managed to get through my state-of-the-art security system.

Nate turned. The giant pineapple on the front of his shirt was impossible not to look at.

"You have the weirdest shirts."

His eyebrows lifted. "They're vintage. And thank you." He patted his chest and the pineapple covering it. His face darkened. "I should've shot him."

"I'm glad you didn't," I whispered, shivering. I would likely hear the sound of that gun going off over and over again for months. The amount of fear I felt when I heard it shocked me.

Not the fear itself, silly.

If a person didn't feel fear when an intruder fired a gun inside their house, then they were probably highly overmedicated.

Or insane.

I was neither.

The fear I felt wasn't for me, though. It was for Nate. That spoke a lot about how I felt about him. About losing him.

"Hey." His voice was so close it made me shiver. I liked how sometimes it was gruff and deep. More serious. "C'mon. You're cold." Without any kind of hesitation, he draped an arm over my shoulder and pulled me into his side.

At the front door (which was still wide open), he stopped abruptly, then moved swiftly, swinging me up in his arms.

Squealing, my wrists looped around his neck automatically. "What are you doing?"

He stopped again and gazed down at me with bright-green eyes. "You saw me in nothing by my skivvies. In some countries, that would make us married. I'm just doing my husbandly duty, carrying my new bride over the threshold."

I blinked.

Blinked again.

"Put me down!" I wailed.

Nate snickered. "There's glass on the floor, princess. I don't want you to cut your feet."

I stopped wiggling around. His words made me melt. *He's still thinking about me.* "What about your feet?"

"Mine are already cut."

Gasping, I grabbed the front of his pineapple shirt. "Why didn't you say something?"

"I was busy," he said, as if it were obvious.

When we got to the stairs, I practically jumped out of his arms and grabbed his hand. "Come on."

I led him back toward his room but through it and into the adjoining bath. I patted the long counter with two sinks on each end. "Sit."

He obliged without any kind of snarky comment, which made me wonder exactly what I would find when I looked at the bottom of his feet. After laying aside the first aid kit, I gestured to his foot. "Let's see it."

"It's not that bad," he argued.

Wrapping my palm around his heel, I lifted. Red smeared the bottom, and I made a sound of distress. "Nate," I said, part sadness, part frustration.

"I'll take care of it. Go check on Cheeto."

"Cheeto's fine. He's still in bed." I flipped open the kit and turned on one of the sinks. "Put your foot over here," I instructed.

He winced when the water rushed over his bare foot, and I felt bad, but not bad enough to stop. Once it was clean, I wrapped it in a clean cloth and repeated the process with his other foot, which was also cut.

"What do you think they wanted?" I whispered. Some of the adrenaline I'd been drawing on started to ebb away, leaving behind a woman who was tired and afraid.

"Cops said they probably didn't know you were here and wanted an easy payday."

"You don't believe that." It wasn't a question. I could feel his doubt.

He didn't say anything as I drew out a pair of tweezers and lifted the foot that still had some glass in it.

"No. I don't."

"How come?"

"Ow!" he howled when I pulled out a sliver of glass.

"Hold still!" I scolded and went back for another.

"Just leave it in there!"

"It will get infected."

"That's what antibiotics are for."

"Don't be an idiot," I admonished and pulled out the last two slivers. The cuts with the glass were bleeding again, so I grabbed up some peroxide and a cotton pad.

He glared at me as I cleaned the cuts and scrapes, added some ointment to the worst ones, and placed a couple Band-Aids over the still-bleeding areas.

"You gonna answer my question?" My voice was soft as I reached for his other foot.

He sighed. "They knew you were home, A."

My face jerked up. "They did?"

He nodded. His lips were a hard line. "They were going upstairs for you."

The liquid in the bottle sloshed around when I lifted it.

"You don't need to do this right now," Nate said, reaching out and covering my hand with his.

"I want to."

"You're shaking." His fingers tightened around mine.

"Just let me."

His hands left mine, and he lifted his foot, offering it.

This one had no glass in it, so I just cleaned it up and added some ointment. When I was done, I busied myself putting away the supplies and hanging the soiled towels on a nearby rack. I felt his eyes the entire time I worked.

He said nothing. I said nothing. The room wasn't quiet, though, because the sound of my thundering heart was so loud.

When there was nothing left for me to do, Nate's hand closed gently around my upper arm and drew me close, fitting my body between his legs.

"Thank you." The words rushed out breathlessly.

"For what?" His hand left my arm and tucked some hair behind my ear.

"For saving my life. Because you probably did."

The corner of his mouth lifted. "You would have given them hell if I hadn't been here."

I ducked my head, suddenly so ashamed. "I'm not as strong as I pretend to be."

His fingers were gentle when they pushed my chin up so his eyes could search mine. "I think you are."

He didn't understand. I didn't expect him to. I was a toad, but he saw a princess.

I wasn't sure if I should love him or hate him for it.

*I think I probably want to love him.*

"Thank you," I repeated.

His eyes warmed. "You're welcome." I couldn't pull my gaze from his. I felt physically chained by something that wasn't even physical.

Then he went and ruined it.

"You owe me."

The words slapped me like frigid water. "Excuse me?"

He opened his mouth, but I cut him off.

"You think 'cause you saved my life, you have some sort of claim on it now?" I crossed my arms over my chest and glared.

I should have known he was just like everyone else… I was stupid. *Stupid.*

He made a face. "No…" He moved, somehow sticking his bandaged foot right in my face. "I meant because I let you dig glass out of my foot."

It took a minute for his words to sink past my anger.

He wiggled his toes, and a laugh bubbled out of me. Those thoughts of love I'd been thinking came back in a rush. "I did that for you," I pointed out.

"I need something for the pain."

I frowned. "How bad does it hurt? I have some pain reliever—"

In one movement, Nate hopped down off the counter but lifted me to where he'd just been. "I don't want pills, princess."

Tiny shivers shot up and down my spine. "No?"

He shook his head.

"What do you want?"

He tapped his lips with a single finger. The bottom fell out of my belly. A soft buzzing sound filled my head.

"Kiss me, Aerie."

"W-what?" I murmured, staring at his lips.

He smiled, a knowing light in his eyes. "Can I kiss you?"

I nodded, not really hearing him, but understanding what he wanted. Both arms slipped around me, dragging my ass across the counter toward him. Automatically, my legs wound around his waist and our chests bumped.

His mouth crashed over mine instantly. Kissing Nate was a full-contact sport. He was unapologetic in the way his mouth moved over mine, the way he nibbled my lips and tangled our tongues.

The buzzing in my head grew heavy, just like my limbs. A small moan vibrated the back of my throat. He kissed deeper.

The next thing I knew, I was off the counter completely and he was carrying me into the bedroom toward his bed. Our lips didn't part when we hit the mattress. One minute I was in his arms; the next his body was lowering over mine.

I sank into the sheets, noting they carried his scent. Remembering my previous regret, I trailed my hands up the back of his neck, delving my fingers into his hair. The strands were thick and cool, wrapping around my fingers like a satin blanket. A satin blanket made of fire.

He moved against me, eliciting an instant rush of need so strong I arched against him. He made a soft sound as his hand slid over my shoulder and down my arm. His lips captured mine in a renewed kiss at the same moment his fingers entwined with mine.

*Oh my heart. Oh, it was in danger.*

He felt the change in me—the slight tensing of my muscles, the way the vulnerability I felt under his touch scared the crap out of me. He didn't leave, but his lips pulled back. He lifted, allowing his body to hover over mine.

My eyes fluttered open. As much as I didn't want to look, I couldn't deny the call. I thought I would find smugness. Power. Some kind of satisfaction in his stare.

I was wrong.

His eyes glimmered like emeralds under a summer sun. Warmth radiated off him. Hunger, too.

Nate smiled down at me.

He dropped a kiss to the tip of my nose, then rolled away and sat up. On the nightstand, his phone went off.

He didn't look at it, but he did groan.

I lifted my head off the pillow. "Nate?"

"I have to go."

"Go?" My brain was having trouble keeping up.

He made a sound. "I was going to tell you yesterday…"

I'd spent the entire day hiding in my room. I pushed up into a sitting position. "You're leaving?"

Everything inside me crumbled.

He made a sound. "*We're* leaving."

"What?"

He stood, towering over me from beside the bed. "There's no way in hell I'm leaving you here alone with a shitty security system and those assholes."

"There are assholes here?" I wondered out loud.

He glowered down. "Pack a bag, princess. You're coming with me."

I lifted my chin. "What if I don't want to?"

He dropped down, planting his palms on the mattress and bringing us eye to eye. "You do."

I could have the windows replaced, the house cleaned up, and the security system fixed and upgraded while I was gone. When I came home, everything would be good as new. Safer.

No one would know where I was this time. No one expected me to run off with Nate.

*Not even Will.*

These were perfectly good reasons to go with Nate. He was right, though. I *wanted* to go with him.

"Where are we going?" I asked.

A slow smile took over his face. "New York."

I faltered. He lived in New York. "You're going home?"

"Yep. And you're coming with me."

"But why?"

"I have some shit to get in order, and it won't wait. But I *can't* leave you here, princess." He paused, tilting his head, and turned back to me. "Actually, I could leave you here, but I don't *want* to. Now go pack."

I hid my smile until he turned away to get his bag.

"What about Cheeto?" I asked, almost as though it were some kind of test.

"He's coming, too."

My smile turned into a grin.

Maybe Nate wasn't just like everyone else after all.

He was much better.

# twenty-one

## *Nate*

Flying back to Blaylock wasn't what I wanted. I gave my word, though, so I was going. A man wasn't much if he couldn't keep his promises.

It was getting harder to compartmentalize my life. It felt more and more like I was living a double one. Like a secret agent. Maybe in my past life, I was Tom Cruise.

A better-looking version, of course.

Much as I hated to admit it, I was beginning to see my dad's point. I couldn't have both. I couldn't remain at Blaylock *and* start my career. Truth was my career had already started the day Ten announced I was songwriting with him. I knew the songs were going to be a hit—hell, even sit at the top of the charts. That was the power of Ten.

I didn't imagine it would basically put me in the middle of a bidding war between labels.

I could do this. Be a songwriter. One who made good money. A man who could do what he loved on his terms.

Yeah, maybe I could have still managed that while being a student at Blaylock, at least until I graduated… but Aerie.

I wasn't willing to work remotely from her. All it took was one week, a stray kitten, and a threat to her life.

I had to make a choice now:

My career or Blaylock. Being at her side or being at home.

My dad was going to be hella pissed.

I didn't expect Aerie to give in so easily when I told her to pack a bag. Her words—*I'm not as strong as I pretend to be*—echoed through my mind as I watched her from across the plane.

She had her knees tucked into her chest, chin resting atop her leggings, and those thick, tall socks with bows pulled up to just beneath her knees. She'd tossed off her boots the second we stepped on the plane (Ten's private jet. Thanks, cuz!) and sunk into the leather seat near the small window. Currently, streaks of sun shone through, lighting the strands of dark hair falling around her face with chestnut-colored features.

"Princess," I said, just wanting to say her name. Wanting to watch her look at me.

Her head swiveled around.

"You haven't told me how you're doing." We'd barely spoken at all about what happened, other than when she was cleaning up my feet.

She shrugged.

"Come here."

Aerie pushed out of the chair. Halfway to me, her cell went off. She frowned and went back. "I should have turned this thing off."

"Shut it off now."

"I don't recognize the number… It could be the police," she murmured.

Aerie swayed on her feet. I caught her around the waist, plucked the phone out of her hand, and hit DECLINE. Then I shut off the device completely.

"No more phone, A," I ordered and tossed it over toward my crap. It was probably the fucking press calling to stress her out even more.

Assholes.

She didn't say anything, just stared off into space. I walked backward, taking her with me, and sat on the couch-style seat, pulling her into my lap.

She curled into my chest, balancing her feet on the seat beside my leg. "Nate?"

I made a sound, acknowledging her.

"I'm glad I came."

I smiled into her hair. "Me, too."

Yeah, there was no way in hell I would walk away from her right now.

Maybe not ever.

# twenty-two

## *Aerie*

When Nate pulled his bright-blue Ford Focus into the driveway of a brick townhome, the reality of what I was doing stabbed me like a knife.

"I know it's probably not what you're used to," he said, turning off the engine.

I gasped, ripped my eyes off the quaint home, and turned to him. Without thought, my hand covered his. "I think it's lovely."

He gave me a look as if he thought I was lying. But I wasn't.

Clearing my throat, an image of my childhood flashed in my mind. "I wasn't always famous or rich, you know. There was a time when I had less... a lot less." I glanced back at the place he called home. "I like it."

Beneath my hand, Nate flipped his over, linking our fingers. "Fair warning. It's a bachelor pad inside."

My fingers tightened around his. "You live with your dad."

He nodded.

"I hadn't really thought of that before... I've been so preoccupied." I lifted my eyes to his. "He has no idea I'm coming."

Nate shrugged. "It's not a big deal. He won't mind."

I wasn't sure I believed him. Watching him now, I wasn't sure *he* believed him.

"I can stay at a hotel." I offered. "Just take me to the closest one."

His mouth flattened. "No. You're staying with me."

"But—"

"You're staying." With those final words, he got out of the car and slammed the door before I could argue further.

Inside his carrier, Cheeto meowed.

I glanced over my shoulder at it on the backseat. "It's okay," I told him. "We're here."

"C'mon, princess," Nate said from the open hatch in the back.

I got out of the car with Cheeto, and Nate loaded himself down with our bags. I followed him through the garage and to a door that led into the house.

He was barely through when a voice carried out to me. "You're late."

"Dad! I missed you too," Nate exclaimed, dropping all the bags and flinging himself at a man standing in the kitchen.

He chuckled, and I smiled. Nate had a way with everyone. He endeared himself so effortlessly.

"Good to see you, son," his father said and slapped him on the back. I moved a little farther into the doorway, and his eyes flashed to mine.

Nate's father was younger-looking than I expected. He had close-cropped dark hair (not red) and light-colored eyes (not green, though). He was slightly taller than his son and wider. He was dressed in a pair of jeans and a T-shirt, a green flannel open over them.

"Who's this?" he asked, still staring at me.

I was used to staring, but he made me nervous. I wanted him to like me, and it seemed I was going to have to work for it. Something I was *not* used to.

"Dad, this is Aerie Boone," Nate said, coming back toward me to take the carrier I was holding. When his back was turned to his father, he winked at me. "And this guy in here is Cheeto."

"You brought home a girl *and* a cat." His father stared.

"Aerie, this is my dad, Derek. He's head of the music department at Blaylock."

"It's nice to meet you, sir," I said. "Music is something we have in common. I—"

"I know who you are," he spoke, cutting me off.

See? Work for it.

"Aerie's having some work done on her house, so I figured she could stay here while we work on her album."

"Album?"

Nate nodded enthusiastically. "Turns out it's not just one song they hired me for. It's an entire album."

Honestly, Derek looked a lot less excited and proud than I thought he'd be. Nate always talked about his dad like they had a great relationship, but it sure didn't seem like it right now.

"How's that going to work with school?" he asked.

"I'll make it work," Nate replied.

Derek didn't say anything. An awkward silence filled the air for a long pause.

I cleared my throat. "I know it's probably a surprise that I'm here. I'm happy to go to a hotel—"

"You are *not* going to a hotel, A." Nate's tone rang with finality, as if anyone would dare say otherwise.

Derek cleared his throat. "Of course not," he said and came forward, offering his hand to me. "Nice to meet you."

I took his hand and smiled. "Nate has told me a lot about you." Derek seemed surprised. I smiled. "All good, of course."

Cheeto meowed. I made a sound and went over to Nate, opened the carrier, and pulled out the kitten.

"That thing is tiny," Derek said.

"Nate found him on the side of the road," I explained. "We sort of adopted him."

"You two adopted him," he echoed.

Nate's hand settled on the small of my back. "C'mon. Let's get him some food, show him his room."

I let him lead me into a room with a twin bed on each side. It looked like a space where a war was going on. A war between a child and an adult.

"Is this your room?" I asked, gazing around. A warm feeling filled me.

"Since I was born," he replied. "It's your room while you're here, too."

I gaped at him.

He chuckled and pointed to one of the beds. "That's usually Ten's, but he won't mind if you borrow it."

"Ten sleeps here?"

He made a face. "I washed the sheets."

We were going to be sharing a room. Nate and I in the same space… all night long. Butterflies filled my belly and my limbs tingled.

Cheeto squirmed around, and I set him down. He moved around the room, sniffing and checking everything out cautiously.

"I feel like I shouldn't be here," I confessed quietly.

Nate dropped the bags he was holding and moved to shut the door. Coming back to where I was, he grabbed my hands and stared down. "I want you here, princess. Don't take my dad's lack of… welcome personal. He's, ah, pissed at me because he wants me to finish school."

"I kinda got the impression he wasn't happy about the album."

Nate sighed, sinking down on his bed. He seemed too big for it, and I smiled a little, kind of excited to watch him squish himself in it tonight. "Ten's career changed him, almost destroyed him."

I nodded. I knew all about Ten and what fame could do to a person.

"Dad thinks it's going to do the same to me, too."

I shook my head, adamant. "It won't."

He cocked his head to the side. "How do you know?"

"You aren't like anyone I've ever met. You're… solid. You know who you are. I don't think anything can corrupt you."

Nate shoved off the bed and stalked across the room with intent. His hands felt familiar at my waist, and I tipped my chin back, knowing he was coming.

The kiss didn't linger, though I wish it had. Instead, he pulled back, rested his forehead on mine, and sighed. "Sometimes I think he wants me to stay a little kid forever."

I cupped his face, letting my thumbs stroke his cheeks. "I can't really blame him. I wouldn't want to let go of you either."

He kissed me again. This time it was longer. This time he didn't pull away until my lungs absolutely burned for air.

A sudden knock on the bedroom door made me jump back.

"Yeah?" Nate called out.

"You guys wanna go to dinner?"

He lifted an eyebrow to me in silent question. I nodded.

"Be right there!" he answered.

The sound of Derek retreating echoed into the room.

"I need to set up Cheeto's stuff, and then I'll change."

"You don't need to change," he murmured, nuzzling the side of my neck. He made me feel drunk. "I like those socks. They kind of drive me crazy."

I wrinkled my nose. "My socks?" They were just knee socks. Cozy ones I usually wore when I was alone.

He growled, kissing under my jaw.

"I look a mess, Nate."

"You could never." He pulled back, leaving me slightly dizzy. Enough that I had to grab the front of his shirt to steady myself.

His hand covered mine. "Hey, you sure you're up for dinner? A lot's happened today. You haven't really said how you are."

*You're here. I'm fine.* I nodded. "I'm up for it."

Cheeto made a sound, and I glanced around, bursting out laughing. He came out from beneath Nate's bed, a pair of boxers draped over his back.

"Hey, I was wondering where those went," he quipped.

I rolled my eyes. "You're gross."

The nervousness I'd felt when we first arrived was still there, but now it wasn't at the forefront. Instead, there was curiosity. I was excited to be here at Blaylock, to see Nate's home.

Excited to learn everything I could about him.

# twenty-three

*Nate*

Small sounds from across the room woke me.

Aerie was whimpering in her sleep.

Without hesitation, I shoved off the blankets and nearly fell out of the bed and onto my ass. I'd gotten used to sleeping in a bigger bed at her place… I really needed to get rid of this children's furniture and get a bigger one.

*I really need my own place.*

She made another sound, and my chest lurched. Moving restlessly under the blankets, she was likely dreaming about what happened just last night.

I sat on the edge of her bed and took her hand. "Aerie," I whispered, rubbing my thumb over her skin. "Wake up."

Her eyes shot open, and she gasped.

"Hey," I murmured, grabbing her other hand, now holding both. "It was just a dream."

She sniffled and drew in a ragged breath.

"You're safe," I whispered.

Aerie tugged her hands from mine, lifting the top of the covers, inviting me in.

I slipped beneath without hesitation. Before I was even on my back, she was fitting herself against me, pressing her face near my neck and tucking her arm around me.

I froze for a moment, lying against the pillows, and stared up at the black ceiling. She was cuddling up to me. This was unfamiliar territory… I wasn't usually the guy who got the cuddles.

I wasn't a virgin, but this kind of intimacy wasn't something I was used to.

I liked it.

A whole hell of a lot.

I didn't know what to do. Did I just lie there and not move? What if I rolled on her? What if I started sweating… Oh shit, what if I farted?

*Do not fuck this up, Roth.*

Aerie made a small sound and curled closer. Just like that, I was unfrozen. My body relaxed into the mattress, my arms closed around her, and I took a chance and gently pushed my leg between hers.

She sighed, content, and then her breathing turned steady.

Cheeto jumped up on the bed. Where he came from I had no clue. He walked around for a few seconds, then settled against us.

I smiled into the dark before I fell asleep.

My alarm went off too soon. And from across the damn room. It went off and off before it silenced itself. I only had five minutes before it started going off again, but hey, five minutes was five minutes.

Aerie stretched against me, her long, lean body arched into me, and a sound vibrated her throat. I rolled from beneath her and onto my side, lining up our bodies so we were face to face.

Her eyes cracked open, and she smiled. "Hi."

"Hi."

"I had a nightmare."

I pushed a strand of hair off her cheek. "I was just thinking you should have one again tonight."

She ducked her head, but not before I saw the full smile transform her face.

"You have classes, don't you?" she asked after a moment.

"There is literally no other reason I would set that alarm."

Her lips turned up again.

Reaching out, I brushed a finger over her mouth. "You're smiley in the morning, princess. I like it."

"Guess I slept well."

Her eyes drifted closed when I leaned forward, then sprang right back open when my stupid alarm started squawking again.

"Worst timing ever," I growled and went to shut the thing up once and for all. In the few short moments I was gone, Cheeto took advantage of the spot I'd just vacated.

"Traitor," I told him, glaring down with the cell clutched in my hand.

I heard Dad out in the kitchen, and I sighed. "I'm going to grab a quick shower and some breakfast. You can go back to sleep."

"'Kay," she murmured, snuggling beneath the blankets.

Geez, she didn't have to rub it in. Or look that comfortable without me in the bed with her.

I grumbled about it the whole way to the bathroom and halfway through my shower. Getting ready for class was the norm. My reality. Getting up, showering, traipsing across campus—those were all things I did on the daily.

Spring break had only been a week and a half (well, two for me 'cause I skipped out early), so this routine should feel normal to me. Like putting on a well-worn pair of jeans.

It didn't. It felt foreign. Strange. Like I was suddenly living someone else's life.

This didn't feel like me anymore. As if some switch inside me had been flipped, and there was no way to flip it back.

Once I was dressed in my usual jeans and a Green Day T-shirt, I made a beeline for the Fruity Pebbles. I dumped half the box in my bowl and added some milk. I groaned in fruity bliss as I crunched on the huge spoonful in my mouth while I made a mug of coffee.

Dad stepped in, dressed for work. "Morning, son."

I said good morning around the cereal. It didn't really sound like anything but loud chewing.

"If you have a chance while you're on campus today, stop by my office."

I swallowed. "Sure thing."

"I have an early meeting…" He began as he poured himself a travel mug of coffee. "So I'll see you later?"

I nodded and shoved another huge bite of cereal in my mouth.

When he was gone, I added some more to my bowl, tucked the near-empty box beneath my arm, and carried the coffee and cereal back into my room.

Aerie was looking pretty adorable in bed with the cat, so I set the mug on the bedside table, plopped down on the edge of the mattress, and shoveled more cereal into my mouth.

A moment later, her head turned in my direction. "What on earth are you doing?"

"Breakfast," I answered, chewing loudly.

She groaned. "I thought you said I could go back to sleep."

"I changed my mind," I told her and dumped the rest of the box into the bowl. "So good." I groaned.

She sat up, leaning against the headboard. Her hair was all disheveled, and her eyes were still sleepy. "Did you eat that entire box?" she asked, pointing to the empty cardboard at my feet.

"I was having withdrawals."

She made a sound, and I took a moment to point to the mug with my spoon. "Brought you some coffee."

"You brought me coffee?"

"I'll make you breakfast before I go. Wouldn't want you to burn the place down while I'm gone."

"Har-har," she intoned, picking up the coffee and taking a sip. Her eyebrows lifted, and her expression changed to one of surprise. "You know how I take my coffee?"

"Duh," I said, polishing off the cereal.

"How?"

My spoon clattered into the empty bowl. "I pay attention to you, princess."

She seemed touched that I knew her coffee preference. I didn't think it was that big of a deal. Hell, I'd been cooking with her for a week.

Brushing it off, I glanced into my empty bowl. "So sad."

She laughed.

My backpack was still in the corner where I'd tossed it before I left, right beside my BU hoodie and sneakers. Aerie watched me as she sipped her coffee. Her eyes felt like a physical caress, and the more she stared, the more tempted I was to crawl back into her bed and blow off all my classes.

"I can hang out here while you're gone?" she asked, clearly not understanding the effect she had on me.

I nodded. "I'll bring you some lunch in a few hours."

"I need my phone before you leave."

I glanced at her sharply.

"I have to make sure the repairs are getting done at my house."

I gave her the cell, but I wasn't happy about it. "If he calls, don't answer."

"I won't." She vowed.

I dragged my feet as long as I could, actually longer than I should have. By the time I kissed her on the head and left the house, I had to practically run from the parking lot to my class just so I wouldn't be late.

I sat in classes all morning, my mind lost in beats and lyrics. Ideas… and *her*. I glanced around every class, feeling like an imposter each time. Feeling I'd somehow outgrown… or just flat-out moved on from here.

I knew some of it had to do with Aerie, but she wasn't the reason.

The catalyst?

Perhaps.

It was me, plain and simple. I didn't want to be here anymore. These walls weren't inspiring. Instead, I felt stifled. Trapped. I wanted to be out there living. Creating.

The more classes I trudged to, the heavier each footstep became.

It didn't matter how I justified the feelings. How I tried to brush them off. By the time my last class let out, I knew they weren't going to change. They couldn't because I had.

Dread filled me up inside, swirled around me like the dark rain clouds moving in overhead. You'd think a man would be happier when he figured out his path.

How could I be happy about something that would leave my father anything but?

# twenty-four

*Aerie*

It was strange being here because I didn't feel out of place.

I felt out of place most everywhere I went... sometimes even my own home. I always thought maybe something was wrong with me, like perhaps I didn't belong anywhere at all.

Then Nate walked into my life, rooting around in my bag for Lifesavers, wearing random T-shirts, making stupid jokes, saving kittens, and creating songs with me that seriously stirred my soul.

He was completely my opposite but everything I sort of wished I was. Maybe the old part of me, the part I thought got lost in all the fame, recognized him.

Maybe it reminded me of who I might have been if this life hadn't changed me.

Even when Derek gave me long, calculating looks out of the corner of his eye and his body language sort of told me he wasn't thrilled I was here, I still felt in place.

Cradling the mug of coffee Nate made, the warmth seeping into my palms, I glanced down at Cheeto, a little orange puffball of fur. Was this what peace felt like? A settled calm, quietness that draped over everything beneath my skin like a thick, warm blanket on a snowy day. No urgency, no stress.

Sipping the brew, I rested my head back against the headboard, smiling at the fact I was a girl sitting in the center of an all-boy room. The blanket was plaid, sports posters cluttered the walls, and none of the furniture matched. I glanced over at Nate's small bed, a bed he hadn't even bothered to make. The blankets were rumpled, the pillow lumpy.

He'd only spent half the night in there. The rest he'd spent with me.

I sipped at the coffee a few moments longer, basically daydreaming about what it had been like to share a bed with Nate. It wasn't the first time I'd shared a bed, but this feeling was brand new. We hadn't been two bodies in a single bed.

We'd been a couple… intertwined.

Daydreaming was nice. I could even write a song about it. But it wasn't reality.

Lifting the phone from the folds of the blankets, I starting making the calls I couldn't put off. My home couldn't sit unprotected, and we'd left sort of in a rush.

I still couldn't believe Nate refused to leave me there…

Mac answered and pulled me back into the present. "Ms. Boone, is everything okay?"

"Hey, Mac. Everything's fine,"

"Are you coming back to L.A.?"

"No, not yet. I'm actually not even in Tennessee at the moment." I went on to explain what happened and asked him to get a team together and fly to my house to upgrade the security and do a sweep of the property. It was going to cost me a pretty penny, but really, I had no choice.

He agreed, and after we hammered out a few details, I let him go. I trusted him to do what needed to be done. He was one of the few people I'd met during the past few years that I actually knew would keep his word and truly wanted to protect me.

Once we got off the phone, I had to make calls to my cleaning crew, house manager, and groundskeeper. By the time I was done, I felt I'd relived it all and wanted to pull the plaid covers over my head and hide.

Instead, I pulled up my big girl panties and phoned the officer in charge of my case. It was depressing. He had no new information to relay, and the man they took into custody lawyered up with some fancy counsel and made bail.

Apparently, it left the entire department scratching their heads on how a criminal could afford such a good attorney. Clearly, ripping other people off paid well.

The case wasn't over, of course, but there wasn't anything I could do today. Before I disconnected the call, I made sure he knew I was having work done on my property, and he generously offered to go out there a few times and make sure everything was going the way it should.

With that done, I melted in the covers, but Cheeto had other ideas. He appeared out of nowhere, a string in his mouth.

Laughing, I slid onto the floor and spent some time playing.

After I took a shower (in a bathroom that was totally maintained by boys), I went back into the bedroom to get dressed. The flicker of my cell phone screen caught my eye, and I picked it up. I had three missed calls.

Back to back.

Before I could even pull up the caller ID, it rang again.

Will's name flashed on the screen, and my stomach twisted. Those missed calls must have been from him, and clearly, he didn't like being ignored. That meant he would just keep calling.

Against my better judgement, I answered the call. "Hello?"

"Jesus Christ, Aerie! You couldn't have answered your phone the first ten times I called?"

"Actually, it was only three."

My calm, sardonic reply made him pause. He cleared his throat. "Are you okay?"

"Why wouldn't I be?"

"Because your front door is open, the windows are smashed in, and your place looks like a tornado hit it. And because you *aren't fucking here!*"

My hand tightened around the cell. "You're at my house?"

"That's what I just said. Are you somewhere in the house, hiding? It's okay now, babe. I'm here. I'll protect you."

And odd feeling creeped up the back of my neck. It felt like a long-legged spider on the prowl.

"What are you doing at my house, Will?"

"I heard about what happened. I couldn't get here fast enough. I knew you needed me."

"What did you hear?" I asked.

"Some guys broke in, trashed the place… tried to kidnap you. You're safe now. Just come out. I'll protect you, just like I always do."

*The only person I need protection from is you.*

"How did you hear about this?" I tried to remain calm, even though my heart was thundering.

"News travels fast, babe. You know that. Of course someone called me. You're my wife."

Swift, pungent denial shot through me. "We are *not* married."

"You can't argue with a marriage license, babe."

"My name is Aerie," I ground out.

"Aerie." He corrected, placating me. "Where are you? Tell me so I can come get you."

"I'm not hiding."

"Are you staying at a local hotel? Which one?"

"I'm not there at all. I left town."

"What?" The shock in his voice practically echoed.

"I left." I enunciated the words dramatically. "I don't need you to save me, Will. I can take care of myself."

"You're scared. Rightfully so. You didn't know what to do. It was good you got out of here. My God, Aerie. This place is trashed. Where did you run to? I'll bring the jet, bring you back to L.A. where you belong."

It was like he wasn't listening, as if he had his own agenda…

*Like he wants me to be afraid.*

I gasped.

"Babe?"

Shock rendered me silent for long moments. Not even I could believe the thoughts suddenly filling my head.

"It was you," I whispered.

The fancy lawyer, making bail... how Will "heard" about what happened. He had planned this.

"You hired those men to break in. To hurt me... You knew. You told them exactly what kind of security I had. You practically handed them a key."

"You're exhausted, not making any sense." His voice was tighter than before.

"I'm not exhausted!" I yelled, shrill. My hands were shaking. "You're sick. He had a gun, Will! I could have been killed. Nate could hav—"

"Roth was there?" Will growled into my ear.

*Holy shit!*

"Ah, did your hired thugs forget to tell you that?" I mused. "Maybe that high-powered attorney you hired advised them to not say a word, even to you."

I could hear his ragged breathing. "Where are you?"

"You think I would tell *you*? You told the world I cheated on you, that I have an STD. You branded me a toad." I paced across the carpet, my mind whirling. "But this... *this*, Will. Your days of controlling me are over. Hear me? I'm not running back to you. I won't. Not ever again."

"You're going to lose it all. The only person who can save your tattered reputation is me."

I laughed.

Then I disconnected the call.

He tore me down, scared me, isolated me—all in the name of control.

This was over. I was older now. Stronger. I had resources, ways to help myself that I didn't used to have. I was only a victim if I allowed it, and I was done allowing it.

Will might be the prince of the music industry… But I was a princess.

That put us on even ground. Didn't it?

I wasn't about to give up my crown without a fight.

# Nate

Ten: *You back in town for classes?*
Me: *You know I am.*
Ten: *Pizza at Vi's?*
Me: *Free food. I'm in.*

Classes were over for the day, and I felt like they'd lasted about fifteen years. Even though I'd stopped in during my lunch break, I was ready to see Aerie's face again. I wasn't really sure how it was possible, but I missed her.

I wasn't a grumpy guy, but I was grumpy.

I parked crooked in the driveway when I got home and burst in the house like maybe my ass was on fire. (I looked to make sure it wasn't.)

"Princess!" I hollered, shutting the door leading out the garage.

She appeared in the doorway of my bedroom a second later. I forgot about my shoes, about the hat on my head. I flipped the bag that was slung over my shoulder onto the floor as I swiftly closed the distance between us.

Her eyes widened a bit as I went, but I didn't stop. "If you don't want me to kiss you, you better run now."

I plowed into her, wrapping my arms around her waist and swooping down to claim her mouth, growling as my tongue swept inside her. My hands glided up her back.

All my attention condensed down into her. The way her full lips were soft pillows against mine. The way her tongue was slightly rough but also sweet.

I started to draw back, but she made a sound, and I crashed into her again, both of us kissing with renewed force.

When she finally pulled away, she compensated by reaching up to flip the hat off my head and run her fingers through my hair.

I nipped at her lower lip, and she giggled.

Suddenly, I wasn't so grumpy anymore.

Retreating out of the doorway, I went back into the kitchen and found an unopened box of cereal, then poured half of it into a bowl. Crunching as I went, I said, "We're invited to pizza with Ten tonight."

"When?"

I shrugged. "Now."

"But you're eating," she pointed out.

I stopped mid-chew. "There's always room for Fruity Pebbles, princess."

She came forward and looked into my bowl. "Is that stuff magic or something?"

My spoon clattered. "You haven't ever eaten it?"

She shook her head.

"I'm shook!"

She burst out laughing. "You're shook?"

I nodded, my eyes wide.

"Do you even know what it means?"

I shrugged one shoulder. "Girls say it all the time around campus."

She laughed again.

I scowled. "Listen here, princess. No girl of mine is going to be walkin' around without ever tasting the greatest food ever bestowed upon man."

Her laugh died, lips pressed together, and then her dark eyes found mine. "Your girl?"

Nervous energy zapped me, and I hoped my cheeks weren't betraying me by turning red. Curse of a ginger... My face always gave me away. I hadn't really meant to say that out loud. I didn't think she was ready. Or know if she ever would be.

So I did what I always do. Made a comeback.

"Well, you aren't now. Fruity Pebbles traitor." I hugged the bowl into my chest and shoveled some into my face.

Aerie pursed her lips, then took another step forward, opening her mouth.

"Oh, you want a bite, do you?"

Her eyebrows waggled at me.

"I don't really like to share."

She poked me in the stomach. Hard.

I made a sound, then scooped up a giant bite and held it out.

She recoiled. "My mouth is not that big!"

I ate half off the spoon, then pushed it toward her again. I thought she would refuse it 'cause, ya know, I just ate off it.

Without hesitation, she took the bite. I was transfixed as her lips slid off the spoon as she drew back.

The spoon stayed suspended between us as I watched her mouth while she chewed. I wasn't thinking about the cereal anymore. I was thinking about kissing her and how I wanted more.

"Crunchy," she said, bringing me back.

I shoved some more in my mouth. "You gotta chew it like this," I said, smacking my lips and keeping my mouth open. "Enhances the flavor."

She mimicked me, then giggled. "It tastes the same."

"I know. I just wanted to see if you'd do it. No manners."

She gasped, then lunged forward and stole another bite.

"I knew it! You love it!"

She stepped back and made a so-so gesture with her hand.

"Cereal is no laughing matter," I told her, quite serious. "Tell me you love it."

"I like it," she allowed.

"Boo," I said and inhaled the rest of the bowl.

Cheeto came over and rubbed up against my leg, so I traded him for the bowl and scratched his head. "What'd you do this afternoon?"

"I used the shower. I hope that's okay."

I nodded. "Mi casa es su casa."

Her nose wrinkled.

I made a sound, then went over and sat on her bed. There was some girly magazine lying there, so I picked it up and started flipping through it. Was this the kind of stuff chicks read? *How to braid your hair like a pro!*

*How to make it look like you aren't wearing makeup! Men: things he will never tell you.*

I snorted. "These articles are stupid." I turned the page. "Ooh, a quiz!" I snagged the pen out of my jeans and started to fill it out.

"So where's Ten?" Aerie picked up Cheeto and sat on the end of the bed.

I glanced up. "He's at Violet's place. She has a dorm on campus. He mostly stays there when he's in town."

She didn't say anything as I continued on with the quiz.

"You up for heading over there?" I asked.

"Sure."

I finished up the quiz and scowled. "It says I'm gay. Why the hell does everyone always think I'm gay?"

I threw the magazine on the floor and made a rude sound. I should have known better than to read something that advised women on how to wear makeup without looking like they were wearing it.

Its, uh, called *don't put any on.*

Aerie laughed. "Who thinks you're gay?"

I leapt forward, pressing her into the mattress. "You don't think I'm gay, do you?"

Her eyes bounced back and forth between mine, a smile playing on her lips. "Maybe it's because everyone wants a piece of you."

I grinned wide and chuckled. "I like the way you think."

I rolled again, taking her with me, pulling her on top of me. Her legs straddled my waist. The weight of her above me pretty much proved to anyone who might care that I was most definitely *not* gay.

I couldn't not touch her. I barely even thought about stopping myself. I rested my palms flat on her legs, just above her knees. I itched to inch farther up, but I wouldn't. Not until I knew she wanted me to.

"You gonna tell me what's wrong?"

She glanced away. "Who says anything's wrong?"

I gave her legs a gentle squeeze. "I pay attention. Remember?"

She shook her head. "Nothing. I guess dealing with all the phone calls, all the cleanup work of my house, reminded me of what happened."

"It just happened," I murmured and pushed up onto my elbows, bringing myself closer to her. "You wanna talk about it?"

"You're sweet." She smiled, kinda sad. It was sort of like the kiss of death. "But I really don't."

I shook my head, adamant. "I'm not sweet."

Her lips curved up. Her hair was down. It waved around her face and skimmed her collarbone every time she moved her head. Her face was bare of any kind of makeup.

The girls in that dumb magazine had nothing on her.

"What's wrong with being sweet?"

"Gay guys are sweet." I made a face.

She laughed. "You have something against being gay?"

I made a sound. "Not at all. But you're not a guy."

Her face softened completely, and her teeth sank into her lower lip. Then she took a page out of my book and tried to lighten things up. "So…" She smiled cheekily. "If I were a guy, would you be gay for me, Nate?"

For once, I wasn't into making jokes. "Yes."

Her breath caught.

She wasn't expecting that, was she? *Way to keep her on her toes, Nate.*

"We're gonna have to talk sometime, sweetheart," I told her, brushing the back of my hand down her jean-clad leg.

Her hand flattened on my chest, and I fell back. Her lips descended right onto mine.

I opened my eyes, not quite sure it had happened.

She kissed me.

All on her own.

I guess telling a girl you'd be gay for her was a good way to get some sugar.

I groaned and followed her lead. It was hard. I wanted to roll and pin her under me. I wanted to do a hell of a lot more than kiss. Again, I held back. This seemed like a big thing, the fact she initiated contact like this.

My hands dove into her hair, fingers flexing to tangle them as much as humanly possible. Tentatively, her tongue slipped across my mouth. I smiled and answered with a lick of my own. Her chest sank onto mine. Through our shirts, I felt the way her nipples stiffened, and my eyes popped open again.

I sucked in a deep breath through my nose as our lips kept moving, as I stared at her in wonder.

One of her eyes cracked open. Then the other. Against mine, her lips stilled, then lifted just a fraction. "Why are you staring at me?"

"Honestly?" I murmured, flexing my fingers in her hair. "Because I can't believe what a lucky bastard I am right now."

She pushed up. Her cheeks were pink and her lips were slightly swollen. "What am I going to do with you?"

I wagged my eyebrows and thrust my hips upward. "I can think of a few things."

Laughing lightly, she climbed off me.

Let's all take a moment of silence for the moment I just got to experience…

…

…

…

It was beautiful.

"Don't we have somewhere to be?" she asked.

I reached out, and she towed me up. "I guess if you like pizza," I muttered.

She laughed. "Don't you?"

"C'mon, princess. If we don't get over there soon, Ten will inhale it all."

She ignored me and snuggled Cheeto.

It was kinda cute, but I made an impatient sound from the doorway.

"Is it cold out?" she said, stopping halfway to me.

I took in her simple T-shirt, jeans, and glitter-covered sneakers. "I got you covered."

She went on past, and before I shut the bedroom door, I snagged my Blaylock hoodie.

She probably thought she'd gotten out of telling me about whatever was bothering her, because I knew it wasn't just what happened the other night.

There was more.

I didn't really want to push her, but I was beginning to think I would have to.

# twenty-six

## *Aerie*

"Nate, bro," Ten said before the door was barely even open.

The second it was, Ten's expression shifted to mild surprise when he saw he wasn't alone. Swiftly, his stare bounced between me and Nate, a mix of emotion crossing his face at rapid speed.

"You brought a date," he said, settling into a wide, half-teasing, half-knowing grin.

I didn't know Ten all that well, but we'd met on several occasions. We always frequented the same events and parties because we were both signed under the same label, just with different producers, etc.

I wasn't surprised how the media turned on him and the way he reacted. Okay, I was a little surprised by some of the stuff he pulled, but who was I to judge? I admired him, though, because I knew he had his act together now. I also knew how very hard that must have been for him. Even more, from what I understood, Ten had settled into a relationship with someone who was far removed from the spotlight.

I had to admit I was ever so curious about how that was working out.

"You're not going to try and steal this one, are you?" Nate cracked.

Ten chuckled. "I already got the one I want."

"You steal his dates?" I asked, incredulous.

Nate made a sound, casually draping his arm across my shoulders. "Don't worry, princess. Ten could only steal the ones I was willing to let him have. You are *not* on that list."

Ten coughed, once again his gaze bouncing between us.

I thought about kicking Nate right then and there. Clearly, he hadn't told Ten I was coming.

"Nate brought a date?" A voice came from inside the room. "This I have to see."

Ten slid over, and a short blond came to the door. Just as casually as Nate had touched me, Ten wrapped his arm around her waist.

"Oh," the girl said, "You're…"

"Are you gonna make us stand in the hallway all night?" Nate wondered. "Seriously, you invited us over for pizza, not to gawk at us in the doorway."

"Of course!" the blonde exclaimed and waved us in.

The door was barely shut, and she offered her hand to me. "I'm Violet. I'd apologize for my appearance, but well, I always look like this."

A genuine grin split my face, and I took her offered hand. Her shake was light and soft, but it wasn't insincere. She had a calming vibe about her, almost innocent. I liked her instantly, which was something that almost never happened.

She was dressed in a pair of black leggings, fuzzy slippers, and a burgundy Blaylock hoodie that looked really familiar…

Nate was stepping by, and I noted the same sweatshirt in his hand. I snatched it. The second my head cleared the neck hole, I told Violet, "Now we match!"

"I hope I don't get cold," Nate said as he flipped open the top of a nearby pizza box.

We ignored him.

"You're Aerie Boone, right?" Violet asked.

I nodded, a queasy feeling shaking my stomach. God only knew what she'd heard about me.

"She wouldn't know that if I hadn't told her Nate was working with you. Vi doesn't follow the current music trends," Ten said, coming to stand close beside her. Screwing up his face, he added, "She listens to classical."

Violet poked him in the side and laughed. Her head tilted back when she gazed up at him. "I listen to your stuff, too, now."

He kissed her on the forehead and tugged the messy bun at the base of her neck.

I could feel the energy around them. The way they looked at each other made it absolutely clear they were in love. All those reports saying Ten's relationship was just a ploy to get good publicity, they were obviously false.

"He's right. I don't really follow the celebrity world."

"I'm actually relieved to hear it," I told her honestly.

"So you came to town with Nate." Ten began.

I nodded. "To work on the album."

"Where are you staying?" I could practically hear the wheels in his brain turning. The expression on his face remained passive, which made it hard to tell what he was thinking. Though, I could guess.

"I gave her your bed," Nate said, chomping on a huge slice of pizza. "You know, since you never use it anymore."

"Vi's bed is more comfortable," Ten quipped and pointed to the pizza boxes "Toss me a slice, man," he called out to Nate.

Nate picked up a smaller box, and Ten shook his head. "That one's Vi's."

"You're eating something other than rabbit food tonight?" Nate exclaimed. "Is the world ending?"

"Must be because you brought a date," Vi shot back, then glanced at me apologetically. "Sorry," she said soft. "I gotta tease him when I can."

I giggled.

Nate put his hand over his heart and shook his head. "Didn't I show you a good time on our date?"

"It wasn't a date," Ten barked.

Violet rolled her eyes and caught my hand. "Come on in. It's not a very big space, but you don't have to stand by the door. And if you don't get some food now, you won't get any with these two around."

Nate winked at me on his way to the couch, carrying a box of pizza. Violet handed me a paper plate from the counter and pointed to a box. "That one's the one you want."

My eyes slid to the smaller box near it. Noticing, Violet replied, "That one is gluten free. I, ah, don't eat gluten."

"Or anything else good," Nate quipped.

Ten slapped him on the back of the head.

"I don't have to take this abuse!"

"Grab the controllers," Ten said, motioning toward a gaming unit near a flat-screen hanging on the wall. It looked oddly out of place there. "I want to try out this new game."

The two guys got into some deep conversation about weapons and upgrades, and my brain shut off.

"I didn't even have a TV," Violet said, amused, "until he started staying here. He acted like I was a cavewoman, for crying out loud. God forbid he not be able to play video games."

I laughed and slid a slice of pizza onto my plate. I couldn't remember the last time I had pizza. My trainer would probably kill me if he knew I was about to eat this. It was going to make it taste even better.

"You're an artist?" I asked, gazing around at all the paintings and drawings lining the walls and floor.

Violet nodded and handed me a bottle of water. "I'm an art major."

"She did the art for *Butterfly*," Ten put in.

My eyes lit up. "That was you? I didn't realize. It's gorgeous. Everyone is loving it."

She smiled. "Thank you."

Violet slid a slice of the gluten-free pizza in her mouth and groaned. After a moment, she glanced at me and blushed. "Why does it have to taste so good?"

I knew Violet had some kind of illness or something. I remembered seeing the headlines.

*Ten's girl—incurable!*

*Will Ten's money get his girl better treatment?*

I didn't know what was wrong with her exactly, though. I never bothered to read the articles. They were probably all lies anyway. Obviously, though, she had some kind of dietary restrictions.

I wasn't about to pry. I knew what that felt like. She probably just wanted someone to see her for her and not for what might or might not be wrong.

"I wish I knew," I replied, taking a huge bite and groaning, too.

"Are you two making a porn over there?" Nate quipped. "That's a lot of moaning."

"What the fuck did you just say to my girl?" Ten growled.

Violet widened her eyes at me, and we laughed.

"I take it he's very… um, protective?" I said after a minute.

"You have no idea." Violet sighed.

For some reason, an image of Nate standing over the intruder in my house, brandishing a gun and a dark look, came to mind. Along with it came an intense wave of longing. I wanted to be protected like that. To feel safe with someone.

"You died!" Nate intoned. "Why did you die?"

"I need more pizza," Ten replied, standing from the couch. His dark hair was messy, and he was dressed casually in a pair of sweats and a T-shirt.

He was more relaxed than I'd ever seen him before. It looked good on him. I wondered how it would look on me.

"Violet, get over here," Nate called out. "Come play with me."

"I don't know how to play that game."

"I'll teach you." He cajoled.

"Go sit down, baby," Ten said, reaching around her for some pizza. "Take your cardboard with cheese."

"It's good. Try it." She held it up.

He blanched.

"Please, Stark," she said sweetly.

His face softened, and he opened his mouth. She put the pizza in, and he took a big bite. She smiled while he chewed. "See! It's good, isn't it?"

"Soo good." He agreed, trying not to make a face.

"Violet!" Nate hollered.

She took her plate to the couch.

"She calls you Stark?"

Ten nodded once. "I'm not Ten with her."

"Who's Stark?" I asked quietly.

"Me."

Nate made a sound and dropped back onto the couch. "Violet! You're terrible at this game."

She threw her napkin at him. "I told you I couldn't play!"

"Look, look," he said, sitting up and holding the controller out in front of her. He began explaining each button, and she just laughed.

I watched them, my throat tight. "They're so…"

"Real?" Ten finished.

I glanced at him and nodded. "Normal."

He half smiled. "It's strange, right?"

"Entirely."

"You get used to it. And then when you're around everyone else, you wonder how you never realized just how fake they all are."

"Oh, I know," I murmured. "Can't trust anyone."

The lid to the pizza box closed. "That why you here with Nate?"

I glanced around at him.

He made a face. "I know it's not just work."

"No." I admitted. "It's not. I needed somewhere to—"

"Hide?"

"Something like that."

"I've seen the headlines. What the hell is going on with you and Will Solberg?"

"Nothing," I said swiftly.

He gave me a quiet look, a look that called me out on my bullshit.

I glanced away.

Ten shifted, leaned in closer, and spoke low. "I know Nate acts like an idiot—"

Instantly offended, I demanded, "He's not!"

Ten smiled slow. "So that's the way it is, huh?"

"It's not any way."

He made a bland face. "I know all too well the draw of someone like Nate. The chance to be someone other than who you are."

My eyes flashed up to his. Was he warning me off his cousin? "I'm not trying to be anyone else."

He raised an eyebrow. "Right now, it sure as hell looks like you're trying to be single when we both know you're married."

I felt all the blood drain from my face. "It's complicated."

Ten held up a hand. "You don't have to explain to me. I understand complicated."

"Then why bring it up?"

His stare went over my shoulder, toward the laughing pair on the couch. "Because he's my family. Because I know what it feels like to hurt someone you love with lies you never meant to tell."

I bristled.

Ten reached out, laying his hand on mine. I stilled and looked down. He pulled back, knowing he had my attention once more. "All I'm saying is you two look familiar."

I blinked, confused.

Ten chuckled. "You should talk to him. Tell him all the shit you're scared to say. Starting with that douche Solberg."

I felt my shoulders sag. "It's all such a mess."

His hand covered mine again, but this time he didn't pull it away. "Sometimes it's easier to clean up a mess when you have extra hands."

I glanced down, avoiding his eyes. "I don't have anyone," I whispered.

He squeezed my hand. "Yes. You do."

"He's not going to stick around once he knows how weak I am."

A rude sound ripped from his throat. "I see the way he looks at you. He's not going anywhere."

He made it sound easier than it was. My past was a lot more complicated than peeing on a crowd and a stint in rehab.

"What the fuck is this?" Nate's voice boomed close behind me. I jumped, surprised, not realizing he was so near. His arm shot out past my body, pointing with accusation at where Ten held my hand. "That's a hell no!"

Ten smirked and didn't withdraw his hand.

Nate lunged forward as though he were going to go over the tiny island and tackle him. I made a sound of distress and yanked my hand from under Ten's, placing both on Nate's chest, pushing him back. "Stop!"

Nate rocked back on his heels and glanced down at where I touched him. Jade eyes bounced between mine, and beneath my palm, I felt his heart hammering.

"That was for asking Vi out on a date." Ten seemed amused.

I really didn't think this was funny. Clearly, Ten had no idea what Nate was capable of.

"Oh my God, Stark! Get over it already!" Violet exclaimed.

"Not cool," Nate told him. His voice was all rumbly. It made my insides tingle.

I started to pull back, but he moved swiftly, covering my hands with one of his, effectively pinning them against his chest. "You know I was just trying to help you out."

Clearly, I really needed the story behind Nate and Violet's "date."

"That's exactly what I'm doing right now," Ten answered quietly.

Nate's stare came back to mine. "What's he talking about, princess?"

I worried my lower lip as I wondered what to say. Nate reached out, tugging my lip from the confines of my teeth. "Don't do that."

"We should talk," I finally said.

Maybe Ten was right. Maybe I should just spill everything once and for all. Then I'd really find out if Nate could still think of me as a princess, or if, after everything, he too would see me as a toad.

# twenty-seven

## Nate

Ten wasn't interested in Aerie. He was all in with Violet.

But dude better keep his hands to himself.

"We should go," I said, taking Aerie's hand and lacing my fingers with hers.

"You don't have to leave." Violet fretted, shifting from foot to foot.

I stopped but kept hold of Aerie. "It's all good." I assured her, giving her a one-armed hug. "We'll hang later."

"But—"

"They need to talk," Ten told her gently, tucking her into his side. The pair exchanged a glance. Then Violet nodded.

"It was nice to meet you," she told Aerie. "If you ever need a break from Nate, you can come over anytime. He can give you my number."

"No one ever needs a break from me." I reminded Violet.

She made an unladylike sound.

How rude.

"I'll call you," Aerie told her as I towed her toward the door.

She said she wanted to talk. It was the first time I'd heard that come out of her mouth, and I wasn't about to fool around and wait for her to change her mind. Especially not since, up until a few minutes ago, I thought I was going to have to push her into telling me anything at all.

Whatever Ten said to her must have had some effect.

That pissed me off, too.

Out in the hall, reluctantly, I released her hand. "I'll be right there."

She nodded and went a little farther, knowing I wanted to talk to my cousin. Violet hung back in the room, and Ten propped himself in the doorway.

"What the hell did you say to her?" I demanded.

"Nothing much."

The stony look on my face told him what I thought about that.

He made a sound. "I just told her she needed to level with you."

"About?"

"About everything. She's not like the girls here at Blaylock. She's from a whole different world, man. A complicated one."

"I'm well aware," I answered, flat.

"I'm not sure you do."

"Really? 'Cause I thought the night I stared down a gun, then knocked some would-be kidnapper down the stairs, was proof enough."

Ten reacted. His body stiffened, and he shot forward. "What the fuck!"

"I handled it."

"It's too late to tell you to not get involved, isn't it?"

I stepped closer and hitched a chin toward the room. "If someone told you that about Violet…?"

He sighed.

"I thought so. Thanks for looking out for me," I told him. I actually really appreciated it. It was sort of proof that the old Ten was back, and he was here to stay. I'd missed him all those years he'd been gone. "But I won't walk away from this. From her."

"Which is why I told her to talk to you," Ten said quietly.

"Next time you wanna talk to her, do it while keeping your hands to yourself." I warned.

He laughed. "You need anything, just call." He held out a hand, and we shook. "By the way," he added, "she got pissed when I called you an idiot."

That made me grin.

She was totally into me.

I jogged down the hallway to her side, and we fell into step together.

"Is everything okay?" she asked, curious.

"'Course."

Inside my Ford, Aerie started to tug off my hoodie. I reached over and stopped her. "Leave it on."

"Aren't we just going to your house?"

I shook my head. "Nope. We're going to talk. And you're gonna need that where we're going."

"Where's that?"

I smiled and turned onto the road, heading away from my house.

"You'll see."

# twenty-eight

## *Aerie*

Headlights bounced off a chain-link fence, an empty, overgrown parking lot, and not much else. The sky was dark and not a lot of stars shone overhead.

"Is this the part where you kill me?" I joked.

He said nothing as he turned off the engine, climbed out, and came around to the passenger door. Once it was open, he leaned into the opening and offered me his hand.

"This is the part where I ask you if you trust me."

I did. I didn't even have to ask myself or question if my trust in him was misplaced. Slipping my hand into his, I allowed him to tug me out of the car and slam the door behind us.

Quickly, Nate jumped the fence, making all the metal clang and wobble. I stared from the other side. "You want me to do that?"

"Come on, then." He beckoned.

I put my foot into one of the links and hoisted myself over. Nate held out his hand again, offering balance, and I took it. He caught me when I leapt off the fence, both his arms wrapping around me.

I laughed as he took my hand and pulled me along. "Seriously, where are we going?"

"You don't see it?"

I glanced all around. There wasn't much to see. Grass dotted here and there with stray litter.

We continued, and a few moments later, a dark shape loomed up ahead. My steps faltered. He gave my hand a squeeze. "Trust me."

As we got closer, I could make out the shapes. "It isn't…?" I whispered, my steps quickening.

Nate stopped walking, jolting me to a stop. I looked back, impatient. With a warm chuckle, he came in front, bending low, offering his back.

I leapt on, draping my arms around his neck. My body bounced against his as he jogged, giving me a piggyback ride toward the dark destination.

"This is amazing!" I said when he stopped in front of the short fence surrounding it.

"You ain't seen nothing yet," he quipped, setting me down and then hopping that fence.

I got a little nervous when he disappeared from sight, but the feeling evaporated the second I heard him throw what I guessed was a heavy switch.

Lights burst across the grass and livened up the dark. Music began playing softly, slowly, almost as if, given a fresh battery, the song would speed up and be clearer.

It didn't matter, though.

Nate had brought me to life in the center of this dead field.

Covering my mouth with my hands, I felt my eyes grow wide as I watched the painted animals begin to bob up and down as the entire structure slowly turned.

Lights blinked and music played. I watched the carousel turn slowly. As it did, Nate came around with it, standing in the center of a few bobbing horses. His hair blew playfully when he jumped off the platform, walked to a gate in the small fence, and opened it wide. I ran through, taking his hand, and he swung me up onto the ride, jumping up behind me.

I didn't see the fading, somewhat chipped paint or notice how a few of the lights blinked on and off instead of staying lit. All I saw was magic.

Nate pointed to a white horse with a blue saddle, and I rushed forward, wrapping my hand around the brass pole. He palmed my waist and lifted, and I scrambled onto the horse as it was rising.

Beside the white horse was a black one with a red saddle and a white mane. Nate climbed on, and together we rode a few turns without saying anything at all.

"What is this place?" I finally asked, gazing out into the dark.

"Used to be a fairground. They had carnivals here every spring, and sometimes the circus would come to town. In the summer, they'd set up a county fair, and this place would be packed."

"They don't do it anymore?"

He shook his head. "Nah. Not sure why they stopped, but no one ever took down the carousel."

"I love it," I said, leaning my cheek against the pole as the horse dipped down.

"I thought you might."

"We probably aren't supposed to be here, are we?"

He smiled. "I won't tell if you won't."

"I like your friends," I said after a moment as the horse I was on rose toward the ceiling.

"You have any friends, princess?"

I swallowed the lump suddenly stuck in my throat. It hurt going down, as though I'd swallowed a shard of glass. "The closest thing I have to a friend is Mac, and I pay him to be around."

His voice was soft, not demanding. Just curious. "Why are you so isolated?"

I gazed out past the carousel and into the night. It felt as if we were on our own little planet and beyond us was an empty galaxy. Like we were the only two people in the world.

"I didn't notice it was happening at first, but after, it just seemed easier that way," I replied.

The horse Nate sat on creaked and squeaked as he got off. I turned toward him as he stepped up so close he brushed the side of my horse and my leg. The intensity of his stare made my stomach wobble and my fingers tremble. He didn't say anything, but our eyes locked. His stare followed mine as the horse rose, carrying me away from him.

Saying nothing, his hands wrapped around my waist, and I let go of the pole. Without any effort, he lifted me off the seat and stepped back to make room as he slid me down the front of his body.

I shivered with the contact. His closeness made me feel lightheaded.

"Are you cold?" His brows drew together, and he reached for my hand.

I started to tell him I wasn't, but the second our fingers brushed, he winced. "Shit, princess. Your hands are like ice."

I hadn't even noticed. I'd been too preoccupied with him.

"I'm sorry," I murmured, trying to tug my hand free.

"What are you apologizing for?" he asked, snatching my hand back. "Let's warm them up."

I frowned, wondering what he meant, when suddenly, Nate lifted the hem of his T-shirt and pressed my icy hand to his midsection. His skin was sinfully warm, and I had a momentary flashback to the night at my house when he'd be wearing only boxers. My palm flattened as blissful heat wrapped around me.

He made a sound, then yelled, "Yikes, woman!"

I jerked away, but he only laughed and towed me back. Grabbing my other hand, he added it beneath his shirt, tugged down the hem, and rubbed his hands briskly over mine.

"You really don't have to do that," I murmured. Will always winced when I touched him with cold hands. He certainly never offered to warm them up with his own body heat.

His voice brushed over me, and goose bumps pricked my skin. "Any opportunity to get you close, princess, is an opportunity I'm going to take."

"Even at the expense of my freezing hands?" I tried to tease, but the words sounded more awed than anything.

He smiled. It was such a genuine one, the skin around his eyes crinkled. "Even then. Besides, you don't feel so cold anymore."

Against his stomach, my fingers flexed. He was right. I warmed right up.

That's how I knew. How I knew one hundred percent I could tell him my secrets.

"I'm ready to talk now," I whispered, nerves colliding inside me as though we were in bumper cars and not standing on a carousel.

Nate took my hand and led me carefully between horses, under twinkling lights, with slightly wonky music floating around us. On the outer edge of the ride, there were a few sleighs where more than one person could sit together. Nate stopped beside one and held my hand as I stepped in and settled on the wooden bench. Settling beside me, I noticed his legs were much longer than mine. His knees nearly bumped the front, while mine weren't even close.

In front of the sleigh, a couple horses led the way. The leads connecting them to our seat had long since fallen away, but it was charming just the same.

It seemed safe here somehow. Even though we were in the middle of some old field on a ride everyone had forgotten about that was chipping and weathered. I wasn't scared, and all the fear I had about telling Nate the things I didn't want to say didn't seem as pronounced.

If this piece of left-behind history could withstand time, then perhaps all the things I thought I'd lost of myself were still there after all. Weathered but still there.

"Tell me," he said, settling back against the bench, making the wood groan a bit.

I sighed. "I don't even know where to start."

"At the beginning, princess. I want to hear it all."

"You're not going to like me so much." I worried.

Nate put a hand to his chest, feigning hurt. "You think so little of me."

I smiled wistfully. "Actually, it's quite the opposite. Which is exactly why I'm worried."

Nate's arm fell between us. Delving between our bodies, he found my hand, pulled it into his lap, and wrapped it tightly in his.

"Tell me," he said again.

I took a deep breath. When I exhaled, so did everything else I'd been holding inside.

# twenty-nine

## Nate

"When I was five, my father went to jail. For armed robbery and attempted murder."

Of all the things she could have started with, that wasn't even on my radar. I thought perhaps the beginning was a few years ago, when she first came onto the music scene. Or maybe the first night she met Will.

But five years old?

No wonder at times she seemed incredibly unwilling to trust anyone. Clearly, she didn't have much practice.

I didn't know what to say, so I said nothing at all. Aerie glanced down at where I held her hand, then cleared her throat and went on. "When I was ten, my mother died of an overdose."

My body jerked before I could control it. A low curse slipped through my lips and hung in the air between us. First her father, then her mother? A lot of celebrities, a lot of brilliantly talented people, came from humble backgrounds. It wasn't exactly anything uncommon. But she lost *both* her mother and father by the age of ten. Not only that, but judging from what happened to her parents, those first ten years of life couldn't have been easy.

What did a guy say when words failed him and a funny one-liner was totally inappropriate? "I'm sorry, princess." It was probably the lamest thing I could have said, yet in that moment, it was all I could come up with.

Again, she glanced down at our linked hands.

A sense of knowing washed over me. "I'm not letting go." I assured her quietly.

Her eyes snapped up to mine. I saw the naked doubt in her stare. I wondered how many people had let go of her.

Every single one of them was a dumbass.

Lifting our joined hands, I kissed the back of hers.

As she stared off into the empty field, her voice was soft, yet it still carried over the music. "I didn't know her that well, my mother. She had a lot of, um, problems. My grandmother used to tell me some people were born with demons they just couldn't shake."

"Drugs were one of those problems, huh?" I asked.

"Drugs, alcohol, men…" Her voice faded away. "Sometimes I still can't understand how a person could have so many addictions when she was raised by a caring woman who never touched a drop."

"Your grandmother?" I asked, rubbing my thumb over the back of her hand.

She nodded, glancing up at me with a warm light in her dark eyes. "She raised me. She was my best friend."

My stomach sank when she said "was." "Did she pass away?" I asked as gently as I could.

Aerie nodded once. Her hand gripped mine tightly for a long moment before relaxing. "I grew up in Tennessee. That land my house is on? It was Grammy's. The land has been in my family for generations. I used to be quite the tomboy. I ran every inch of that place for years." She glanced up at me with a twinkle in her eye. "You ever need to climb a tree, I'm your girl."

I chuckled.

"We had this three-bedroom house. It was nearly as old as the land. The roof leaked every time it rained, the windows were drafty, and sometimes birds flew down the chimney and chased us around the house until we could shoo them out the door." She laughed, the far-off look in her eyes spoke of returning to a different place and time.

"She homeschooled me at first because the bus didn't come as far out as we lived and it was a pain to drive. But then later... I didn't want to go to school. Kids can be cruel, especially when your dad is in jail, your mom's the town joke, and none of your clothes are on trend."

"What about your grandfather?"

"He wasn't around," she said, finality in her voice. "Grammy always said she didn't want or need a man anyway because she wanted to live her life the way she wanted and not according to anyone else."

"Stubborn," I mused. "Now I know where you get that trait from."

Playfully, she bumped into my side. "You're kinda easy to talk to, Nate."

"Listening is easy when the topic is something you're really interested in."

"I haven't told you everything yet." She warned.

"The plot thickens." I wagged my eyebrows.

Aerie leaned her head onto my shoulder. The second she moved, so did I, automatically shifting so she would be comfortable.

"We didn't have a TV, but we had this old radio. Grammy sang all the time. She had such a beautiful voice. So naturally, I sang a lot with her. When I was seventeen, she got sick. It started as the flu that never quite went away. Finally, I convinced her to go to the hospital."

My stomach tightened. I knew what was coming, and I almost told her not to tell me. I didn't want her to live it twice. Instead, I tucked my arm around her and held her close.

"She had cancer, and it wasn't in the early stages. The doctors didn't seem very optimistic, but I refused to believe she wouldn't get better. I still remember their looks of pity when I asked about treatment options and medicine. 'These treatments cost a lot of money. You can't afford this,' they would say. Money shouldn't be the deciding factor of whether a person lives or dies."

"No," I said, thinking of my own mother. Thinking of watching her die. I knew all too well the dark days Aerie experienced and the frustration of knowing you couldn't do a damn thing to help the person you loved. Dad had insurance, though. My mom wasn't faced with not getting the treatment she desperately needed.

Though, in the end, those treatments didn't save her.

Didn't mean they weren't worth trying. Any effort to save the life of someone you love is worthy, and A was right. It shouldn't come down to money.

"So what happened?" I asked. The echo of my mother's laugh rang through the back of mind. Sometimes I forgot what it sounded like, but tonight, I heard it clearly.

"They sent us home. Said without the cash to pay for any kind of treatment, there was nothing they could do beyond keeping her comfortable. It was raining, and I remember when we walked through the door that day, this overwhelming sense of anger overcame me. It wasn't fair that the only person who ever loved me, a good woman who raised me when my own mother wouldn't, was dealt such a shitty hand in life. I watched water drip through the roof, noted the dwindling pile of firewood by the hearth, and covered her with a million blankets to protect her from the draft." She lifted her head. Eyes dark as night, round as saucers, fell on mine, and in them she pleaded with me to understand. "I couldn't let her die that way. It was too unfair."

Smoothing my hand down the back of her head, I nodded and pulled her into my chest. My breath ruffled her hair when I spoke. "I know you couldn't."

"I went to town to apply for any job I could get. While I was there, I saw a flyer for a singing competition in Nashville. The cash prize was ten thousand dollars. I couldn't believe it. Singing was something I grew up doing, and to get that kind of money for it…? I was shook."

I grinned. "Do you even know what that word means?"

"No, but this guy I know says it all the time." She teased.

"It was one time. *One*." I corrected.

A laugh bubbled out of her, and it felt like a win. See? There was reason behind my madness, intent behind my goofy ways. It was always something to fall back on. Always something there to soften any kind of situation.

Or to make a beautiful woman smile.

"Naturally, you entered the contest, won, and got the cash." I surmised, wanting to know the rest of the story.

"*After* I hitchhiked to Nashville." She corrected.

I made a sound. "You did what?"

She glanced up, noting the anger in my voice. "There was no way our car would make it that far. Besides, what if there was an emergency and Grammy needed it?"

"Jesus," I muttered. "Do you have any idea how dangerous that was?"

Her eyes narrowed, chin jutting out. "I did what I had to do."

I bit back any kind of demand that she never do something that stupid or reckless again. I wanted her to talk to me. Not yell. And if I started telling her what to do, her voice was bound to rise.

I'd just save the lecture about transportation safety for later.

I gestured for her to continue because I still didn't trust myself to speak.

"After I hitchhiked to the club…" She glanced up at me through her lashes, and I growled under my breath. "I entered the contest, sang my Grammy's favorite country song, and lost the competition."

My feet slapped against the floorboards of the sleigh when I sat up abruptly. "You lost!"

She nodded. "There are a lot of talented singers out there, and the girl that won had the whole package. Hair, makeup… the right people behind her."

I growled again.

"But." She put her palm against my chest, pushing me back into the seat. "Before I left the club, I was approached by a man."

"I swear to God, Aerie, if you tell me you hitched a ride back with the that nut wagon…"

She drew up short. "What's a nut wagon?"

I made a dismissive gesture with my hand, still pissed about all these dangerous things she did. "You know, some douche who carts his balls around like they're God's gift to women."

She giggled, pressed her lips together, then giggled again. "Well, that *nut wagon* was Byron Ryan."

I grimaced. "I think it's best if we just don't tell him what I said."

Aerie nodded definitively. "*Any*way," she enunciated and patted me on the leg. "He gave me his card, told me that even though I didn't win, he liked my voice. He had a song they were trying to find the right voice for, and he thought mine could be it."

"'The Telltale Heart?'" I asked, thinking of her first single, which basically turned her into an overnight success.

She seemed surprised. "You know my first song?"

"I know all your songs."

She melted against the seat, her body turning so she faced me. "That's really sweet."

"Sweet, but *not* gay." I reminded her.

"Definitely not." She concurred. "I didn't know who he was at the time, or that Time Track was the biggest player in the industry. All I knew was I was willing to take any work that might help pay for medicine. I met Byron at a studio in Nashville the next day—"

I held up my hand, cutting her off, and scowled. "Did you hitch again?"

"He sent a car for me."

"He's definitely not a nut wagon. I need to shake that man's hand."

Aerie rolled her eyes. "I spent most of the day in the studio with him and his producers. And by the end of it, he pulled out a contract and offered me a recording deal. I signed it right there. I didn't even know what I was getting myself into really. I just knew he was offering me an advance, and I desperately needed the money."

I nodded, completely understanding, yet at the same time, inside I was cringing. She could have signed her life away, gotten some hideous deal, and totally been screwed. I wasn't kidding when I said I needed to shake Byron's hand. Thank God for him. I needed to send him an Edible Arrangement.

"The money helped with Grammy?" I asked, even though there was a whispering warning in the back of my mind that this story wasn't over yet.

She nodded slowly, and the warning in my head turned to a full-blown suspicion. "It did. Until it ran out."

"Ah, princess," I murmured, reaching for her.

Aerie evaded my touch, though, sitting back and regarding me with the same wary look she'd given me when we first sat down. "And that's how I got involved with Will."

# thirty

*Aerie*

I wondered if he knew.

If Nate knew just how much of an anchor he was sitting here holding on to me. If he let go, I might surely float out into the galaxy surrounding us and simply disappear.

Admitting how much of an uncharmed life I'd lived was one of the most difficult things. Second only to actually living through it. Some people would say I should be proud because of all the things I'd "overcome." I didn't see it that way, though.

I didn't overcome my father's criminal record or my mother's overdose. I still lived with the heart-wrenching pain of losing the only woman who ever loved me to a disease I hated more than anything in the entire world.

Overcoming something means to rise above it. I never rose above anything. I wasn't better than I'd been before. Being famous just opened a door for more heartache.

I'd actually never told anyone this much about myself, not even Will. I suspected he knew everything about me because that's what Will did. He paid people to know things. I never actually laid it all out like this for him, for anyone.

This was a leap. A risk. Sort of my one "all-in" shot with someone. I hoped Ten had been right when he said Nate wasn't going anywhere. If he left me after all this, I might never recover.

I was very afraid I was falling in love with him. The longer he sat here and held my hand, the more kisses he pressed to my hairline, and the more stupid jokes he cracked, I would fall deeper and deeper… until every last piece of my heart lay unprotected in his hands.

"I wondered when we'd get to him." Nate made a face like he'd swallowed a rotten egg.

"I'm pretty ashamed." I ducked my head.

"Why would you be ashamed, princess?" His hand was in my lap. I stared down at the contrast between our fingers.

"Because everything I just told you sucks, but none of it was really anything I did wrong, you know? Like I had no control over my shitty parents or that I grew up in what I now realize was poverty."

He made a sound, and I lifted my chin. "That's how you know you were raised by one of the good ones, sweetheart. You didn't know you were poor until you were old enough to really look around."

I smiled. Warmth suffused my chest. It was probably the nicest thing anyone had ever said about my grandmother. "You're right. I didn't realize how much I didn't have because Grammy always made it feel like we had everything."

I didn't realize I was crying until Nate swiped a tear from the corner of my eye.

"The stuff with Will?" I continued. "Everything that's happened, I had control over... I was just too weak to stop it."

"Stop what? The marriage?" The muscles in his jaw ticked when he said that. I never wanted to marry Will, but that feeling was even stronger now. Now I knew it bothered Nate.

"The marriage is just the last in a long line of bad decisions when it comes to Will." I admitted. "Remember when I said I got an advance from Byron?"

Nate nodded.

"I spent it all on treatments and medicine for Grammy. She stayed in a care facility while I was working on my first single. I was scared to leave her home alone."

He nodded encouragingly.

"Between signing the contract and when I started working on the single, there was a period of time. It wasn't like an overnight thing. But the networking started right away. Byron started taking me around to parties and events, introducing me as his newest discovered star. I was so awed by it all. I'd never seen so much glamour in all my life."

"That's understandable, princess."

I took a breath, feeling the familiar cramp in my stomach I always felt when I thought about how I first met Will. If I only knew then what I knew now...

"Will was at one of the parties. He was tall and handsome, rich, and everyone vied for his attention."

Nate coughed. *"Douche canoe."*

"I was shy and overwhelmed. Innocent in a lot of ways. Will introduced himself. I couldn't believe he even noticed me."

"I bet everyone in that room noticed you," Nate rebutted, tucking my hair behind my ear.

"We talked. He was a nice guy. I liked being around him because he was my opposite. I was so shy, and he was the life of the party. Anyway, he started showing up at all the events I was at, and then one night, he asked for my number." I laughed lightly, remembering how shocked I'd been. "I didn't even have a phone. The look on his face…" I laughed.

Nate made a sound, and his expression… Let's just say he wasn't enjoying this conversation about Will. At all.

I pressed my lips together, afraid I'd made a mistake. "I'm sorry."

He blew out a breath and pushed a hand through his hair. "Don't be sorry. I just don't like thinking about you with him. With anyone."

I nodded, understanding. I wouldn't be thrilled to sit and listen to him tell me about his relationship with another woman. "I wouldn't tell you. I just…" I glanced up, held his stare. "I just want you to understand."

Cupping my jaw, he leaned forward and pressed his lips to mine. I took solace in the kiss, in his warmth. It was short, more comforting than anything. When he pulled away, his palm remained. "I'm listening."

"He became my friend, something I'd never really had before. He got me a phone, called me every day.

He sent flowers on my birthday and helped me learn about the industry." I fell silent a moment, hoping Nate could understand, even just a little, what small gestures like that meant for me. I'd never had anyone's attention like that before. Especially not a rich, handsome, powerful man. "One day, Will called, and he could tell I'd been crying. Up until that point, I hadn't told him about Grammy. I'd just been trying to make it 'til my single came out and I had some money again. He could tell something was wrong, and I confided in him."

Nate's mouth flattened, and he stared out over my head, past the horses and the lights, into the darkness. "Go on," he murmured.

"The facility Grammy was staying in while she got her treatments was kicking her out. I was out of money, and with no insurance, they weren't about to let her stay. I took her home, and just a day after we got there, Will showed up. I don't know how he found us. I never even asked.

"He looked around and said he couldn't stand the thought of me and Grammy in such an unsavory place. He said he'd made arrangements with the best doctors in L.A. He had lined up all the treatments and medicines that I couldn't afford. Even better than the ones I'd been able to pay for. Specialists all made room on their calendars for her, and suddenly, all these doors were open." I glanced up at Nate, begging him to understand. "I couldn't say no. How could I say no?"

He wrapped his arm around me and tugged me into his chest. I let out a sob into his shirt and fisted my hands at his chest.

"She was everything to me. All I could see then was making sure she wasn't in pain." My words were muffled against his chest, but I knew he heard them because he answered.

"I know, sweetheart. It's okay. You did the only thing you could. You thought he was a friend."

I wrenched away and swiped at my cheeks. "I did. I trusted him. He was so good to me. To Grammy. He paid for all her treatments and came to her appointments. He held my hand when I cried."

Nate's voice was the tightest I'd ever heard when he asked, "What happened?"

"Grammy lived a year longer than the doctors said she would. There at the end..." I paused as pain lanced through me. "At the end, she was so weak and sick. The treatments that tried to save her life left her drained. It was so selfish of me, Nate. So selfish to try and save her. I did all that because I didn't want to have no one. Because she was the only person who ever loved me... So I clung to her. They pumped her full of medicine and chemicals, all to prolong her life... but what kind of life was it really?"

"No," he intoned, pulling me back and staring into my face. "You are not selfish. And I never met your Grammy, but I know without a shadow of a doubt that she's probably shaking her finger at you from up above."

I laughed a little at the image he conjured up. I could totally see her wagging her finger at me for something she didn't like.

Nate continued. "I've never been the one in the hospital bed, but my mother was. The treatments pretty much did the same to her—prolonged her life, but didn't save it. I remember one night..." he said, his eyes sort of drifting. I knew he was looking into his mind, seeing the past as clearly as I could. "I'd gone to get something from the vending machine. When I came back, I heard my parents talking from outside the door. My mother was crying, but I still remember what she said." He blinked and focused on me again. "She said, 'I may be stuck in this bed, but any day that I'm still here and can see you and my son, even for just one more hour, it's worth it.'"

"Oh, Nate." I sighed and slid into his arms. We hugged each other for a while, just going around on the carousel, listening to the music that didn't play at the correct speed.

"You aren't selfish for wanting to keep someone you love in your life. You aren't, and you never will be." He insisted.

I felt as though this invisible weight I hadn't realized I was carrying was suddenly no longer there. It was easier to breathe. "I did get to take her to the ocean. She'd never seen it before." I smiled at the memory. It was painful to remember that day, but it was also wonderful. "She was more impressed with the palm trees than the ocean, though." I snickered.

"Seriously, though, those trees grow coconuts!"

I laughed. "That's what she said!"

"Smart lady."

After a moment, my smile faded. "After she passed away, I was devastated. Will was there through everything. I promised I'd pay him back for everything he did, but he insisted he didn't want my money. He said my love was more than enough."

"He wanted you." Nate surmised, then made a disgusted sound. "That stupid fucker. Your love is priceless, certainly worth more than some medical bills."

Lifting my head off his shoulder, I stared at him in awe. "You think my love is priceless?"

His forehead collided with mine. "I think anyone who's lucky enough to be loved by you has everything." After kissing the tip of my nose, he swiftly pulled back and scowled. "Love isn't a bargaining chip. And it's not something you can pay for."

My heart swelled. It had never felt so full before. No one ever acted as though me loving them was something special. Except Will… But Nate was right. If Will had really thought it was that precious, he wouldn't have tried to put a price on it.

Tucking my cheek against his shoulder once more, I detailed, "After the funeral, he told me he loved me and he wanted a life with me."

Nate's body tightened. His hands balled into fists.

"My entire world changed overnight. My single was an instant success. I started making a ton of money, was on the cover of every magazine. Will paraded me around on his arm like a trophy, and we became official." I paused, turning thoughtful. "Well, I thought we'd just become official, but Will considers all the time I thought we were just friends as us being together, too."

Nate snorted. I laid my hand on his thigh and whispered, "It was a whirlwind, but it was good. Until he changed."

"Didn't like your success, did he?" Nate asked. "Probably made his ego feel about the size of his dick."

"Oh, no. He liked my success. The more successful I became, the tighter he tried to hold on to me. I became more of a possession instead of a girlfriend. He started being photographed with other women, criticizing what I wore, or making comments to remind me I'd come from nothing and he helped make me who I was. I didn't like it, but I didn't know what to do. He was all I had. Literally. The friends I'd try to make when I moved to L.A. permanently, he'd find a way to get between us. And then I signed a contract for an album with Time Track. Up until that point, it had only been a few singles. You know, just to test to see how I'd do."

"Will thought you would sign with Solberg."

I nodded. "I knew that would be a huge mistake, though. Things with Will were already going downhill. He controlled almost everything. My career was the one thing he hadn't been able to get ahold of. We got in a huge fight when he found out. He, ah… smacked me." I'd actually forgotten about that. *Or maybe I blocked it out of my mind.* I guessed the last time hadn't been the first time, and I knew if I didn't stay far away from him, it wouldn't be the last.

Nate sucked in a sharp breath, and I looked away, wanting to just finish. "I got my own place, and we broke up for a while. But he came back… and I forgave him. Every time I tried to walk away, he would remind me of what he did for Grammy and how I owed him. He claims he's the reason my career is so hot, never mind Byron Ryan and Time Track."

"How the fuck did you end up married to him, Aerie?"

I made a distressed sound. "I wish I knew."

Nate surged up and paced out of the sled, between two bobbing horses.

"Please." I rushed after him. "Believe me. Will and I have a messed-up relationship." He turned instantly, his eyes boring into mine. I cringed. "*Had.*" I corrected. "We had a relationship. I've been trying to get away from him since before I met you."

"Do you love him?" His tone was accusatory, but his eyes were wounded.

I gasped. "No!" Rushing forward, I nearly fell into him, but he caught me. "I thought I loved him… back when Grammy passed, after everything he'd done and how good he'd been to us."

"He's nothing but a con man with cash." Nate fumed.

"I know. It took me a while to figure it out, but I know that. I never loved him. Never. I didn't realize it until…" My lips snapped shut with an audible sound.

"Until?" he asked, his gaze sharpening. The hurt in his stare gave way to hope.

*Until you.* I wanted to say it out loud. But I was afraid. I straightened and shook my head slightly. "I could never love someone who calls me a toad in the media, who makes fun of my 'hick' name, flinches when my hands are cold, and tries to control me with fear… I—"

"Control you with fear? How?" he demanded.

My shoulders sagged. I felt as if I'd been pouring my heart out to him for ages, yet there was still more to tell. I couldn't expect him to stick around and listen much longer. Why would he?

I swallowed. "Will called me today."

"You answered?"

Instead of trying to explain why I made another dumb move, I decided to get right to the point. "He was at my house in Tennessee. He knew about the break-in."

He jolted upright, reached out, and grabbed one of the brass poles for support. "What?"

"He said he was there to take me home where I belonged. Where he could protect me."

"That no-good, dirty son of a bitch," Nate intoned. His chest nearly vibrated with the words as they rumbled out of them. His green eyes flashed, and the air around him grew frigid. "He sent those men after you."

I nodded. "He wouldn't admit it. But I know. He's trying to scare me back to L.A. Trying to control me with fear."

"Make himself the only one you can rely on…" Nate murmured.

"Yes."

"What did you tell him?"

"I told him I'd left town. I refused to say where I'd gone."

"Good, that's good." His voice was thoughtful.

"But, Nate?"

He glanced up.

"When I realized what he'd done, I reacted. I yelled at him because you could have gotten shot."

Nate blinked. Then a slow smile spread over his features. "You yelled at him about me?"

I nodded, forlorn. "Now he knows you were with me."

His eyebrows lifted. "Ah. So he's beyond pissed."

I nodded again, twisting my hands in front of me. The very last thing I wanted was to drag Nate into the crosshairs.

"I'm getting in his way, aren't I?" he mused, proud of himself.

"That's not something to be proud of," I pointed out. "He's obviously willing to go to extremes to get me back under his thumb, and he has the money to do it."

Nate's eyes narrowed at the same time there was a horrible sound of grinding metal. The carousel lurched, began moving, then lurched again. I fell forward with the movement, knocking into Nate.

We fell onto the floor as the carousel stopped altogether. The music sounded even more wonky than before. The lights stayed lit, but the horses went still around us.

I was lying over his chest, him having broken my fall.

"Guess the ride's over," he quipped. I looked down, and we both laughed. He caught my face with his hands. "You okay? You hurt?"

I fell on him, and he was worried about me. "I'm okay," I whispered.

"I'm actually surprised the old girl went as long as she did." He patted the dirty metal floor.

"We've been here a long time," I commented, gazing around. The horse beside my head had a chipped hoof.

"You talk a lot."

I gasped, and he laughed. "C'mon, up." Even though I was on top of him, he somehow managed to help us both to our feet. "Stay right here," he told me and disappeared around the side of the ride.

A second later, the music died and the lights went out. Eerie silence pressed in around me. Standing on a broken carousel ride in complete darkness was suddenly not so romantic.

Nate appeared, the beam of the light from his phone leading the way.

"C'mon. Let's get out of here." He took my hand, led me to the edge, and jumped down. Before I could follow suit, he lifted me off the platform, setting me gently on my feet.

We were quiet during the walk to the car, something I might not have normally minded. That is, of course, when I haven't just literally poured out my life story. I'd been sort of hoping I'd get some kind of response.

And not the kind where he declares it's time to leave.

*It's too much to handle. He probably lost all respect for you. You're weak. You let someone control you.*

Drawing the keys out of his jeans, Nate walked to the passenger door first, opening it up for me. I tugged my hand free from his and stepped around, careful not to touch him anywhere.

*Now he thinks you're a toad, too.*

"Where do you think you're going?" he asked, close behind.

Glancing over my shoulder, I gave him a curious stare. "Um, the car?"

The sound of his car keys hitting the driver's seat with a thud filled the silence between us. "Not yet, you're not."

Nate's hand wrapped around my wrist and tugged me back around. Strong arms encircled me, holding me against his chest. I inhaled, recognizing his scent instantly, comforted by it.

The palm of his hand settled on my head. He turned just enough to press his lips against my temple. My eyes sliding closed, his voice filled my ear. "Thank you for letting me discover you tonight, Miss Aerie Boone."

My fingers flexed in the muscles of his back, and I clung to him a little tighter. My stomach was haywire, bouncing and twitching all over the place. I could barely breathe, and I could honestly say I had never, not ever, felt this way with anyone else.

I shifted just enough so he could hear me ask, "What exactly did you discover?"

He pulled back and smiled down at me. "That I was right all along."

I rolled my eyes, but still I couldn't help but want to know. "Right about what?"

"You're not a toad. You're a princess."

# thirty-one

## *Nate*

Will Solberg was slime.

Wait. No.

That was an insult to yogurt everywhere.

Will Solberg was a shitty human being.

Not only was he an abusive dick, he also took advantage of my girl when she was literally at her lowest and needed a friend. Sure, he might have pretended to be one, held her hand and picked up some mega medical bills, but…

That did not make him a knight on a white horse. Oh, hell no. He didn't do any of that out of the kindness of his heart. Dude had a lump of coal in its place. He did all that as a down payment on what he knew was going to be a major star in the music industry.

To Will, Aerie wasn't a person with feelings. She was dollar signs, prestige. A means to an end. Arm candy.

You know, she was the kind of respect and beauty a man tried to buy when he couldn't get those things on his own.

I was pretty much boiling on the inside, knowing how badly he manipulated and used her. Only the worst kind of trash used a loved one's death to get what he wanted.

The kicker? Aerie blamed herself for it. That was classic mental abuse right there. Made me want to *physically* abuse him. In the face. With a chair.

Too graphic?

I didn't think so, either.

As I drove, headlights slashed over the dark pavement, and I wondered how the fuck he managed to get her to marry him. Clump nugget new she was just searching for a way to get away from him, and he managed to chain her even tighter.

How the hell I was going to get him out of her life once and for all? Because, *oh*, he was on his way out. Jackass sent men to scare her, possibly hurt her. Game over for him.

Game on for me.

I had no idea what I was going to do, and it would be so easy to get lost inside my head right now, trying to figure it out. I couldn't, though. As much as I wanted to plot, there was something more important than getting that sleaze out of Aerie's life.

Aerie.

She didn't know what to make of my silence. I could tell by the way she fidgeted in her seat, by the way she looked astonished when I told her I still thought of her as a princess.

I had no idea what to say. I didn't have a lot of experience with girl drama. Hell, I didn't even watch reality TV. Not that I thought she was being dramatic. If I had, I probably could have come up with something to say.

This shit was real. And she trusted me enough to spill it all, something she clearly didn't have much experience with. I felt I was creeping around on tiptoes, worried I would say the wrong thing and blow the gift she gave me.

Truth was I wanted her. Everything about her.

Except her husband. Him… I'd have to do away with.

Geesh, no, I wasn't going to murder him.

Though the thought did cross my mind.

I didn't care where she came from or how she got here. All I needed were the words to tell her. A way to make her really believe.

"Wasn't that the turn to your house?" she asked, tapping on the window as we went past.

"We're not going home just yet."

"Why?"

"Because I want to be alone with you."

"You do?" she whispered.

I smiled.

A few minutes later, I pulled onto the street where the music department was located on Blaylock's campus.

"This is your school?" she asked, face pressed to the window.

"Yep."

"It's beautiful," she murmured. "I never went to college."

"Is that something you wanna do?" I asked, curious.

"I'm really not sure."

I parked behind the building near a side door only staff used. The back of the building was filled with shadows. Most of the lights were at the front and in the parking lot.

"Let's go." I gestured, getting out of the car. I had a key to the department, courtesy of my father (with approval from the dean), from when I'd been working here with Ten. We liked to come at night when no one else was around. The acoustics with the piano in the auditorium were pretty good.

"Are we allowed to be here?" she whispered as I unlocked the door and ushered her inside.

"I have a key, don't I?"

"Why doesn't that make me feel better?"

I chuckled and took her hand. "I wouldn't do anything that would put you in danger, okay?"

She nodded.

Our footsteps echoed down the hall. I switched on the lights as we went. Toward the end, I tugged her around to a large wooden door and pulled her inside. It was dark, but I was familiar with the space. Keeping hold of her hand, I led her to where I wanted.

"Stay here."

"Why are you always bringing me to dark places and then leaving me alone?" she quipped. "I'm starting to think you're super weird, Nate."

"It's part of my charm," I called out, then flipped a switch.

I heard her gasp and smiled. Her back was to me when I came up behind her. She didn't even hear me. She was too busy looking out over the empty auditorium.

"Still think I'm weird?" I murmured in her ear, sliding my arms around her from behind.

The way she sank back into me actually gave me butterflies. I'd never admit it out loud, though. But just so you know, guys get butterflies, too.

"This is beautiful," she murmured.

"Yeah. It's one of the newer buildings. It's even nicer when it's all lit up."

"I like it the way it is," she mused, glancing up at the vaulted ceilings overhead.

From our position on the stage, we could see equipment and ropes, all the behind-the-scenes stuff that people in the audience couldn't. As a backdrop, there were heavy velvet drapes in the university's primary burgundy color.

The only lights I turned on hung from the ceiling on long black chains, looking sort of like oversized lightbulbs. The hardwood underfoot was glossy and shiny where the light hit, and in the center of the majestic stage was a wooden grand piano.

Sitting down on the long, tufted-velvet bench, I hit a few keys, playing a simple melody. Aerie smiled and sat beside me, close enough that her leg and hip pressed against mine.

I still had no idea twhat to say to her. Finding words wasn't always easy... so I thought perhaps I'd try it this way.

My fingers moved over the keys, not as graceful as I would like, but skilled enough. I played a song I knew by heart, then segued into a few things I'd written, but didn't have any lyrics for. Aerie laid her head on my shoulder. I heard her sigh beside my ear. Her hand moved to rest on the top of my thigh, making my fingers stumble on the keys.

She giggled a little, and it was prettier than the music I played. I thought back to the morning in her living room when we were both by the fire. The moment the attraction between us became undeniable. The moment we connected. Automatically, my fingers began playing the song I'd been working on, the song she'd added to without any difficulty at all.

The melody was a little different on the piano than the guitar, but she recognized it.

Lifting her cheek off my shoulder, she looked at me. I still played, but my eyes collided with hers.

*"Sometimes it feels like you were just a dream,*
*"A wish floating through reality.*
*"At night, I wait for sleep to claim me,*
*"To hear your voice, remember your face,*
*"but when I open my eyes, you're gone without a trace."*

Aerie's voice picked up when mine faded away. My heart turned over as she sang, because she remembered the words from that day.

She remembered *our* song.

A song not really about us, but our song just the same.

*"Lost in the past, nonexistent in the future.*
*"Which is worse? I'm just not sure.*
*"Looking in the mirror, a reflection gazes back,*
*"But it isn't me.*
*"It isn't me.*
*"It's how I know you weren't a dream,*
*"A wish floating through reality.*
*"Memories are hard to keep*

*"But you're always there, aren't you?*
*"Buried down deep, always there when I've had too much reality."*

When the last of the music echoed out into the audience, my fingers stayed perched over the ivory for a few moments before retreating into my lap.

"You know you can't go back to him, right?" I told her quietly.

"I don't want him."

Gazing down into my lap, I watched her hand slowly glide over the side of my leg, fingers extending toward mine. Opening my hand, palm up, I waited for her to arrive.

"I don't care that you're married. About the rumors, where you grew up, or even that you like yogurt."

She made a sound between a groan and a laugh. "Everything I just told you—"

I cut her off. "Doesn't change how I feel. I told you back at your house. I'm telling you now. I'm just going to keep saying it."

"How *do* you feel?" she whispered.

Suddenly, I knew what all those guys on TV felt like. You know, the ones in charge of choosing the red or blue wire? Cutting the wrong one would blow up everyone. I was so nervous my hands were getting clammy.

Without thinking, I let go of her hand and wiped my palms down the thighs of my jeans.

"You make me nervous." The words spilled out, and I wanted to bang my head on the keys.

She giggled. "You make me nervous, too."

Everything inside me quieted. My head whipped around. "I do?" I'd never made anyone nervous before.

Not in a good way anyway. I cocked my head to the side. "In a good way?"

A small smile played on her lips. "Depends on what your answer is to that question I asked you."

I rubbed my hands on my jeans again. "I think maybe I'm in love with you."

Her breath caught. It was sort of a gasp, sort of a choked sound.

*Great.* I was choking her.

An edible arrangement probably wasn't going to fix this.

"It's a really good kind of way."

My head shot up. "Really?"

She laughed, but it was cut off when I pressed my mouth to hers. Aerie grabbed my wrists as I held her face and the kiss stretched on and on.

Desire flooded my system so hard and so fast nothing else mattered. I grabbed her, pulling her into my lap. Her legs wrapped around my waist, bringing her core right up against me.

Deep in my jeans, my balls tingled and my cock jerked. She must have felt the stony length because she rocked against it, and I groaned. Kissing her still, I grabbed her hips and made her rock into me again… and again.

Pulling back just enough, I sucked her lower lip into my mouth, then nibbled at it with my teeth. Her hips thrust again, and mine arched up to meet her.

Aerie ripped her mouth away and I tried to follow, but she laid a palm on my chest and said my name.

I blinked, trying to think with my head and not my dick, but it was really, really hard (both thinking *and* my dick).

"Nate," she said again.

"Hm?" I managed.

Her smile could light up an entire room, but since I was the only one in this room, it was entirely for me.

"You're so beautiful," I told her, "so fucking beautiful."

"There's still a part of me you haven't discovered tonight," she said, her fingers playing with the hem of my shirt.

My mouth ran dry. "Don't say shit like that to me, princess."

"Why not?"

"Because I'll lay you out on this piano and play your body like a guitar."

"I was kinda hoping you would."

I stood up so fast the bench beneath us clattered to the stage. Her arms gripped my shoulders; her legs locked around my waist. Her ass hit the top of the piano at the same time her feet hit the keys, making the space echo with sound.

I pulled off her shoes and threw them behind me, then caught her stare and held it. "If we do this, you're officially mine."

"I was officially yours before our first kiss."

Need hammered inside me so hard. Harder than it ever had before. I lifted the hem of my hoodie—the one that looked hella better on her than me—and tugged it over her head.

When it was gone, I lowered it and said, "I don't share."

"Neither do I."

Holy shit, the way she arched her brow and said that made it physically painful to wear these jeans. I spread the hoodie out on top of the piano. Aerie ripped at my shirt until it disappeared somewhere with her shoes.

I knew I wasn't nearly as buff as any of the men she was used to seeing, but when her eyes scraped down my body, I saw only want. It kinda blew my mind.

More music filled the auditorium when I pulled off her jeans and tossed them over my shoulder. Leaning down, I kissed the inside of her knee. She made a sound, and I smiled, licking farther up the inside of her leg. Her knees fell open, giving me some space.

Gliding my fingertips up her calf, around the outside of her knee, and then up to caress the side of her hip, my fingers played with the edge of her panties as my lips drew dangerously close to her inner thigh.

"Nate," she whispered. The quiver to her voice only spurred me on.

"Lie back, princess," I said, using my free hand to push her down against the hoodie.

Once she was spread out, her knees bent, feet still resting on the keys, I pushed her legs wide and had a perfect view of her entrance.

As I climbed my hands up the insides of her legs, she shivered a little, her hands gripping the edge of the piano. Her panties were pale pink, trimmed with lace. Dipping under the edges, I caressed the area where her legs met her body. I trailed my fingers around the sides of her opening, teasing the silky skin then slipping away made her squirm.

Pulling back, I swiped my hand up her center over her panties. She gasped and her legs started to close.

Chuckling, I pushed her legs open again and kissed all the way up to her inner thigh. One of her hands found its way into my hair, tangling in the strands and urging me on. I sucked deeply at the softness of her inner thigh, then dipped beneath her panties again.

She was soaked. Her body clearly liked the sweet torture I was making her endure.

Unable to stop myself, I tugged down the underwear, baring her completely. Palming her inner thighs, I pushed, feeling as if I were pulling back the curtains to reveal a beautiful day. Aerie whispered my name the second I dipped into her wetness, swirled my slick finger around her swollen clit, then pushed two fingers into her tight, warm body.

She arched up off the piano, and I pushed her back down, descending upon her center with my mouth.

The first lick made me high; the second made me an addict. I could feel my heart pounding against my ribs as I licked and teased her body, all the while fucking her with my fingers and feeling her legs quiver around my head.

Her hand tightened in my hair, almost to the point of pain. With one last lick up her center, I pulled away.

"Don't go," she whispered, reaching for me but meeting air.

All my clothes met the floor, and I climbed on the piano, caging her in with my body.

Her hands started running over my naked form, exploring and driving me wild. Dipping my head, I made love to her with my tongue. The taste of her sweetness lingered between us and reminded me there was so much more of her I had left to taste.

"Shirt," I told her, and she immediately tossed it away.

The second she was on her back, her hips thrust upward, seeking mine, but I made a sound and worked my way down her body, kissing and stroking until my lips closed around one of her swollen nipples.

Aerie cried out, but I kept sucking, then moved on to the next. Her legs locked around my hips, and I thrust toward her, allowing my hard dick to slide over her opening, but not penetrate.

The feel of her silk sliding over me caused my entire body to shudder. My head lifted, no longer able to just kiss her. All train of thought condensed into getting inside her body.

Aerie reached between us, wrapping her hand around my length and stroking upward. I sank down on top of her, my body pressing her into the piano. "I want you so much," I whispered in her ear.

Her palm flattened on my shoulder, and she shoved up.

I moved instantly, thinking my weight was too much for her to take. When I glanced down to apologize, I noted how dilated her eyes were and how unfocused her stare was. "I want you."

I practically leapt off the piano and fished around in my jeans until I found what I needed. Ripping open the packet with my teeth, I rolled the condom over my length in record time.

The second I came over her again, Aerie pulled me down so we were chest to chest. "I'm covered." I assured her, and she smiled. Her head lifted off my hoodie beneath her, and we kissed.

With a single plunge, we joined, and everything else ceased, even our kiss. Keeping myself still, I gazed down through heavy-lidded eyes. Holding my gaze, she moved, stroking my dick with her tight, warm walls.

I moaned and started to move, thrusting into her over and over. She met my thrusts with some of her own. Her enthusiasm only fueled my desire and made me want to give her more.

Sweat beaded my back. My body screamed for release, but I denied myself and thrust as deep as I could go.

"Look at me," I demanded.

Her eyes opened, and she smiled.

"I don't *maybe* love you. I fucking do."

"I love you, too, Nate."

It was as if she lit a flare in the middle of the darkest night. Waved a red flag in front of an already incensed bull.

"Say it again," I growled and pushed into her again.

Her body slid up the piano with my thrust. Her hands wrapped around my biceps for an anchor.

"I love you."

The little bit of control I managed to hold on to snapped. My hand wrapped around the edge of the piano above her head, and I used it as leverage as I thrust inside her again.

"There." She gasped, her eyes opening wide.

I rocked, and her eyes rolled back in her head. Her moans of pleasure coupled with the feel of her nails biting into my back sent me over the edge. I shuddered and cried out as I exploded into her body.

Even after I came down from the high of being inside her, I stayed where I was, buried deep. My arms were quivering, but it didn't matter. I kissed her temple, along her hairline, and then the corner of her eye.

Her arms slipped around my waist and tugged me down. After a moment, I shifted, rolling so she was atop me and I was bearing her weight.

Air brushed over our bare skin, and for the first time since we got here, I wondered if maybe a bed with blankets would have been better for our first time.

"You're really good at this," she purred.

I couldn't help but grin up at the ceiling. I totally rocked her world.

"You seem surprised." My voice rumbled out of me, sounding a lot rougher than normal.

"I really shouldn't be anymore. Everything about you surprises me."

Gently, I pulled my hand through the strands of her tangled hair.

"I didn't know men like you actually existed." She confided as if she'd just discovered some sacred secret.

My chest swelled with love. And pride.

"They don't," I quipped. "I'm limited edition."

"I really think you are," she responded, snuggling her cheek into my chest a little bit farther.

My stomach flipped. Those damn butterflies in there were misbehaving. "I meant it, you know. It wasn't just the heat of the moment."

Propping her chin on my chest, she asked, "What?"

"I love you." I'd never said that to anyone before. I honestly never knew love had the power to overwhelm anyone this much. But it did. *She* did.

Her face softened. "I really love you, too."

Priceless. Hearing that. Having her love. It was absolutely priceless.

I kissed her quick. "We should probably get dressed. If the janitor comes in here and sees my girl in the buff, I'll have to take him out."

She gasped and sat up, covering her perfect breasts with her arms. "The janitor!"

I chuckled. "So gullible. I'd never strip you down if I thought there was even a chance someone else might see."

She stuck out her tongue at me, and renewed desire caught fire inside my body.

Leaping down off the piano, I gathered all our clothes and laid hers on the piano. After I tossed the rubber and put on my jeans, I helped her get dressed, letting my fingers linger on her skin.

Abruptly, she spun, fell against my chest, and kissed me wholeheartedly.

I could get used to this.

I *was* used to it.

Aerie was mine, and I wasn't about to give her up.

But if I was honest, *totally* honest, she wasn't one hundred percent mine.

She couldn't be.

Not while she was legally someone else's wife.

# thirty-two

*Aerie*

"Aerie?"

"Yeah?"

"Why did you marry him?"

My heart ached because of the question. It ached because of the answer. I was owned by him but promised to someone else.

"It doesn't make any sense," I whispered into the dark. "I wish I could remember."

I felt his head lift off the pillow behind me. It was so dark in here, the middle of the night. But neither of us was asleep. "You can't remember?"

Glancing over my shoulder, I said, "We went to Vegas, and I woke up in the hotel room the next day with a ring on my finger."

"Why'd you go to Vegas?"

"The tabloids had just printed a new story about me. They were relentless, as always. I was stressed. Will suggested we get out of town for a getaway... to relax and be out of the spotlight."

"And he thought Vegas was a good place to do that?" Nate asked, clearly not impressed with Will's choice.

"We stayed at Yellow, the ultra-private and exclusive hotel. The staff there is sworn to secrecy, and no cameras or press are allowed inside."

"It's still stupid."

I smiled into the night. It was stupid, and looking back at it now, I realized it was just another way for Will to control me. To get something he wanted. *He'd probably planned it all along.* My smile faded. "I should have stayed home."

Nate tightened his arms around my waist, and I snuggled firmer against his body and sighed. "Were you drinking? Did you black out?" he asked.

I sifted through the fuzzy, hazy memories from that night. Trying to recall what happened. "I wasn't hungover the next day. I had a headache, was tired. And thirsty. My brain was filled with fog. But it wasn't like a hangover."

Nate lurched up suddenly, propping on his elbow, and looked down at me. Hair fell into his face. His jaw was set. Gently, he took my chin and turned my face to look up at him. "Did he drug you?"

My lip quivered. "I don't know."

"*Shit,*" he swore beneath his breath. Squeezing his eyes shut, he cut off the way his irises glittered. Letting go of my chin, his fingers stroked my cheek as he took a deep breath. His eyes reopened as he exhaled slowly. "The last thing I want to do is upset you."

"You have a right to know, Nate. I just wish I could tell you more. I wish I knew what I'd been thinking that night."

"You weren't." He allowed.

"No. I wasn't. If I had been, I would never have married him. Please say you believe me."

The feeling I got when he dipped his head and I had long moments to anticipate the touch of his lips against mine was like finally arriving at the top of a roller coaster and getting ready to plummet down.

The kiss was full contact, totally grounding, and settled all that jittery excitement inside me. I'd never known anyone who could rile me up then calm me right back down. I'd never known both those emotions could be equally addicting.

"I believe you," he murmured against my lips. "I never had any doubt."

Gazing up and him, I pressed my lips together and searched his eyes. "Why?" I asked.

He lifted a brow.

I smiled. He was so handsome. Definitely a limited edition. "The rumors, the articles, my quickie wedding, and the way I treated you when we first met. I gave you so many reasons to believe I was exactly who everyone else said I was. Why didn't you?"

"You have really nice legs," he deadpanned.

Gasping, I reached up and yanked his hair.

"Ow!" he howled. Beside us, Cheeto perked up to stare. "Save yourself while you can!" Nate told him.

"Shush." I admonished, reaching out to scratch the kitten behind his ear. Loud purring filled the room.

"Traitor." Nate mumbled and settled back beside me. "Maybe because of Ten. Because I knew behind that media perception, there was a person, someone who was probably entirely different than what everyone believed."

"It was because of Ten?" I was considerably underwhelmed by this response.

"That and the fact that when you ran into me in the hallway—"

"You ran into me!" I exclaimed.

He patted my hip as though he were humoring me. "I just knew. I felt something… like a tingle of awareness or something. You felt it, too."

I nodded. "I felt it."

"Then when I came to your place and you finished my song, it kinda felt like it wasn't just the song you were completing… but me, too."

Well. That answer was so much better.

"I called my lawyer again today. I left him a less-than-friendly message." I made a rude sound. "They said he was in a meeting, but he was probably afraid to pick up the phone." Taking Nate's face in my palms, I looked into his eyes, holding his stare. "I am getting this annulment."

Under my palms, his jaw muscles jumped. "He's going to keep fighting you."

"He won't win."

"Can't you just say you weren't of sound mind? You were so drunk you can't even remember that night?"

Frustration welled inside me. "I need to be able to prove it. How can I prove something I don't even remember?"

He pulled me into his arms, meaning to comfort me. It was hard to find comfort when I felt trapped.

"I need to just confront him." I concluded. "Force him to tell me what happened that night."

"No." His voice was hard and finite. "You stay the hell away from him, Aerie. He's an abusive bastard, and if he even so much as breathes on you, I swear to god—"

I pressed my hand over his mouth, cutting off his words. I could feel the hard hammering of his heart beneath his ribs.

He fell silent, and after a moment, I lifted my fingers away. "He'd just lie to you anyway. Can't believe a freaking thing that comes out of his mouth."

I knew Nate was right, yet I still needed proof.

I just had to figure out where to get it.

# thirty-three

## *Nate*

The sound of Dad moving around in the kitchen was like the loudest, shrillest alarm there ever was. My eyes popped open, and awareness slammed into me.

*Shit.*

Forget lying here in this too-small bed in bliss; I was waking up beside the girl of my dreams.

Nope. No bliss for me today.

Kicking at the covers, I lurched out of bed and fell onto my ass. "Ow!" I muttered and rubbed my back. Another low sound from the kitchen had me scrambling toward the door.

"Nate?" Aerie asked, her voice still thick with slumber.

Reversing my scramble, I went back to the bed and dropped a few rapid kisses to her forehead and cheeks. She giggled, and my groin tightened. "I'll be in the kitchen." Then I took off again.

As I ran, I adjusted my junk, realized I had no shirt on, cursed, and grabbed my hoodie as I went out the door. Pulling the material over my bare chest, the scent of my girl enveloped me. Damn, she smelled good. She was going to have to wear this shirt more often.

Making sure it was somewhat covering my still rocking boner (guess trying to hide it with something that was scented with the object of my desire wasn't a bright idea), I stepped into the kitchen.

Dad had his back to me, but his shoulders stiffened the minute I showed up. I grimaced. I fucked up. Big time. The guilt I felt was only compounded by the tautness of his back and the way his neck sort of bunched.

"Dad."

He turned, holding a bowl of cereal. (Not Fruity Pebbles. He ate Raisin Bran. Which, thinking about it, could probably explain some of his mood.)

"Son," he intoned.

*Yikes.*

"You forgot something yesterday."

My shoulders sagged, and I moved farther into the kitchen, standing beside the basic brown dining table. "I'm sorry. I was on my way to your office, like you asked. Then Ten texted, and I got distracted…" The excuse sounded pathetic even to my own ears.

"I don't ask much of you."

Without thinking, I made a sound. "No, you just want me to live here forever, not have a life, and spend all my time at school."

His spoon clattered into the bowl. Milk splashed up and hit his shirt, but he ignored it. "Finishing school will *give* you a life. A good one."

"I'm sorry. I didn't mean to blow you off."

He set aside the bowl and regarded me. Already dressed for work, he had on a pair of dark jeans, dark shoes, and a dress shirt. My dad had that kind of shape all the girls swooned over. You know, the wide shoulders that tapered into a narrow waist. The way he dressed only seemed to accentuate that. Despite the fact I knew he could probably be a ladies' man, he barely dated. I never asked him why. I figured it was because no one could measure up to my mom.

I got my red hair from her.

"So why did you?" He crossed his arms over his chest.

"I just forgot. I was coming, but then Ten texted, and Aerie needed me. I lost track of time. I'm here now, though. We can talk."

"I thought she was married."

"It's complicated."

"She's either someone's wife or she isn't."

Temper flashed through me. "She's mine." I was really, *really* starting to fucking hate Solberg.

He seemed surprised, banked it, then cocked his head to the side. "I thought I raised you better than to fool around with someone else's—"

"If you say she belongs to someone else one more time," I snarled. "And I'm not *fooling* around."

He raised an eyebrow, something I did quite a lot, but it never seemed to be so condescending when I did it. "You have a cat with her."

"I love her," I snapped, then cleared my throat. In a much more serious tone, I said, "I'm in love with her."

His arms fell away from his chest. "It's been two weeks."

"I don't think it matters." I knew it didn't. My head might read the calendar, but my heart had its own timetable. I fell hard. I fell fast. I wasn't going to apologize for it.

"How much could you know about her? I mean, I've read the press, Nate. This girl—"

"This girl is going to be in my life for a long, *long* time. And I know more than you think. Stop reading that media trash. If you want to know something about her, ask me. Ask her."

"Are you the guy her husband is claiming she cheated with?"

"What the fuck, Dad?" I burst out. I could barely believe he just fucking asked me that. The judgement in his voice was fucking outrageous. "First off..." I held up a finger. "The fact you even read that garbage has me concerned. You know exactly what the press did to Ten. You know exactly how untrue that shit was."

"Not everything they said about your cousin was a lie."

"I'm not him!" I yelled and spread my arms wide. "I'm not some kid sensation whose life changed overnight and I couldn't handle it."

"I know that."

I held up another finger and cut him off. "Second of all, Will Solberg is a lying piece of shit who not only hits Aerie, but somehow forced her into a marriage. When she tried to walk away, he sent men with guns to her house in the middle of the night. If I hadn't been there—"

"Wait. What?" Dad shoved off the counter, fists balled at his sides.

"About that... Maybe you and I could get some target practice in at the range."

"This is *not* a joke!" he yelled.

I held up my hands. "I know."

Concern darkened his features. "What happened?"

I told him about the night at Aerie's and the real reason I'd brought her here with me. Well, besides the fact I didn't want to be away from her.

"This is a matter for the police," he said, sounding very much like a sensible father.

"The police are involved. Along with all of Solberg's money and lawyers," I muttered darkly.

"This is exactly why I don't want you involved in that life. Why you need to drop this all, stay home, and finish college. You can have a good life, son, a quiet life."

I smacked my hands on the table and stood up. "I don't want *your* life!" I yelled.

"There something wrong with my life?"

I slumped. "Of course not, Dad. I know it probably hasn't been easy raising me without Mom. It's probably not what you imagined for yourself. I'm not trying to sound ungrateful. Or even unhappy. But I want more."

He shook his head once. "I don't want you involved with her. With any of it."

"I am. And I'm not walking away… from any of it. They're paying me a million dollars to write her album. A million! There are songwriters in L.A. that have been doing this for a decade and still haven't been able to score this kind of deal. I'm not just some goofball whose dad heads a music department. I'm good at this." I paced away from him, frustrated and pissed. I wished he could see that. I wished he could be proud of me, impressed with everything I'd accomplished.

Instead, all he saw was tabloid drama and the kid he used to have to tutor.

"You think I'm not proud of you?" he asked, his voice much quieter.

I spun and pinned him with a stare. "Considering all you've done is tell me you don't think I can do this and lecture me about being involved with a 'married' woman," I spat.

"I never said you couldn't do it."

I scoffed. "No, just that you practically forbid it. And you walk around all frowny faced." I lowered my voice to impersonate him. "*School is life, Nate. School is the be-all end-all of the world.*"

His lips twitched. "I do not sound like that."

"Yeah. You do."

He came to stand just in front of me. "I know how talented you are. Sometimes it blows my mind. I used to lie awake at night when you were younger and worry that you were going to somehow be discovered. I always tried to figure out how I could protect you from it."

I drew back. "Seriously?"

He nodded once. "It was Ten instead, though. I saw you boys drifting apart as Hollywood pulled at him. I didn't do anything to stop it. I didn't support him the way I could have. Maybe if I had, he wouldn't have had such a rough time."

My mind was blown. I had no idea he thought this. But shocked as I was, I still knew one thing. "What went down with Ten wasn't your fault."

"I had to make a choice. You or him. I was worried if I stepped into that life with him, you would get pulled down, too. So I stayed out of it. And I watched your cousin, who was more like your brother, drift away…"

I tackle-hugged him. His body swayed when I slammed into him, patting him on the back. "That's some deep shit, dad!"

He made a sound between a laugh and a groan, and I pulled back.

"I made a promise to your mother, Nathan."

My eyes widened. He *never* used my full name. Hell, sometimes I forgot that was my full name.

"I promised her on her deathbed that I would watch out for you. That I would raise you right and would keep you safe. It's all she wanted."

I sniffled, using the sleeve of the hoodie to swipe at my face. The scent of my girl wrapped around me, drawing me up short.

For a long time, I only ever saw it from my point of view. A kid who lost his mom too early. A boy who sometimes wished he still had the love of his mother.

Now I was older. Now I was standing in front of a man who made a deathbed promise to a woman he still hadn't moved on from. Even after all these years.

I thought of Aerie lying in the bedroom, beneath the blankets, where she'd just been in my arms. I put myself in my father's shoes… in the perspective of a man in love.

The instant terror and pain I felt drew me up short.

My mother was his Aerie. He had to watch her die, unable to do anything to stop the cancer that attacked her from the inside out.

I couldn't even imagine. The thought of never seeing Aerie again left me cold, my hands shaking and fear clawing at the back of my throat.

And then to be faced with the absolution of her not surviving and being left with something—with someone who was a living piece of her. I'd protect that piece with my dying breath.

I was that piece, the last remaining portion my father had of my mother.

"I'm sorry, Dad," I said, sincerity ringing in my tone. "I understand now, in a way I never could have before. You just want to protect me, and by doing that, you protect her."

He blinked. "You really are in love with her."

I nodded slowly. "I really am."

He sighed and paced away, staring down at the half-eaten, likely mushy cereal in his bowl. Silence was loud through the kitchen as we both stood there digesting.

We were at an impasse, weren't we? I felt stuck. Stuck between the woman my father loved and the woman I loved.

"Your mother would be so proud of you." He spoke, not turning around. "Of everything you've accomplished and of everything you will."

"I'll finish school," I said as heaviness wrapped around me, making it a little hard to breathe. Was this what doing the right thing felt like? Heavy?

"Yes. You will." He turned from the counter. "But not until after you write this album."

My mouth fell open.

"And get that scumbag away from your girl."

I pointed to the fact that my mouth fell open.

Dad chuckled and rolled his eyes. "You remind me of your mother."

A small ache pierced through some of the awe I was feeling. My mouth snapped shut, and I took a step forward. "Dad."

"Don't Dad me," he said sternly. "This is what you wanted."

I nodded, feeling guilty. It was what I wanted, but I didn't want my own happiness to come at his expense.

He sighed, as if knowing the direction my thoughts were taking me. "You're twenty-two years old, son. A grown man. I know I treat you like you aren't, but I know better. Maybe clinging to your life was easier for me than facing my own."

"It's okay to be happy again," I said quietly. Even as I spoke, the words hurt. I couldn't help seeing Aerie in my mind. I ached for her. If this conversation wasn't so important, I would rush back down the hall and lock myself in the room with her.

"I know, and I am. But it's time to let you be the man I raised you to be." He smiled, albeit sadly. "I kept my promise to your mom. You turned out better than either of us could have imagined."

"Gee, thanks," I muttered.

He laughed. "Keep the job. Make a name for yourself in music. They're lucky to have you. You're the best damn songwriter they're ever gonna see."

"But school." I objected. My, how quickly things changed. I went from trying to get away from it to trying to keep it close.

He waved a hand. "Don't worry about it. I can probably get the rest of the semester credited to you since you'll be writing an album."

"Seriously?"

"You will probably have to come back and take the final exams in each class." He warned.

"I can do that." I nodded vigorously.

"We'll work out something for your final semester, then. Maybe online classes. Or once the album is done, you and Aerie can come back here while you finish."

"Aerie, too?"

"If she's special enough for you to love, then I know I'll love her, too."

I rushed forward and hugged him.

I was a huggy kind of guy.

"I love you, Dad."

He chuckled and hugged me back. "I love you, too, son."

I pulled back. "You sure you're okay with this?"

"I am."

I hugged him again. The weight of a thousand pounds lifted off me. Having his approval meant more than anything. Now that I had it, I knew I could rock this album.

"Hey, Dad?"

"What now?"

I looked at him seriously. Now that I knew things were going to be okay between us, I wanted that for him and Ten. "Some of that stuff you just told me? You should tell Ten."

"Ten?"

I nodded. "He thinks you're embarrassed of him. He thinks you don't want people to know you're related."

My father's eyes widened in shock, and then a look of what could only be described as regret filled his face. "Thanks for letting me know."

I nodded, about to say something else, but Dad cleared his throat and patted me on the shoulder. I turned, seeing Aerie hovering in the doorway.

I grinned wide, about to fill her in, but the smile died before it barely formed.

"What's wrong?" I asked, closing the distance between us.

Her eyes searched mine. They were apprehensive, and her skin was colorless. "The hearing for the annulment has been set. I have to go back to L.A."

# thirty-four

*Aerie*

The law offices of Bright & Wilde were located in downtown L.A., not far from Solberg Records. We used a private car service to get there and the confidentially located back entrance that was off the street, away from prying, busybody eyes.

Nate sat beside me, black shades wrapped around his eyes and a baseball cap turned backward on his head, hiding his beautiful red hair. We weren't exactly sneaking around, but we were hiding from the press.

If Nate's father suggested he was the one I was "cheating" with, then it would be far too easy for the rest of the world to come to that stupid conclusion as well.

As much as Seth wanted a statement of some kind for the press, I deferred, deciding I was going to do exactly what Byron Ryan wanted and keep my mouth shut. I planned to let speculation mount, rumors swirl, and conspiracy theories abound. I'd say it all in the music and give an exclusive interview *after* it released.

Maybe it was the coward's way. I mean, I definitely didn't want to say anything about my life. Not that I wanted people to think I was a cheater with a raging STD either (aka a frog with warts), but choices had to be made.

I was choosing me.

To hell with what everyone else thought.

And on a business side, it would be good for album sales.

Seth was a little put off when I informed him of the decision. For two reasons:

1. His phone was never going to stop ringing.

And…

2. Like the rest of them, he wanted to know what was going on.

Maybe I'd take Nate's suggestion and send him an edible arrangement. He seemed to think that was like the best thing since Fruity Pebbles. Well, that and corndogs.

Mac knocked on the heavily tinted window, and I reached for Nate's hand. Lifting mine, he kissed the back of it and then moved beside me. "I'm going first." He cautioned, popped open the door, and started out.

Expecting me, Mac had his hand out. Nate glanced at it and then slid his into it. "Wow, this is really full service."

I giggled.

"Sir," Mac said. "That was meant for Aerie."

Shedding his jokes, Nate turned to the bodyguard. "I won't put her out of a car ahead of me. What kind of man do you think I am?" His eyes bored into Mac's.

Finally, Mac inclined his chin. "A good one, sir."

"Call me Nate. Sir is for stuffy people." Nate reached in and helped me out of the SUV. Tucking his arm around me, we went quickly into the elevator Ben was holding open.

The receptionist didn't even bother to get up when I strode into the lobby. She glanced up. Then her eyes slid right to Nate. I felt myself bristle, but he gave my side a squeeze.

"He's expecting you," the receptionist said, still looking at Nate.

I paused, my heels going quiet so my voice could be heard. "Do you have something in your eye?" I asked sweetly.

She pulled her stare from Nate and looked at me. "Uh, no."

"Would you like to?" I intoned, feeling my freshly painted nails dig into my palm.

Nate made a sound and ushered me away. Glancing back over his shoulder, he told the girl, "I'm limited edition."

I rolled my eyes.

The door to Walter's office was open when we approached. I told Mac and Ben they could wait outside, so they took up position by the door, and Nate shut it behind us when we went inside.

"Ms. Boone," Walter said, standing from behind his desk and smiling. I had to give it to him. He only slid a cursory glance at Nate before returning all attention back to me. "Thank you for coming in."

"The annulment hearing is in two days. Of course I'm going to be here," I said, blunt. It wasn't like this was some social call.

"Yes, well. There are just a few things I wanted to go over with you before we meet at the judge's office."

"So it's not a court thing?" Nate asked.

Walter glanced at him. "And you would be…?"

"Nate Roth," he replied, sticking his hand out for a shake.

Walter returned it but seemed confused. "And why are you here?"

I opened my mouth, but Nate beat me to it. "Because Aerie is." Then, as if he realized he wasn't done speaking, he said, "And because I'm here to make sure you do your job and don't screw her over."

I pressed my lips together.

Walter bristled. "This firm is not in the habit of screwing people over."

"Then why isn't this thing done already?" he commanded.

Apparently, that intensity he used to make me want him… He could also channel it into intimidation.

I had no idea he could be so…. *alpha.*

Well. Not true. I guess he proved that the night he fought the men with that gun.

Suffice it to say, I liked this side of him. Nate Roth was a complete package. Every quality that could make a girl swoon was wrapped up right there beneath his skin, just behind his emerald eyes.

"I don't discuss legal cases with people who are not my clients."

"Who's paying whom?" Nate wondered.

Walter blanched, and I hid a smile.

"Forget it." Nate went on, his tone completely changing. "I want some answers."

I straightened, stepping in front of Nate.

"He can still see me, princess. I'm taller."

Over my shoulder, I delivered a withering stare.

He held up his hands. "Fine. Go ahead."

"You have my permission to speak freely in front of Nate. He's my… support system."

But, oh, he was so much more than that.

"Very well." Walter went back behind his desk. "As you are well aware…" He began, sitting down. "Will Solberg has been actively fighting the petition for annulment."

Nate made a rude sound and sat down. I took the chair beside him.

"I finally managed to get a hearing set, as you requested. And I managed to do it slightly before the mandatory thirty-day waiting period here in California."

I hadn't known about the thirty-day thing.

Walter seemed to read it on my face and sniffed. "As you can see, my firm and I have been doing everything possible to get this matter cleared up quickly."

I sat back, feeling a little guilty. I had been pretty, erm, rude to him before. "I'm sorry, Walter—"

"Nope," Nate said, putting his arm out across me as if we were about to be in a collision and he was going to protect me. "You're not apologizing, not for being clear on what you want. This is a shitty mess, and you have every right to be upset."

"But—"

"Isn't that right, Walter?" Nate intoned.

He met Nate's eyes, then looked back at me. "Of course."

"Anyway." Walter cleared his throat. Nate's arm dropped, and his hand reached for mine. "The day the hearing was set, I received a notification from Mr. Solberg's attorney. He has a witness who will be testifying that you were indeed of sound mind to agree to matrimony."

I gasped. "He's lying!"

"Can you prove that?" Walter asked.

Tears filled my eyes, and I shook my head.

"What kind of proof do you need?" Nate asked, the voice of reason while I was falling apart.

"Something to discredit this witness… or proof that you were indeed incapacitated. A blood test from the next day, a breathalyzer. Something that would prove you were under the influence."

"I don't have that!" I exclaimed.

"It's okay, princess." Nate said softly, then turned back to my lawyer. "Who is this witness anyway? A friend of theirs? Maybe we can talk to them—"

"You cannot do that. It will only make her look guiltier."

"Guilty of what?" I gasped, a hiccup rocking my body.

"Of lying. Of trying to manipulate the courts regarding something you did and changed your mind about."

I gasped again.

Nate surged to his feet, planting his body in front me. "Let's get one thing straight right now, Walter," he snarled. "You work for *her,* and as such, you don't suggest she's lying or insult her. If you do anything of the sort ever again, all of California is going to know what a crook you are."

"I'm no such thing!" he spat.

"Maybe not. But the idea will be out there. And as a lawyer, you know all about reasonable doubt."

Silence filled the room, and I brushed at the tears falling down my cheeks. Ugh. I needed to be better than this. Stronger. Falling apart now was not an option. It wasn't crown worthy either.

I took a deep breath and stood. Nate reached for my hand, and his fingers slid through mine.

"I certainly never meant to imply you are lying, Ms. Boone."

"I understand, Walter," I said, my voice strong. "You're just telling me how it looks. I can assure you, whoever this witness is, Will is paying them to lie."

"Without proof—" Walter began.

"Yes. I know. Who is this witness? Are you at least allowed to tell me his name?"

"He's from the chapel where you got married. I believe he's the man who actually performed the ceremony."

My stomach sank. I lifted my chin. "I don't even know where the ceremony took place. Do you know the name?"

"I have it right here," he said, opening a folder. "It will be listed on your marriage certificate."

I recalled the day in the office Will showed it to me. Though, it was more of a flash. I'd barely had a chance to look at it.

"Could I see that, please?" I asked, reaching for it.

Walter picked up the paper and handed it over.

*The Palisades Sands of Time Chapel,* the certificate read. What a stupid name for a chapel. My eyes blurred a little as I looked down, realizing how much this piece of paper had cost me.

*What a stupid mistake.*

*What was I thinking?*

"J.," Nate said. "What's your middle name?"

"What?" I asked, glancing at him.

He pointed to my signature on the certificate. "What's your middle name?"

"Oh. It's Joeline." I gasped. Lifting the paper closer to my face, I stared at the signature. Right there in black ink was my name.... Aerie J. Boone.

Except that was *not* my signature.

"I didn't sign this," I announced. My finger stabbed at the paper, and I looked at my lawyer. "This is not my signature."

"I'm afraid I'm not following," He replied.

"That's why he didn't let me look at it closely. It's why he never showed it to me again!" I mused, excitement making my voice high.

"What's going on, princess?" Nate asked. I felt his palm on the small of my back.

I turned to him and smiled wide. "I didn't sign this paper. That is not my signature." I turned back to Walter. "That nullifies this entire marriage. I didn't even sign!"

"Could you please explain? Is your legal name not Aerie J. Boone?"

"Yes, it is. But I *never* sign my middle initial. Never."

"Perhaps you did that night and don't remember? Your memory seems to be a little spotty." He suggested.

"Watch your mouth," Nate growled.

"I really don't have to take these threats." Walter sniffed.

"Then stop saying stupid shit," Nate retorted. "And people say I'm the moron."

"Memory or not, I can guarantee you that I did not sign this. It's all wrong. Even if for some reason I did put a J., I don't write them that way."

I handed the certificate to Nate and leaned over Walter's desk to grab a piece of paper and a pen. In one second flat, I scrawled my signature, the one I always used, on the paper and then just below it, signed again, this time using the letter J.

"See!" I said, triumphant. I took the certificate from Nate and laid it right beside the one I'd just written, pointing to the two signatures.

"That is not mine."

Walter stared down, and Nate leaned over the desk so he could do the same.

"They *are* different." Nate observed. The second the words left his mouth, he burst up with a huge grin on his face. "You aren't married. You never even got married!"

He came at me, wrapped his arms around my waist, and spun me around. I laughed. Nate stopped turning and let me slide down his body, green eyes boring into mine.

"You've always been mine," he whispered, then kissed me.

Everything felt right in the world in that moment. It was perfect.

Until Walter cleared his throat.

"I'm sorry to interrupt this happy moment, but this isn't going to be enough."

"What!" Nate and I both said at the same time.

"I can see the signatures are different. However, without proof that you actually didn't sign…"

"What about a handwriting expert? They can prove it wasn't me. Will probably drugged me, took me to the chapel, and then forged my signature!"

"I can definitely get a handwriting expert to concur with your allegations."

I made a sound of distress.

"But?" Nate demanded.

"But that will take several weeks. The hearing in two days will have to be postponed. It will give Mr. Solberg more time to find witnesses…"

"So you're saying he can legally trap me into a marriage I didn't even participate in?" I exclaimed.

"Oh, hell no," Nate growled.

"For now at least. Possibly enough to make an annulment inviable. There is always divorce…"

"No!" Nate and I both shouted.

Walter sank into his desk chair as though he were tired.

Yeah, well, buddy, join the club.

"You can question the witness, get him to admit he's lying." I encouraged.

"I can do that. But if he doesn't admit it, it still comes down to your word against his."

Nate made a frustrated sound and paced to the window, fists at his sides.

"I don't have to remind you that confronting Will Solberg about any of this can only be used against you at the hearing."

I nodded, understanding.

"And that if you and your boyfriend here are seen anywhere together, it will make it look like you're trying to get out of the marriage because you *are* having an affair and don't want to split assets or be liable for alimony."

"Dudes who take alimony are lame," Nate intoned from his position by the window.

"Yes, well, Mr. Solberg's alimony would be millions of dollars," Walter quipped.

Nate cursed. It was pretty creative, and even Walter smiled.

I sank back into a chair. Not only was Will controlling me, threatening my future, my bank account, and my reputation (what was left of it), but now he was keeping Nate and me apart.

"What do you suggest, Mr. Bright?" I asked, defeated.

"I know this is very hard—"

"No." Nate turned from the window. "You have no fucking idea."

The lawyer swallowed. "I will call in a handwriting expert and see how fast I can get an analysis." He gestured to the certificate and my actual signature. "But it will be a few weeks."

I opened my mouth, but he held up his hand.

"I understand you want this done yesterday. I will hold off on having the hearing postponed for another twenty-four hours. Perhaps reach out to the chapel where you got married. See if anyone remembers you. You're very famous. That makes you memorable. See if you can find someone who was there that night at the chapel. Someone who can corroborate your story. If you can find someone in the twenty-four hours and get them back here, we can proceed with the hearing. If you can't find anyone, we'll go ahead with the handwriting analysis."

A witness. Just one person. One person who could speak on my behalf. I could do it.

I glanced at Nate.

I *had* to do it.

I stood and nodded. "Thank you for your time today, Walter. I will find you a witness, and I'll be in touch."

"Call me the minute you have something."

I nodded.

Nate put his arm at my waist as we walked to the door.

Behind us, Walter called out, "And don't forget. The press cannot get wind of your relationship. And under no circumstance can Mr. Roth be at the hearing."

Nate's hand tightened at my side. I felt his frustration and anger.

"We understand." I confirmed.

The second the doors to Walter's office opened, Nate dropped his arm from around me and put a little distance between us.

A rift opened up in my chest, but I knew the pain of him only standing beside me would be nothing compared to the feeling I would know if I had to remain "married" to Will for any longer than two more days.

We walked down to the SUV, the entire time barely looking at each other, certainly not touching.

It was the longest walk of my life.

Once we made it to the car, I pulled out my phone.

"Who you calling, princess?" he asked quietly.

"Ten," I replied, focused. "I need to borrow his plane."

# thirty-five

## *Nate*

I'd rather never eat Fruity Pebbles again than pretend my girl wasn't my girl.

Yet here I was… riding the Nate Train solo.

I mean, it was a pretend solo trip, but I hated it.

And I hated Will Solberg.

Yeah, yeah, hating someone was wrong. Well, if hating that douchebag was wrong, then I didn't want to be right.

We flew together to Vegas, thanks to my cousin and his private plane. But we departed the plane separate and took separate cars from the airport in Vegas to the hotel.

Aerie was already inside the exclusive hotel, Yellow. The place where she woke up married. I didn't want to stay here. I didn't even want to look at this building, but the fact it was exclusive, had no cameras, no press, and the staff was all sworn to secrecy made it the only place in Vegas we could stay. That is if we wanted to see each other.

And I wanted to see her.

Letting her come to Vegas without me was not in the cards. As in, over my dead body. My instinct to protect her was in overdrive right now, and I was beginning to think it might never be anything but.

Still, we had to be cautious because the last thing I wanted was for us to be photographed together and give Will even more ammunition against her.

Someday that guy was going to get what was coming to him, and I sure as hell couldn't wait.

A while after Aerie was checked in, I pulled my rental into the private tunnel where guests entered. There were no signs or indications that it led to any sort of hotel, and the building itself was half a mile from the entrance. It too had no kind of identification on it. From what Aerie said, a lot of the locals all thought it was just a high-rise of office buildings. To keep up with the façade, the first two levels of the building did house offices, which were accessible from the street, but the third floor was sealed off from the lower portion.

After driving for what felt like forever, the tunnel opened into a space that felt as if I'd just arrived at the swankiest parking garage ever. I mean, the space was actually like a hotel for cars. The floors were polished, there was art on the walls, and all the lighting was crystal sconces. There were even velvet drapes at the valet station.

"Guest of Yellow, sir?" The man in a full-on tuxedo asked when I stopped the car and rolled down the window.

"Yes," I said, keeping my eyes trained ahead. I was wearing dark Ray Bans and a baseball hat.

He handed me a ticket and then held his hand out for my keys.

"You don't need my name?" I asked.

"We don't do that here, sir."

I took the ticket, he put a corresponding one on the dash, and then I got out of the car, giving him the keys. I didn't have a bag, and he didn't ask me if I did. He simply got in the car and drove off.

Across from the valet station was a huge glass rotating door trimmed in crystals. I went through and was instantly transported into easily the most luxurious, most moneyed place I'd ever been.

I'm talking crystals that shimmered like diamonds, gold and silver trim everywhere. White marble. Art I was pretty sure belonged in museums and a bar literally serving free Cristal from a fountain.

I sincerely tried not to gape as I gazed around for the elevators. It became almost impossible when the white marble wall slid open, revealing a softly lit car that looked more like some fancy spaceship than an elevator.

What's more was that a very famous actor stepped out of it.

"Dude! I love your movies!" I said, my voice echoing around the hushed, posh environment.

He merely smiled and kept walking.

Quickly, I dove into the elevator as the walls started to slide shut. I typed in the room number Aerie had texted (like for real typed it in; there were no floor buttons here) and barely felt when the car started to slide up.

When it stopped, the doors slid open, revealing basically a very short hallway that led directly to the door to Aerie's suite. There was no stepping off the elevator onto the floor and hunting down your room.

There was just the door to her space and enough room to stand in front of it.

I stepped out, sort of feeling claustrophobic, and rapped lightly on the door with my knuckles. I heard someone on the other side, and then it opened, just enough for a dark eye to peer out.

"Hey, princess," I said, feeling more like I could breathe now.

She opened the door wide and pulled me inside as the elevator behind me shut and disappeared.

"This place is like creepy and amazing all at the same time," I told her.

Aerie wrapped her arms around my waist and pressed close. Holding her with one arm, I shut the door and locked it with the other, then wrapped that one around her tight.

"Everything okay?" I murmured, rubbing her back. "They give you trouble checking in?"

"No, it was fine. You pay cash up front. They don't log you into the system, so there isn't really a record of you being here. It's all very exclusive. No one even knows who's in what room because the elevators stop at each room and not on a floor."

"I noticed." I thought it sounded pretty macabre, but I didn't say it out loud. I was just glad to be with her.

"When you order room service, it's left in that little space between the elevator and the door of the suite. The delivery person doesn't even know who they're delivering to."

"This place is so fancy they probably don't have Fruity Pebbles." Which meant this really wasn't my kind of place.

She lifted her head off my chest, gazing up. "I don't like having to hide you."

I kissed her in reply, sweeping my tongue into her mouth, playing with hers. She sighed, and I picked her up, her legs hooking around my waist. Not breaking the kiss, I carried her into the room, laying her across the bed.

I didn't get many kisses in today because we woke up in New York, flew to L.A., met her lawyer, and then hopped on another flight to Vegas. Quite frankly, I didn't even know what time it was.

All I knew was now we had less than twenty-four hours to find a way to discredit Solberg and his so-called witness.

As I dragged my lips across her jaw and down her neck, she moaned and turned her head, giving me more access to her sensitive skin. I nipped at it, then sucked her earlobe between my lips and massaged it. Her fingers slipped under my T-shirt and caressed my sides and back.

My cock strained against the fly of my jeans, and I thrust my hips against her. Automatically, her legs spread, and I settled between them, dry-humping her like we were a pair of sex-starved teenagers.

Aerie rocked with me, and my blood boiled. My lips went back to hers, making out until I was sure the entire inside of my mouth tasted like her.

I pushed up, hovering over her body and balancing on my arms. Breathing heavy, I stared down into her flushed face and nearly came in my pants. "If I don't get off this bed right now, we're going to be late getting to the chapel."

Her pink tongue slipped out, smoothing over her lower lip. "That place is open twenty-four hours. We have some time."

I groaned, and her hand curled in the front of my shirt, tugging it up. I let her peel it over my head and toss it away before colliding with her body once more.

Her hands were in my hair, on my chest, and grazing down my back. The feel of her tongue wrapping around mine was like a drug I couldn't get enough of. Continuing to kiss, I pushed her shirt up over her breasts. She had one of those flimsy, soft-feeling bras, so it was easy to pull the material down and bare her perky breast.

She sighed into my mouth when I caught the hardened nipple and rolled it around between my fingers. Her lips slipped away from mine, her face falling to the side as I caressed her. My mouth latched onto the place my fingers had been, and I sucked deeply, causing her to arch up off the bed.

My arm slipped under her body, fitting against her back so even when she relaxed, her body remained arched upward at the perfect position for my mouth.

The fabric of her bra was damp by the time I lifted my head. Her chest rose and fell deeply, her hips moving impatiently.

"I love you, princess," I told her as I peeled the clothes off her body.

"Oh, Nate." She sighed. "I never even knew love could be like this until you."

I moved down her body, licking and kissing until I felt her tremble beneath my touch. Grabbing a condom out of my back pocket (I might not have brought extra clothes, but priorities…), I quickly removed all my clothes. When I turned back, she was sitting on the edge of the bed, legs spread, hair all mussed.

I moved toward her, liking the way her eyes slid over my body, a caress that required no physical touch. She took the packet out of my hand and laid it beside her hip before taking my dick in her hand.

I shuddered, and she smiled.

"I think I want to feel you tremble the way you make me."

I opened my mouth, but whatever I was about to say turned into a moan. Aerie's hot little mouth slid down over my length, taking it all.

I felt my tip quiver in her mouth, and I pictured old ladies in their underpants.

What?

A man's gotta do what a man's gotta do.

And this man wasn't about to come early, because I had a lot more of this woman to enjoy.

She made a sound, vibrating against my cock, as she torturously pulled back, dragging her lips over my skin. My hands found their way into her hair, my hips thrust out, forcing me deep into her mouth again.

I froze, thinking maybe it was an asshole thing to do. She felt my reaction and gazed up my body, still keeping my cock in her mouth, and smiled.

After that, I sort of stopped seeing. All I did was feel the way she sucked my rod as if it were coated in honey and honey was her fucking favorite snack.

My balls and legs were indeed trembling when she finally released me.

"I can taste you," she said, pulling my lower lip into her mouth. I made a sound. It was all I could manage. Her fingers delved into the short, springy curls, and she smiled. "Red is definitely your natural hair color."

I picked up the condom and ripped it open. She moved back into the center of the large bed while I rolled it on. When I was done, I went to her, pinned her hands above her head in one of mine, and kissed her while my free hand tested out her readiness. She was drenched, and the second I flicked my thumb over her swollen clit, she shuddered.

Releasing her hands, I moved over her, settling between her knees.

Rising, I pushed her legs wide, staring down at her body stretched out before me. Unable to stop myself, I leaned down, sucking her breast into my mouth. She arched up and whispered my name.

I dipped into her. Slow this time, not all at once. She grabbed at my hips and ass, trying to pull me in deep, but I wouldn't let her. I went little by little... teasing us both.

When I was at last sheathed inside her, I pulled out and plunged back in with one hard stroke.

Her mouth opened, but no sound came out. I did it again and again, pausing only long enough to make sure she was okay with the punishing pace.

"Don't stop." She gasped, digging her nails into my hips.

I went back at her, pumping into her body like my life depended on it.

She was gasping for breath, straining against me, when I leaned down and pinched her nipple lightly. She exploded beneath me. My name echoed around the room as she came apart over and over.

My strokes gentled as she came down, her body sinking into the mattress with a heavy sigh. I kissed her softly, and she smiled against my lips.

I pulled out, then sank back in. Her walls spasmed around me.

Her palm hit my chest and pushed. "Roll over,"

I did, making sure I stayed in her heat. Aerie rose over me like a queen claiming her throne. She sank down deep, wiggled her hips, and smoothed her hands over my chest. Then she linked her hands in mine, stretched them above my head, and rode me like a cowgirl on a wild stallion.

I wished I could say I lasted longer, but *fuck me…* She milked my dick so good it was literally impossible not to explode.

Even as I came, she moved over me, clutching her walls so I was sheathed so tight as I pumped hot seed inside her.

When it was done, she collapsed over my chest and kissed the underside of my jaw.

I was going to marry her someday.

And not in some shitty chapel in Vegas.

I was going to make her mine in every way humanly possible.

Aerie was my forever.

"Wow," she said a short while later.

I laughed, a throaty, cocky sound.

"I guess it's true what they say about redheads," she quipped. "Red in the head, wild in bed."

I grinned. "You don't have red hair, so what's your excuse?"

Gazing down at me, she whispered, "You."

Lifting off the pillow, I kissed her quietly. Tenderly. Then I pulled her back into my chest and wrapped her in my arms. "Come back down here. I'm not done holding you yet."

#  thirty-six

## *Aerie*

Seriously, though, were all redheads this fantastic in bed? Because *damn*.

But that's not what this chapter is about. Sadly.

Let's move on…

"You know you can't come to the chapel with me," I said, still drunk on whatever it was he did to my body.

Seriously, he was like the body whisperer.

That thought made white-hot jealousy rip through me. How many other bodies did he whisper? Just the idea made me sick.

"I'm not letting you go alone."

"How many women have you slept with?" The words literally toppled out of my mouth without any caution at all.

He stilled beneath me. "What?"

Well, the question was out there now. There was no point in backtracking. Besides, I was still insanely jealous.

Lifting off his shoulder, I said, "How many?"

"Why?" His voice was dubious.

"Because I want to know."

"How many men have you slept with?" He countered.

That was easy. "Two, including you."

His green eyes rounded. "Really?"

I nodded, feeling a little self-conscious.

Nate dragged his fingers through my hair. "He was your first." The storm in his eyes proved he didn't like it.

I laid a hand on his chest. "Yes, but it was never like it is with you."

"Girls never forget their first… Do they?"

"Would you rather be a girl's first or her last?"

He grinned fast. "Both."

I pinched his nipple.

Nate laughed, but when it died away, his eyes softened on my face. "Last. Definitely last."

I smiled. "So?"

He sighed. "Same as you."

I couldn't help it. I gaped at him.

He made a sound and tried to roll away.

"Come back here," I demanded and pulled him back beneath me. "Are you embarrassed?"

"Should I be?"

"No!" I said, trying not to smile like I'd won the lottery. I failed. "I'm so glad!"

He scowled. "What's that supposed to mean?"

"It means I don't have to be angry at a bunch of faceless women who came before me."

Realization dawned in his spectacular eyes. "You're jealous?"

"Ragingly jealous." I confirmed.

"There's nothing to be jealous of, sweetheart." He brushed his knuckles over my cheek but ruined his sweetness by grinning wide.

I frowned. "You aren't lying, are you?"

"If I was going to lie, I'd lie about being more experienced."

"You have more natural ability than experience will ever teach some guys."

He raised an eyebrow. "And how would you know?"

"A girl just knows these things." I sniffed.

He laughed.

After a moment, I admitted, "I'm actually surprised, though."

He made a sound. "Me, too."

I laughed.

This was nice. Being in bed with him. Laughing. Feeling safe. It was new for me, but something I didn't ever want to give up.

Turning serious, he said, "It wasn't like I didn't try. Most women see me as a friend or a goofball. I'm not Ten."

"I love you the way you are."

"Thank you."

It pierced my heart in a way nothing else ever could, the fact that he was thanking me for loving him.

Sometimes it surprised me how much we had in common even though we were so very different.

"Now what's this about you thinking I'm going to let you walk outta this hotel without me?"

"You know we can't be seen there together, Nate. There could be press. And it's pretty obvious Will has the place on his payroll. They'll probably call him up the second I walk in the door."

"Which is exactly why you can't go there alone."

"I'll take Mac and Ben."

He growled. "I don't like it."

"I don't either. But I really don't think we have a choice." I shrugged.

"You stay here, and I'll go."

"No!" I said, sitting up and staring at him.

He sat up, too, and nodded. "Yes. I think that's the safest thing. They won't know to call him if I walk in there."

"I am not putting you any more in the middle of this than you already are."

Nate shook his head. "You just said it, princess. I'm already in the middle. It won't matter."

"It matters to me!"

He took my face in his hands, eyes staring into mine. "It's my job to protect you."

"I have to protect myself. Depending on a man is what got me into this mess in the first place."

Hurt flashed in his eyes. "I'm not like Will."

"I know that." I grabbed his hand. "And I love you for wanting to protect me. But I have to do this. I got myself into this mess, and I have to be the one to get myself out."

His eyes bounced between mine for a long time before he sighed. "I don't like this."

Relief filled me. "I don't either, but I'm doing it."

Begrudgingly, he said, "You better call Ben and Mac have them meet you downstairs."

"They're already down there waiting."

"I didn't see them." Nate wondered.

"There's a private lounge for security detail behind one of the walls."

"Of course there is." He scoffed.

I kissed him, then reluctantly reached for my clothes.

The only thing that kept me going was the fact that, very soon, all this could be over.

The Palisades Sands of Time Chapel made me queasy. From the minute I walked in, though, I knew I was at the right place. It felt slimy in here, which was just perfect for a man like Will.

Mac and Ben flanked me. The three of us moved through the gaudy lobby as a single unit. The fact that I even supposedly got married here made my skin crawl. Taking a breath, I reminded myself I wasn't actually married to Will and that's why I was here.

To prove it.

Because it was so late here, there weren't a ton of people (how busy would a place like this be, though?), but as we approached the front desk, a couple who were clearly just married burst out a set of double doors across the room. She was all dressed in white, and the groom was laughing as he carried her.

My stomach tightened. This place might not be my ideal wedding venue, but regardless of the place, that's the way it was *supposed* to be.

Happy. Wanted. Two people in love.

The bride noticed me staring, and a light of recognition came into her eyes. Turning toward the reception desk abruptly, I prayed to God she didn't call out my name. Sensing my discord, Mac and Ben closed in behind me, totally shielding me from view.

Thankfully, the happy couple moved on, getting back to their own happy ending.

A man came out from behind some curtains, stopping short when he saw me there. He knew who I was instantly, and his eyes turned wary. I plastered a catlike smile on my face, rising to my full height.

"Hello," I said, reaching out a hand to shake. He glanced between me and my hand before reluctantly returning the embrace. "I'm Aerie Boone."

"I know who you are," he said coolly. I glanced at Mac and lifted a brow. "Then you know why I'm here?" I asked, turning back to the man.

"I'm afraid not."

"I'm here because a few weeks ago, I was apparently married here in this fine establishment."

He didn't say anything, but he did swallow thickly.

"I'd like to speak with someone who was here that night."

"I wasn't," he said. "And I don't know anyone who was."

Sighing, I pulled out a copy of the marriage certificate and gazed down at it. "Is Mr. Richman here? He's the man who officiated the, um, ceremony." *If you could even call it that.*

"I'm not sure if he's here." The man hedged.

"Would you mind checking? I'll wait."

He excused himself and disappeared behind the same curtains he'd come through. Minutes ticked by, and the more time passed, the more certain I was that

Will paid off everyone in this place. I began to worry. I began to fear. What if I couldn't get what I needed here?

What if I was forced to stay "married" to Will until I could prove that signature wasn't mine—or worse, file for divorce?

When I was good and worked up, the man came back, followed by another. Faint recognition flooded me, along with very hazy pictures of standing with him and Will as he went on about marriage.

I couldn't deny I'd been here that night. That much was clear.

"Ah, Mrs. Solberg, how nice to see you again!" Mr. Richman exclaimed. "How are you enjoying life with your new husband?"

"I'm not," I said, blunt. "And I think you know that."

He seemed taken aback by my frankness, and I took advantage of the fact he was off guard. "How much is Will paying you to fly to California and lie in a court of law about me being in my right mind to consent to the marriage you performed here?"

He sputtered and gripped the edge of the counter. "I beg your pardon?"

"I'll double whatever he's paying if you just tell the truth."

He blanched. Temptation passed behind his eyes, and then all expression left his features. "I'm so sorry to hear you aren't enjoying being a wife. You were so happy that night. So excited. I could barely get the words out fast enough before you were shouting, 'I do!'"

"Why are you doing this?" I asked, miserable.

He wasn't even fazed by the fact that he was ruining my life. "Telling the truth?"

"Is there anyone else here tonight who was there at my wedding?" I asked. Clearly, trying to bargain with him wasn't going to work. Will had his hooks in too deep, and the more I tried, the more it was going to look as though I was trying to tamper with his witness. I probably shouldn't have offered him money, but, well, desperate times and all.

"I'm afraid not," he said with a heavy sigh, as if he were sorry.

I snorted.

"Perhaps you should reconsider," Mac said, leaning on the counter.

"I can't help you." Mr. Richman sniffed, then disappeared behind the curtain.

"Wait!" I burst out and nearly flung myself across the counter after him. Mac caught me around the waist before I could get across and towed me back.

"I wouldn't advise that, Ms. Boone."

I opened my mouth to argue, but Ben caught me around the elbow and led me over toward the front entrance. "Let's take a moment to regroup."

We were standing by a bunch of tall plants—I couldn't tell if they were real or fake—as I tried and failed to catch my breath. "I'm not leaving here without some kind of proof," I said, adamant. "I don't care what that liar says." I pointed to the front desk accusingly. "I'm not the one who signed that damned paper!"

All of a sudden, the plants began rustling around, and a man in a black leather jacket and hat appeared. I screeched and jumped backward. Mac and Ben jerked around.

"It's just me!" Nate whispered.

"Nate!" I gasped, also whispering. "What on earth are you doing here? Were you in that plant?"

He lifted a hand dismissively. "That British guy taught me this trick."

"You aren't supposed to be here!" I hissed. "And what the hell are you wearing?"

He smoothed his hands over the black leather jacket, which sort of looked like a bomber-style coat. On his head was some kind of old man hat, and covering his eyes was a pair of mirrored aviator glasses.

Instead of jeans, he was wearing a rumpled pair of trousers, but his sneakers were still the same.

He looked ridiculous.

"Pretty good, right?" he asked. "There's a thrift shop a block over."

Mac and Ben snickered, and I swear their behavior only egged his on.

"Nate," I said and pointed to the door silently, telling him to leave.

"You don't seem to be having much luck," he murmured.

"I'm just going to wait until someone new takes over the counter. I've got this," I said confidently because I was utterly confident I would get this done.

I had no choice.

"Watch and learn," he remarked, straightening his jacket.

Before I could say anything, Nate strolled across the room as a woman appeared from behind the curtain to stand at the desk.

"Hey there, gorgeous," he said, leaning on the counter, chomping on some gum I didn't even know he had in his mouth.

"Is there something I can help you with, sir?" the woman asked.

Clearing his throat, he rose to his full height and reached into the pocket of his coat. "Actually, yes. I'm Carl Flintstone, a licensed private investigator here in Nevada." He flashed what looked like some kind of badge. "I work very closely with the LVPD."

"You're a police officer?" she asked, interest filling her eyes.

"Unofficially officially, yes." He nodded.

What the hell did that even mean? The woman seemed impressed, however.

"I need the assistance of someone just like you to help me solve my latest case. You think you're up for the job?"

"Well, I can certainly try."

"I've noted that you have security cameras located around the premises." He pointed up to one in the corner, which was focused on the desk. "I'm gonna need to look at the footage from the night of…" He pulled out another piece of paper, glancing at it. "March first."

"I don't think I'm allowed to just show that to anyone."

"Good thing I'm not just anyone." He smiled.

She looked doubtful, and I was about two seconds away from marching over there and demanding to see the footage. Cameras! Why didn't I notice those before?

"Barbara," he said, noting the name on her blouse. "Can I call you Barb?"

"My mother does," she said with a giggle.

"Barb. I could head on down to the LVPD now and get a warrant and make a big to-do of this, possibly interrupting someone's happy day. *Or* you could just be a hero and escort me back to the room with the tapes. You could even help me review the footage. It shouldn't take long."

A moment ticked by. Then another. Suddenly, Barbara nodded. "I don't think it will hurt anything. Cooperating with the police department is always important."

"You, Barb, are a fine citizen and the reason I'm proud to call Las Vegas my home."

I rolled my eyes. He was laying it on thick.

She beamed, and I thought about kicking her. "The cameras are just this way," she said, coming out from behind the counter.

Nate turned to me and motioned for me to come forward. "Just one more favor, Barb. This is Clary. She's a witness in the case I'm working on. Highly confidential. I need her to join us in the back."

Barb squinted. "You look awfully familiar."

"I have one of those faces," I said, smiling. *Please don't recognize me. Please.*

Nate nodded and moved in front of me. "Mm-hmm." He agreed. "I said the same thing. She kinda looks like that there famous country singer. 'Course, this lady here is prettier."

Barb's face lit up. "You're right. And you are prettier than that girl, honey," she told me. "Those famous types all look so fake. I think it's the Botox." She confided.

"Must be," I muttered, utterly insulted.

Nate hid a laugh, and I glared at him when Barb turned to lead us into the back.

Mac and Ben moved to follow, but I waved them back. "*Wait here,*" I mouthed.

They didn't seem too happy about it, but they did as I asked.

Barb led us into this small room with no windows and a bunch of surveillance equipment. Inside the room was a security guard perched on the stool, a soda at his elbow.

"Hey, John." Barb giggled when she saw him. "I need you to pull up some footage from March first."

"Barbara!" he said, nearly knocking over the soda. "I wasn't expecting to see you. You're looking beautiful tonight."

Nate gave me a knowing grin. "Say, are you two dating? 'Cause you make a striking couple."

Barb blushed furiously, and John looked like a deer caught in headlights.

"Ah, no, someone as beautiful as Barbara is out of this old dog's league."

Nate slapped him on the shoulder. "Sometimes a guy gets lucky." He glanced at me when he said it, and his stupid getup and this crazy plan didn't seem crazy anymore. It just seemed incredibly sweet.

"What day did you say you needed?" John asked. He was beginning to blush, too.

"March first. Sometime late in the evening," I said, knowing if Will was pulling something shady that night, it would be at a later hour.

"This might take a minute," John said and got to work.

Nate saw Barb hovering by the still-open door and reacted. "Barb, why don't you come on in? Have a seat right here next to John." He patted an empty stool, then went to pull her away from the door and closed it quickly.

"John, Barb here is a practical hero, helping us out like this."

"She's pretty amazing," he said, glancing her way when she sat beside him. "Oh," he said, looking back at the monitor, "here we go."

I rushed forward to look at the screen, desperate for anything.

Nate smiled and patted John on the back. "Would you two mind just stepping aside while my witness and I review the footage? Shouldn't take too long. Just long enough for you to ask Barb out on a date."

Barb gasped. John coughed. Nate led them over near the closed door. "I hear the show by Brittany is really something."

"Oh, I've never been to that," Barb said.

Hearing the interest in her voice, John spoke up. "I know the security over there. I could get us some tickets."

I stopped listening to their flirting, and Nate returned to my side. Quickly, he pecked a kiss on my cheek, then put his hand on a knob and sped up the footage.

"Where'd you get the badge, *Officer Flintstone?*" I murmured as we both stared at the tape.

"It was a prize in my Fruity Pebbles," he replied. "I keep it in my wallet. Never know when it might come in handy."

I glanced away from the screen to stare at him, astounded. I didn't know what was crazier—the fact that a grown man carried around a fake badge he'd gotten out of a cereal box in case he needed it *or* the fact that it actually was of use.

"Here!" he said, his tone serious, eyes fully focused on the monitor.

I whipped around to see the paused image of me and Will standing at the desk. "Play it," I hissed.

Nate clicked something, and the tape began to roll.

Saying I was "standing" at the desk was a generous statement. I was more half leaning on it, half supported by Will.

"What the hell is wrong with you?" Nate demanded a little too loud.

"Everything okay over there?" John asked.

Nate made an annoyed sound. "Going great. We'll be out of your hair in a moment!"

I watched, horrified, as I teetered on my feet and Will pulled me up, anchoring his arm around me. "He must have drugged me," I said, fear and embarrassment overcoming me.

The monitor blurred a little as unshed tears pushed at the backs of my eyes.

"It's okay, sweetheart," Nate murmured, reaching for my hand. "We've got him now. This tape will clearly prove you weren't... sober."

"I want to see the rest," I said, sniffling.

"Maybe it's best—"

I brushed away Nate's hand and hit the button. We both watched Mr. Richman come out of the back and shake Will's hand. The two men talked for a few minutes, and I pretty much stood there looking lost. Mr. Richman asked me a question, but I didn't answer the first time. When he asked again, Will shook me and I nodded.

"I'm gonna kill him," Nate growled.

"Look," I whisper-exclaimed, my finger bumping the screen when I pointed.

Both of us stared as Mr. Richman pulled a piece of paper out of a stack and slid it across the counter toward Will. Nate hit another button on the control panel and zoomed in.

It was the marriage license, no doubt about it.

I squeezed Nate's hand and leaned in.

It felt as if it took forever for Will to fill it out and scrawl his name at the bottom. Then, Mr. Richman slid the certificate in front of me and held out a pen.

I shook my head.

My teeth sank into my lower lip as I watched.

He offered me the pen again, this time a little more forcefully. I refused it yet again.

Will grew visibly upset, screwed up his face, and said something in my ear. I flinched away from him, but he followed, whispering more words. From the angle of the camera, we could see me turn and look up at him. Even with just the view of my profile, it was obvious I was upset.

Will shoved his face in mine, his mouth moving rapidly. Then he grabbed me around the waist and shook. If he hadn't held on, I would have fallen.

Will turned back to Mr. Richman, and the two men exchanged a few words. After a moment, Mr. Richman nodded, and Will produced a stack of cash. The second the money was in the man's hands, Will picked up the pen and scrawled my name across the certificate.

I gasped, my hand covering my mouth.

Nate hit pause, his mouth grim, his eyes angry. "That dirty son of a bitch."

Reaching out, I grabbed the shoulder of Nate's coat. "I didn't sign it," I said. "Nate. I didn't sign it."

"Who's Nate?" Barb wondered from the back of the room.

"The man on the footage, ma'am," Nate answered without missing a beat. "It appears we got our man."

He turned back to me, worry lines around his eyes. "We got him," he said, drawing me into his chest. I succumbed with a low sob. He rubbed my back, and his breath ruffled my hair when he spoke beside my wear. "I always knew you weren't lying. And now everyone else is going to know it, too."

It took everything I had not to lose it right there. I couldn't. That would just draw attention to us and the situation.

"You say you found what you needed?" John asked, coming closer, and I stiffened.

Nate rubbed my back reassuringly and spoke over my head. "I'm going to need a copy of this."

"Well, I don't know..." John hedged, and I felt a change in Nate's body. He might have been playing the role of good cop matchmaker, but the second he stopped getting what he wanted, I knew the side that not many saw would come out.

"Oh, just give it to him, John," Barb said. "He's with the police department."

"You should listen to your new lady, John," Nate rumbled. "She's a smart cookie."

Barb giggled. I didn't think either of them realized the change that had come over Nate.

"All right, then." John sighed. "If that's what the lady thinks is best."

Ten minutes later, my bodyguards and I walked out of the chapel with the tape in my bag and a plan to never come back to this hellhole ever again. The second the dark SUV Ben was driving turned onto the next block and slowed at a red light, the automatic locks popped up and the back door opened.

I made a sound of alarm, but Nate slid into the seat beside me and shut the door.

"It's me."

I made a sound and flung myself into his arms. Tears I'd been holding back started leaking from my eyes, and he tightened his hold.

"Where to?" Ben asked.

"The airport," Nate instructed. "The sooner we're in the air, the better."

After a moment, I lifted my face from his chest, tears streaking my cheeks. "What about your car?"

"I took care of it."

"What if someone sees us?"

"They won't."

"You weren't supposed to be at the chapel," I said, unable to muster any anger about the fact he'd gone against my wishes.

If he hadn't, I probably would have been shut out completely.

"I told you I was going to protect you," he said, not a hint of apology in his voice. "Besides, you needed me."

"I did." I sniffled and fell back into his chest. "Your plan was stupid," I cried.

"Sometimes stupid works, sweetheart, because no one thinks stupid is a threat."

"Thank you," I said, clutching at him, crying harder.

"Don't thank me," Nate replied. "I did that for me just as much as I did it for you."

"That only makes it even sweeter," I wailed.

He laughed and patted me on the shoulder. "I know."

# thirty-seven

## Nate

I wanted to be there. Unfortunately, the annulment hearing was one place I couldn't just stand outside or hide in a plant. The last thing Aerie (or I) needed was anything fucking up the chance at her permanently separating herself from Solberg.

Side note: I feel it's award worthy every time I refer to Solberg by his name, like an adult, instead of the names I prefer—*douchebag, douche canoe, clump nugget, asswipe, ass face*—and the classic *fucker*—and the ever-popular *dingleberry*. Legit, dude was like a turd that wouldn't stop clinging.

So instead of lurking outside the courthouse like one of those scumbag reporters or trying to hide at Aerie's condo (which was also staked out by reporters), I was here. At Ten's place. It was a pretty good place to wait with its heated pool that looked like a lagoon, wine cellar, chef's kitchen, and private gym. Not that I was enjoying any of it.

Nope.

Currently, I was wearing a hole in the floor with all the pacing I was doing.

I didn't like not being in control, especially regarding something as important as my entire future with Aerie.

She was stressed, and I couldn't blame her. It killed me I couldn't make it easier, but it was out of our hands. We'd found the proof her lawyer was so adamant we find. Now all I could do was wait to hear if it was enough.

*Please, let it be enough.*

It would be. It would. As long as the dingleberry didn't have some other rich-boy trick up his sleeve.

Glancing at the clock for like the millionth time since I got here, I wondered if it was over yet. It should be. I checked my cell, but nothing yet.

It vibrated in my hand, and I nearly left skid marks on the screen opening the text.

Ten: *Is it over yet?*

Me: *Haven't heard anything.*

Ten: *Let me know soon as you hear. Vi is worried sick.*

Me: *Will do. Tell Violet to calm down.*

I didn't like the idea of Violet sitting at home, worrying about this. It wasn't good for her health.

It was just one more thing I could hate Solberg for.

A few minutes later, there was a knock on the front door. Since I was already in the foyer, it didn't take long for me to rush forward and yank it open.

"Please tell me you have good ne—" I said, the words and my smile dying instantly.

"Aww, what's the matter? Not who you expected?"

I blinked, taking a moment to register that it was the dingleberry himself right in front of me.

"What the fuck are you doing here?" I growled.

Instead of replying with words, he lunged.

# thirty-eight

## *Aerie*

I met Walter and one of his associates on the steps of the courthouse and walked with them to the judge's private chambers. Will was already there, looking mighty cocky and a little intimidating in a custom-tailored Versace suit and designer shoes.

I couldn't help but snicker to myself because he probably shined his shoes so glossy so when he looked down, he would be treated to his own reflection.

Nate was right. Will was a douche.

I wasn't overdressed, *like some people*, but I wasn't underdressed either. I decided to keep it classic and wear a subdued and modest black jumper with flowy pants and a faux wrap-around top. It was cut a little low, so I added a white lace shell beneath it and a few gold necklaces. I chose my highest pair of black heels because I wanted to be as tall and un-intimidatable (Is that even a word? It is today!) as possible. I blew my hair out sleekly around my shoulders, the long bob just brushing my collarbones when I turned my head.

As my lawyers and I took our seats inside the office, my eyes searched for Nate, even though I knew he wasn't here. I wished he was, but at the same time, this was something I had to do on my own. I felt a little ashamed he'd had to basically save the day in Vegas and get that footage, but the more I thought about it, the more I decided to give myself a break.

I'd been alone a lot in my life. I'd handled a lot of stuff from the time I was just five years old. It wasn't as if I were completely lacking in courage and strength. Besides, Will was a mistake. A mistake I was rectifying. One I would be rectifying even if I'd never met Nate. It wasn't exactly something to be ashamed of that I actually had someone I could rely on now.

The sound of a throat clearing over me made me jump and glance up. I frowned, seeing it was Will.

"I don't have anything to say to you."

"You still have time to call this off, you know. Save yourself the embarrassment."

"I could say the same to you." I sniffed.

"Heard you made a trip to Vegas." He smirked. "Were you disappointed to find out you really had been jumping at the chance to marry me?"

I thought back to the footage I saw, how even drugged or whatever he'd done to me, I still refused to marry him. I wondered how badly that stung his ego. If that was one of the reasons he was so adamant I didn't get this annulment.

Instead of saying any of that, I turned and looked at Mr. Richman, who was sitting behind Will's team of lawyers. He saw me, and I waved.

He glanced away, looking like he'd swallowed a fly.

Will frowned, noting the way I acted toward his star witness and because he'd failed to get any kind of reaction out of me.

"If you wouldn't mind returning to your seat," I asked, keeping my voice tart. "That cologne you drenched yourself in this morning is giving me a headache."

Will made a sound and adjusted his tie haughtily. "This cologne is designer."

"FYI, just because it's designer doesn't mean it smells good. Or that you need to wear half the bottle."

Walter's associate barked a laugh, then pressed his lips together and coughed.

Will went back to his seat, and seconds later, someone called, "All rise."

Everyone in the room stood while a man with a balding head and a long black robe entered from a door in the back. The second he sat behind his massive desk, everyone else took their seats.

"We're here today regarding the matter of an annulment between Will Solberg and Aerie Boone. The petition was filed by Ms. Boone the day after the wedding took place."

"That's correct, your honor," my lawyer replied.

The judge glanced over at Will and his team. "Mr. Warren, your client is contesting the annulment and claims that Ms. Boone married him of her own free will and that the marriage is valid,"

Mr. Warren stood up. "Yes, Your Honor. The marriage took place at a chapel in Las Vegas. My client has been very forthcoming that both the bride and groom had imbibed on some champagne, as one does on their wedding night, but that both parties were of sound mind and capable of making such a life-altering decision."

"I see." The judge looked at Will. "And you, sir, would like to remain married?"

"Yes, sir. I love my wife very much."

I actually think I threw up in the back of my mouth.

The judge turned to Walter. "Mr. Bright?"

Walter cleared his throat and stood. "Your Honor, thank you for seeing us today. It is of utmost importance to my client that this matter is resolved quickly and quietly. Given her major celebrity, you can understand why something like this could be damaging."

"Get on with it, then." The judge sounded bored.

I wanted to scream at him that this was most definitely not boring. I was over here damn near sweating through my clothes I was so nervous!

"My client is adamant that she did *not* agree to this marriage. In fact, she states that Mr. Solberg had asked her to marry him a few months before the alleged wedding, and she refused."

"Your Honor, the marriage is not alleged. It's a matter of record." Mr. Warren interrupted.

"I'm getting to that," Walter replied.

The judge made a motion for Walter to continue.

"Ms. Boone does not recall the night the marriage allegedly took place. She claims to have woken up the next morning in the hotel with a ring on her finger. She wasn't even aware of the name of the chapel until I told her at one of our meetings."

The judge glanced at me. "Were you drunk?"

I swallowed and shook my head. "No, Your Honor. I think Will drugged me."

"That's insane!" Will burst out.

The judge beat his gavel on his desk. "I'll have order in my court!"

After everyone was settled and Will was quietly seething, the judge looked at me once more. "Do you have proof that you were drugged."

"No, Your Honor."

He made a sound.

Mr. Warren interjected himself into the mix. "Your Honor, I have a witness here, the man who actually married this couple at the chapel. He's taken time off work so he could be here today to testify to the fact that Ms. Boone was in fact of sound mind and that she's now trying to get out of the marriage."

"Why would she want out of the marriage?"

Will sounded pathetic when he replied, "I think she's cheating on me."

I bit the inside of my lip to keep from yelling.

"Do you have proof of this?"

"No."

The judge glanced at me. "Young lady, are you having an affair?"

"No."

"Then why do you want out of a marriage with a man that you—" He paused and looked at the papers in front of him. "Dated willingly for two years?"

Will settled back in his seat as if he'd already won this thing. Anger consumed me. "Because, sir, Will hits me. He has on several occasions. And the only reason he wanted to marry me is because he thought if we were married, he could force me to sign with his father's record label."

"That is not true!" Will yelled, standing from his chair and making it plummet back onto the carpet.

The judge sighed loudly and banged his gavel on his desk.

I was getting a headache.

"Your Honor." Mr. Warren stood. "I think if we just listen to what the witness has to say, it will clear up everything, and we can all go home."

"I think perhaps that would be the thing to do."

"Objection," Walter said, standing. "If it would please Your Honor…" He began and pulled out the recording I gave him. "What I have here will speak much louder than anything the witness will have to say."

"What is this?" Mr. Warren asked, his voice rising. "I wasn't apprised of this."

"It's new evidence that was lately attained by my client that proves there isn't actually anything here to annul because Ms. Boone did not sign the marriage certificate. Her signature is forged."

I actually held back laughter at the shocked expression on Will's face. "Cameras!" He gasped. Suddenly, he lurched up from his seat and turned toward Mr. Richman. "You never told me about any cameras!"

"Mr. Solberg!" the judge yelled.

"I forgot about them," Mr. Richman cried.

With a roar, Will reared back and punched Mr. Richman, which caused him to crumple to the floor.

I gasped and jumped to my feet.

Will swung on me, despite the fact that his lawyers were trying to detain him. "You little bitch." He started forward, and I rushed back.

"Get him out of my chambers!" the judge ordered.

Seconds later, two officers grabbed Will by the arms and escorted him out of the office. Mr. Richman was helped to his feet and given a wad of Kleenex for his bloody nose. I wanted to stick my tongue out at him and tell him he got what he deserved, but I refrained.

"If we have one more outburst like that, I will hold everyone in this room in contempt of court!" the judge declared.

I sat down and folded my hands in my lap, trying to hide the fact that they were shaking.

"Your Honor," Mr. Warren said, obviously shaken. "How do we even know this footage is legally obtained or even genuine?"

"It has the chapel's timestamp and watermark in the corner," Walter told the judge.

"Ms. Boone, how did you obtain this evidence?"

"An employee at the chapel gave it to me," I replied. "Her name is Barbara, but she told me I could call her Barb, you know, because that's what her mother calls her. She took me back to the security room where her new boyfriend John works. He pulled the tapes up, let me have a look, and then made me a copy."

The judge blinked. "And, uh, did any money exchange hands for this evidence?"

"No, sir."

"They gave it to you readily?"

I nodded gravely. "They were just trying to be good citizens."

"This isn't even admissible in court!" Mr. Warren claimed.

"We're in my private chambers, not my courtroom." The judge reminded him. "And I'd like to see what's on the footage."

The tape was played.

It was just as hard to watch the second time around as it had been the first.

When it was done, everyone in the room was silent. A moment stretched into two.

"Bring in Mr. Solberg," the judge instructed one of the officers at the back of the room.

My stomach tightened, and I glanced at Walter frantically. He nodded reassuringly as Will was escorted back in.

"Your Honor, I'd like to apologize—"

"Do not speak unless you are spoken to!" the judge bellowed.

Everyone was quiet.

"In light of the footage that those in this room just witnessed, it is painfully obvious that Ms. Boone did *not* consent to a marriage with Will Solberg. In fact, it is clear a marriage didn't even take place at all."

Will started to speak, but the judge silenced him with a single look.

He turned to me. "Ms. Boone, I cannot grant you an annulment because there is no marriage to annul. I will, however, grant you a restraining order against William Solberg for the obvious threat to your well-being and apparent abuse."

"Thank you," I said, so much relief washing over me.

"You are free to go."

I nodded, wiping the tears from my eyes.

The judge looked back at Will. "You, sir, are ordered by the state of California to remain at least fifty feet from Ms. Boone—her person, all places of her work, and residences—for a period of one year."

"Your Honor, this is ridiculous!" Will burst out.

"I also believe it is in my right to bring you up on forgery charges, lying in court, falsifying a witness, and numerous other counts."

Upon hearing that, Will slumped and looked at his lawyer with alarm.

"Your Honor." Mr. Warren spoke up. "Due to today's events, I would ask that the court bid leniency on my client and also give me a little time to prepare a better defense for his… new crimes."

"You have some nerve asking me for anything," the judge quipped.

I stopped listening as they all went back and forth, arguing amongst themselves. A smile formed on my lips as it sank in that I was finally out of this mess.

Leaning over to my lawyer, who was watching everyone with amusement, I said, "Everything is clear on my end?"

He smiled. "Clear as glass."

"Send me the remainder of my bill."

"I will do that," he said.

I covered his hand with mine. "Thank you, Walter."

"Don't thank me. You got the evidence. I had the easy part."

Nate got the evidence, not me.

A huge smile overtook my face. "I can go now?"

He nodded.

I stood instantly, grabbed my bag, and headed for the door. As I was about to push through, Will stepped in front of it, his face dark.

"Move," I intoned.

He didn't, so I shoved right by him and marched out the door.

"Aerie!" he snarled, following me out into the hall.

I turned around. "You're not supposed to be this close to me."

His face twisted. "This is all his fault."

I batted my eyes. "Whose?"

"Roth."

A dead calm washed over me, and I stepped right up to Will and poked him in the chest. "No, Will. The only person you have to blame for any of this is *yourself*."

He grabbed my hand as I was snatching it back and squeezed.

I kneed him in the balls.

He groaned and doubled over.

"Don't *ever* touch me again," I spat, then turned and walked way, not bothering to glance back, even when he yelled my name.

Outside, I lifted my face to the sun and smiled. An image of Nate filled my head, so I pulled out my cell, anxious to call him, beyond excited to give him the good news.

But as I stared down at my phone, a better idea formed in my head. I'd stop and get a bottle of champagne, then rush over to Ten's and tell him in person. I wanted to see the look in his eyes when I told him.

Finally, I was free.

# thirty-nine

## Nate

I lurched back, narrowly avoiding the fist flying at my face.

"I take it things in court didn't go the way you hoped," I quipped. Instantly, though, I wondered about Aerie. Where was she? Did Will make it here before her? Had he done something to her?

"Where's Aerie?" I demanded and rushed toward the door.

Will's fist plowed into my face. I stumbled back, surprised, but not really.

"What did you do to her?" I spat, tasting blood.

"Relax." Will scoffed. "She's not here. The second she got her freedom, bitch took off and left us both in the lurch."

Like I was going to believe that. But I did feel better that he didn't know where she was. Otherwise, he probably wouldn't be in here with me.

"That's the only free hit you're going to get," I said, swiping the blood off my lip. "I guess you didn't appreciate the gift I sent you."

"Gift?" he said, his eyes going blank.

"You know, that nice basket filled with green lifesavers and plain yogurt?"

His eyes rounded and his nostrils flared. "That was you!"

"I find it a little telling that you actually didn't know it was me. That it could have been a list of people."

"You son of a bitch!" he roared and came at me.

I moved at the last second, and he fell into the entry table, knocking the frames and Ten's Grammy onto the floor.

"You better hope that didn't break," I told him.

With a battle cry, he lunged at me again. This time, I wasn't as quick, and his fist smashed into my jaw. My head snapped back, and a little bit of pain exploded through my face.

"That's for sleeping with my wife!" he spat, shaking out his hand.

"I'm pretty sure the states of California and Nevada have no record of her ever being your wife," I snarled, no longer feeling the sting of his hit.

"You smug little bastard," he growled.

I rushed him, caught him around the waist, and plowed him back. We both hit the wall, but I recovered first, drawing back my fist and burying it in his gut. He made a sound and bent forward. I took advantage and decked him in the face.

Surprise flared in his eyes when his face snapped back. Then he surged at me.

We went down in a flurry of fists and grunts. He was bigger than me, which sucked giant monkey ball sacks, but I wasn't completely lacking. I might have been on the skinny side, but I wasn't small. And I spent my high school years on the wrestling team.

Banking some of the raging anger I felt for this asshole, I breathed in deep and moved, slipping out of his hold and putting him in one of my own.

He bucked and fought me, but I held strong.

"Let me tell you how it's going to be," I intoned, breathing heavily. "Stay the fuck away from Aerie. Keep your mouth shut to the press. Tuck your tail and that tiny dick of yours between your legs and go home to Daddy."

He roared and thrust up, literally standing off the ground with me on his back.

Well then. Maybe I took the insults too far?

I felt him bending as if he were going to whip me over his head and drive me into the floor. Thinking fast, I drove my fist into the side of his head, and he staggered. I leapt off him, landing on my ass, then scrambled up.

Broken glass crunched under his feet when he rushed me again. I grabbed him low, spun around, and put him in another hold.

He ran at the wall, the crazy bastard, bouncing us both off it and disengaging my grip. We both crumpled to the floor in a heap.

I lay there breathing heavily, trying to figure out my next move.

I felt his hand grab my ankle and tow me closer. Glass scraped at my arms as he yanked.

I kicked him with my free foot, and he let go. We both jumped up, and he lunged. We landed on the table, me beneath him. I tried to buck him off, but he outweighed me and he knew it. His eyes lit up with some kind of victory, as though he thought he'd won.

His hands went around my neck, and as they tightened, he taunted, "When I'm done with you, I'm going to go find her… and I'm going to fuck her brains out."

Using all my strength, I drove my knee up toward his groin. I didn't get the full effect of the hit because of the way we were positioned, but it was enough that he let me go. I scrambled out from beneath him and picked up the Grammy that was close by on the floor.

This thing was heavy, and I knew Ten wouldn't mind if I used it to knock a motherfucker out.

Will wasn't paying any attention to me. Instead, he was gazing at the open front door, and a slow, sick smile spread over his features. "Oh, look," Will mused, swiping at his bloody nose. "There she is now."

I ripped my eyes off him only long enough to see Aerie standing in the doorway, clutching a bottle of champagne, a horrified look on her face.

"Run!" I yelled.

A few things happened at once… The sound of the champagne bottle hitting the floor and shattering filled the room, and Will darted in the direction of my girl. With a yell, I pulled my arm back and launched the Grammy at him, using every bit of my remaining energy.

The award slammed into him, knocking him sideways, and he crumpled to the floor.

Mac and Ben rushed into the house around Aerie, and I ran toward her.

"You okay?" I worried, looking her over, making sure she wasn't hurt.

"I'm okay," she answered, but I was beyond hearing.

"There's glass." I fretted. "Jesus, don't cut yourself." I lifted her into my arms so her feet wouldn't touch the ground.

"My face is broken!" Will wailed from his position on the floor. "He broke my face!"

"Don't move," Mac said, his voice leaving no room for pity. "Cops will be here in under five."

"Your arms are shaking," Aerie said, pushing her fingers through my hair. "Put me down. You need to sit."

"I'm fine, princess. It's just the adrenaline," I said, finally realizing she was okay.

"You're bleeding!" She fussed, dabbing at my lip.

"I broke his face," I said, kinda proud of myself.

"Fighting is not the answer." She admonished.

"Guy deserved an ass beating," I said, still trying to catch my breath.

"Mm-hmm." Mac and Ben both agreed.

"Here's a seat, boss," Ben said, placing a chair down and gesturing toward me.

"Make sure there isn't any glass under it. Her feet—"

"He was talking to you," Aerie said gently.

I glanced around at Ben. He nodded and patted the seat.

"Well, I could maybe sit," I said casually.

I carried Aerie over to the chair and sat down, keeping her in my lap.

"I'm gonna sue you for everything you're worth! I'll see you in jail!" Will threatened, his words kinda slurred.

Mac put his foot on him, holding him down.

"What happened?" Aerie turned my face this way and that so she could see what I was sure were several bruises.

"I came over here, and he attacked me!" Will yelled.

Mac made a sound. "Not the way I saw it. Looked to me like you showed up, tried to pick a fight, and Nate here tried to shut the door in your face. You forced your way in and attacked him. He was just defending himself against an intruder."

"That's exactly what happened." I agreed.

"Liar!"

Mac grunted. "Well, feel free to tell your version to the cops. It will be three against one."

"You guards weren't here when I got here," Will demanded.

"Yeah," Aerie said. "I sent them here ahead of me."

All four of us were lying.

All four of us smiled.

"I can't imagine this is going to go over real good when the judge hears about what happened here today. Especially not after you narrowly avoided going to jail for what you pulled on Ms. Boone." Ben taunted.

I turned my stare on my girl.

"I'm all yours," she whispered. "No one else's. Never was… Never will be."

"All mine," I echoed, and she nodded. "That sure makes my face hurt a lot less."

She made a sound and leaned in, kissing me gently on all the places I was hurt.

Sirens carried in the distance, and Will started yelling more threats that no one bothered to listen to.

"The next time someone puts a ring on that finger," I told her, "it's going to be me. And you're sure as hell going to remember."

"That's one ring I'll never take off."

Cops filed into the house, and Mac filled them in on what was going down. Will was handcuffed and pulled to his feet. He swayed crookedly and would have fallen over if it weren't for the officers holding him up.

The whole side of his face was distorted and swollen. I actually had broken his face.

Fucker deserved it.

As the cops towed him out, he turned back and glared at me.

I waved at him with all four fingers and smiled sweetly.

He tried to lunge back into the room, but the cops hauled him out of sight.

"It's finally over," Aerie said, relief making her voice shake.

Gathering her closer, I kissed the top of her head. "No, princess. It's just beginning."

And what a beautiful beginning it was.

# epilogue

## Aerie

*"And the winner for Country Album of the Year is… Aerie Boone!"*

The applause was deafening and so was the thundering of my heart. Even though I heard my name, processing it was something else altogether.

"Princess," Nate said right beside my ear. "That's your cue."

My eyes latched onto his, asking if this was for real, as he stood, pulling me to my feet along with him. The entire row we were sitting in stood, closely followed by everyone else.

"You need me to carry you to the stage?" he asked, smiling wide.

I squealed and kissed him quickly. Ten, Violet, Derek, and even Violet's brother Vance were all here tonight. All people I had come to love. All people who became the family I never had. My eyes filled with tears as they smiled and congratulated me as I moved toward the stage.

Onstage, I was oddly transported out of this epic moment and back to another night when I'd been on a different stage, under lights, and glancing out at an empty auditorium with Nate's arms around me from behind.

That wasn't the night it began for us, but it did define who we became as a couple. Without him and his support, I knew I probably wouldn't be standing here clutching this prestigious award (or any of the other three I'd won earlier in the night—including Country Artist of the Year).

The crowd grew silent when I stepped up to the mic. My eyes sought and found Nate, who was still standing, smiling up at me with pride and love.

"I just want to thank everyone for giving me a chance to say who I really am and for letting me really discover it for myself with this album." There was more applause, and I caught my breath. "To Time Track, for believing in me and staying with me even when the situation was less than ideal. And to the fans who have listened to the music and sent their love."

I looked at Nate again, standing there in a deep-green velvet tuxedo jacket and a stupid bowtie that he somehow made look so freaking sexy.

"And finally, but definitely not least," I said, smiling at him as if he were the only one in the crowd.

"I like being last!" he yelled out, and people laughed.

"You're definitely my last," I told him, putting a hand over my heart. People stopped laughing and awed.

"I couldn't have done any of this without you, Nate, the man who not only helped write *Confessions*, sang background vocals on our song "Reality," but also changed my life and my heart. This album isn't just mine. It's ours. You're the best partner any girl could ask for, and I love you so much. Thank you for seeing a princess when the rest of the world saw a toad."

I turned away from the mic to be escorted offstage by the presenters when the crowd started laughing and applauding. I turned back in time to see Nate bounding up the stairs, two at a time, and rushing across the stage.

The green velvet of his jacket brushed my bare arms and closed me in softness when he swept me close. I laughed. He bent me backward, dipping me toward the floor and kissing me deeply right there in front of everyone.

The applause was deafening. The background music came up, and the presenters around us cheered.

Nate lifted his face, still keeping me captive in his arms. "I'm proud of you, princess. And I love you more than Fruity Pebbles."

I was still beaming when we made it backstage, where Byron Ryan was waiting.

"Aerie." He spread his arms wide. "Way to clean house tonight!"

I felt myself blushing as I smiled. "Thank you for everything, Mr. Ryan."

"Byron." He corrected. "And you did all the hard work. Both of you."

"You were right," I told him. "Telling my side of the story on my album instead of releasing a statement or two was so much more cathartic. And it was a way for me to get out so much without actually having to confirm if it was all true or just part of the song."

People were still speculating, and Will was subject to a lot of the speculation… none of it good. That, along with the legal troubles his daddy bought him out of, insured Will Solberg's reputation was less princely and more… toad.

Giggle.

"Stick with me, kid," Byron said. "Your next album will be even better."

"I'm counting on it."

"And you," he said, turning to Nate. "Be expecting a call from my office on Monday. I'm about to keep you very busy."

Nate nodded, then amended. "As long as you know Aerie is my number one, then I'm down for any work you throw my way."

My heart tripped a little. I liked being someone's top priority above money, success, and fame. For a girl who had been from poverty and alone to rich and popular and back to isolated and broken… I knew a lot about all the different states a woman could live in.

But there was one that topped every single one.

Being loved by Nate.

I took his hand, lacing our fingers, and gave it three little squeezes. *I love you.* He returned the gesture instantly, leaned over, and kissed my head.

Byron stared between us and smiled. "Of course, of course. Wouldn't even try to keep my dream team apart."

I leaned into Nate's side and smiled.

"Now you two go on. Enjoy your success tonight, Aerie. I'll be in touch."

When he was gone, we were treated to what I knew was probably the only minute we were going to get alone for a while.

"So once we blow this joint, what party does my girl wanna hit up first?" he asked, pulling me into his chest.

I wrinkled my nose and pursed my lips. "I think we should get on our new plane and go home."

He raised an eyebrow. "Tennessee?"

I nodded. I barely stayed in L.A. anymore. Nate moved into the ranch house, and now with him and Cheeto there, it was the only place that felt like home. Though, his dad's house was a close second.

My hands slid down his back, and I cupped his butt. "The only party I want to go to is a private one. The only clothes allowed is that bowtie you're wearing."

He smirked. "Chicks dig a bowtie."

I laughed.

"What about the rest of the family?" he asked.

"They can fly down with Ten in the morning. We can all celebrate then."

"I like the way you think, princess," Nate mused, kissing me.

From behind, someone called out my name, and I groaned.

Putting his hand on my lower back, Nate directed me toward the waiting crowd and photographers. "C'mon. Let's do this thing so I can get you alone."

We didn't sleep at all that night. And while it wasn't the best night of our lives (I knew there were even better ones to come), it sure came close.

# author's note

How many of you want to eat Fruity Pebbles now? Ha! I still remember them from when I was younger. They were good eats. Still are.

Cereal aside, Nate is one of my favorite characters I've written in a while. I really like him in the sense that he is sort of fresh, you know? Like he's not some hot, hunky model with bulging biceps and a fat bank account. He's not the most popular guy on campus, doesn't drive a sweet car (well, not for long, lol), and he's goofy. I don't know about you, but I love that. He's real. And if I'm honest, he totally reminds me of Stiles from *Teen Wolf*... which used to be my favorite show. Dylan O'Brien is bomb. But this note isn't about my love of Stiles and Dylan.

Don't get me wrong. Nate (in my opinion) is good-looking, strong, and has a lot of really good attributes. He just isn't the kind of guy that's usually the lead in a romance book. He's more like the sidekick. More guys like him should be the lead, though. Maybe he's right. Maybe he is limited edition.

*Toad* took forever to write even though I knew I wanted to write it when Nate almost took over *Butterfly* (Ten's book). I loved the idea of making the girl the "toad," just as I loved the idea of making the boy the "butterfly." The public enemy angle is fun to write because you can basically break a character down, really flaw them… but then make them lovable. I think I accomplished that with Aerie. At first, she was a bit aloof, sort of bitchy… definitely commanding. But as her layers got peeled back, I think we saw, underneath that exterior, she was really just trying to protect herself from more pain.

I started this book before Thanksgiving, and here I am *after* the New Year (welcome 2018!) finishing it up. Usually, books only take me roughly three weeks to finish—if I'm really into it. No matter how much I loved Nate and Aerie, this one felt like it took forever. The holidays and life made it impossible to really dig in day after day the way I like to write. I think, in the end, though, *Toad* pulled together. Nate and Aerie's story was a little more powerful than I expected, something I hope balances nicely with the lighthearted parts of this book.

Overall, I love this one. I hope you did, too. I want to take a moment to thank YOU as a reader for reading my work, telling your friends to read my work, and leaving reviews. Those things are so very important, and I am truly grateful for any time you spend doing any of it.

Best wishes for a wonderful 2018, and I will see you next book!

XO~
*Cambria*

# about Cambria

Cambria Hebert is an award-winning, bestselling novelist of more than forty books. She went to college for a bachelor's degree, couldn't pick a major, and ended up with a degree in cosmetology. So rest assured her characters will always have good hair.

Besides writing, Cambria loves a caramel latte, staying up late, sleeping in, and watching movies. She considers math human torture and has an irrational fear of birds (including chickens). You can often find her painting her toenails (because she bites her fingernails) or walking her Chihuahuas (the real rulers of the house).

Cambria has written within the young adult and new adult genres, penning many paranormal and contemporary titles. She has also written romantic suspense, science fiction, and most recently, male/male romance. Her favorite genre to read and write is contemporary romance. A few of her most recognized titles are: *The Hashtag Series, GearShark Series, Text, Torch,* and *Tattoo.*

Recent awards include: Author of the Year, Best Contemporary Series (*The Hashtag Series*), Best Contemporary Book of the Year, Best Book Trailer of the Year, Best Contemporary Lead, Best Contemporary Book Cover of the Year. In addition, her most recognized title, *#Nerd,* was listed at Buzzfeed.com as a top fifty summer romance read.

Cambria Hebert owns and operates Cambria Hebert Books, LLC.

You can find out more about Cambria and her titles by visiting her website: www.cambriahebert.com.